Flaming June

By Emma V. Leech

****

Published by: Emma V. Leech.

Copyright (c) Emma V. Leech 2018

Cover Art: Victoria Cooper

ASIN No.: B07DFCS8SG

ISBN No.: 978-1723571725

All rights reserved. Without limiting the rights under copyright reserved above, no part of this publication may be reproduced, stored in or introduced into a retrieval system, or transmitted, in any form, or by any means (electronic, mechanical, photocopying, recording, or otherwise) without the prior written permission of both the copyright owner and the above publisher of this book. This is a work of fiction. Names, characters, places, brands, media, and incidents are either the product of the author's imagination or are used fictitiously. The author acknowledges the trademarked status and trademark owners of various products referenced in this work of fiction, which have been used without permission. The publication/use of these trademarks is not authorized, associated with, or sponsored by the trademark owners. The ebook version and print version are licensed for your personal enjoyment only.

The ebook version may not be re-sold or given away to other people. If you would like to share the ebook with another person, please purchase an additional copy for each person you share it with. No identification with actual persons (living or deceased), places, buildings, and products is inferred.

Table of Contents

Chapter 1	1
Chapter 2	11
Chapter 3	22
Chapter 4	31
Chapter 5	46
Chapter 6	57
Chapter 7	68
Chapter 8	76
Chapter 9	83
Chapter 10	93
Chapter 11	102
Chapter 12	109
Chapter 13	122
Chapter 14	131
Chapter 15	139
Chapter 16	152
Chapter 17	166
Chapter 18	174
Chapter 19	182
Chapter 20	192
Chapter 21	202
Chapter 22	209
Chapter 23	218
Chapter 24	226
Chapter 25	231
Epilogue	237

Charity and the Devil	244
Chapter 1	246
Chapter 2	256
Want more Emma?	265
About Me!	266
Other Works by Emma V. Leech	268
Audio Books	271
To Dare a Duke	272
Dare to be Wicked	274
Dying for a Duke	276
The Key to Erebus	278
The Dark Prince	280
Acknowledgements	282

Chapter 1

"Wherein we meet an unlikely, and unlikable, heroine."

"Not that one, you stupid girl." Isabella snatched the brooch from her abigail and threw it across the room. It landed with a dull thud on the luxurious, thick pile of the carpet in her bedroom. "I said the diamond and pearl brooch. Can't you tell a sapphire from a pearl?"

"Yes, my lady," the maid muttered, scurrying back to the jewellery box and plucking the correct piece with shaking fingers. She returned to her mistress, blinking back tears, and tried to pin it in place.

"Don't stab me with it, you clumsy creature," Isabella shouted with growing impatience. "Oh, give it here. You're worse than useless. I'll do it myself."

Isabella took the brooch from her with a tut and a scowl. She dismissed the girl and watched as she ran for the door as fast as possible.

To her dismay, Isabella found her own hands were shaking just as much as the hapless maid's, and it took several tries to fix the brooch in place.

A deep breath expanded her chest as Isabella stared at herself in the mirror. Her skin was flawless, fine as porcelain, and her expression held about as much warmth. Isabella blinked hard, refusing to give into the tumult of emotions surging through her. A lady never showed an excess of emotion, of any kind. That was a lesson her mother had taught her well. Lady Scranford had slapped hard for laughing, harder for crying. Isabella had received a lifetime of instruction about many such rules. Blushing was inadvisable and avoided at all costs. A lady should look down on those around her with disdain, according to her mother, as if from a great height. A lady was always serene and unruffled, cool and dignified, no matter the circumstance. Serenity was something Isabella was finding harder to feign.

She looked down and smoothed her hands over the ever-increasing curve of her stomach. Fear lanced through her. She could not hide her condition for much longer. It was a wonder she'd managed it this long. Slender of figure, her clothes would not continue to conceal her foolishness. Efforts to hide her burgeoning body from her abigail had become a stressful ritual that was becoming harder each day. The girl studied her with watchful curiosity in her eyes and a guarded expression adding to her already reserved demeanour. That she feared her mistress and her fiery temper was no secret. Isabella didn't doubt that the girl hated her. She would delight in her downfall. Good fortune alone had kept her secret so far as her monthly courses had always been sporadic; five months, however, that was hard to explain.

Whatever was she to do?

The father, the handsome and feckless Viscount Treedle, had made his feelings clear. He'd enjoyed his cruelty. There would be no marriage proposal. He didn't want her, or his bastard, and he cared little what happened to her. She had been an easy conquest and one he would not consider again. He would lose no sleep over her predicament.

Don't cry, don't cry, don't cry. Isabella repeated the words to herself and prepared to go down to dinner. A meal shared with her mother was nothing more than a battle, each of them keeping score and counting the number of barbed and serrated comments that hit home. The past few months had made the confrontations insupportable and her stomach twisted. It was hard enough to eat at all at present, doing it under her mother's icy and judgemental gaze did not encourage her finicky appetite.

Isabella glided down the grand staircase with the regal poise of a queen, ignoring the staff as if they did not exist. A lady never acknowledged the serving classes.

"Good evening, mother."

Isabella steeled her spine, readying herself for the night's battle. The finest Limoges china, crystal glassware and shining silver graced the table. The dining room glowed, bathed in candlelight, beautiful and perfect, at least on the surface.

To her surprise, Isabella discovered that her mother stood waiting for her, and the room was devoid of serving staff. In fact, her mother's expression, always so impassive, almost showed signs of emotion. Anger.

Isabella paused, laying her hand on the back of the chair. The room appeared in stunning clarity, all her senses heightened and on alert. The mahogany chair under her fingers, cool and smooth to the touch; the slight, smoky aroma of recently lit candles and warm wax floated on the air. Isabella gripped the chair a little tighter as her mother moved towards her and placed her bony hand on her stomach.

No matter how long she lived, Isabella would never forget the expression on her mother's face at that moment. It was the first time she had ever seen anything resembling an honest emotional reaction, but the revulsion, the anger, the outrage ... It was blatant.

"You ungrateful little slut."

Isabella jolted but did not react. The urge to cry was strong, but tears would not help her. That this woman had given birth to her seemed incredible, improbable at least. She hadn't anything resembling a maternal instinct and Isabella knew her future was now uncertain. She had hoped that she might have the baby somewhere quiet and isolated and then return as if nothing had happened. They could raise the child as a cousin ... Even as she grasped at straws, Isabella knew it was hopeless.

"You told me to entice him with any means necessary, mother," Isabella replied, though the tone of her voice was weary. This battle was already lost. "You said I wasted this chance at my peril after what happened with Lord Winterbourne. Well ..." Isabella gave a mirthless laugh. "I followed your instructions to the letter."

The slap was hard and fast and stung like the devil. It made her eyes water, too, and Isabella blinked the tears away, careful to keep her head up.

"You weren't supposed to open your legs to him until you got the proposal," her mother snarled, her face screwed up with bitterness. "Even the little nobody who trapped Winterbourne understood that much."

Isabella tried hard to suppress the memory of the night in question, when she'd acted in desperation, forced to behave in such a lowering manner. Her mother had been pushing and pushing. She must do whatever necessary to get the viscount to propose. So, she had.

Pain and discomfort and indignity lingered in her memory. She had hated no one as much as the viscount in that wretched moment, and yet she was desperate to marry him. It wouldn't be worse than her life now. Her mother's constant manoeuvrings left her out of control, shifting her back and forth like nothing more than a pretty, ivory gaming counter. She had never in her life regretted anything more than her actions of that night, but the viscount had promised that if she did ...

What a fool she'd been. Yet she wasn't the first girl ruined by a lie, and she would not be the last.

"Well," her mother said, shaking her head and letting out a breath. "I have no further use for you now. You have ruined yourself and all my hopes and dreams with your stupidity. I have no wish to look upon you for a moment longer. Take your bastard and get out."

The words circled in Isabella's brain, but for a moment she could not comprehend them.

"B-but mother..." Isabella stammered, casting around for reasons she should stay, even though she knew it was hopeless. Her mother never changed her mind. Never. "I could go away until..."

"No."

Isabella watched as her mother seated herself at the dining table, spreading the napkin in her lap with care. Her cold, precise existence would continue unhindered. The decision was made, and Isabella would be cut out of her life with a clean, sharp blade. She would be removed and never spoken of again.

"Your cousin, Jane, is coming to stay with me as my companion," Lady Scranford continued, not looking at her. "I shall see if she can't succeed where you have failed so utterly."

Isabella caught her breath, stunned by the depths of the betrayal. "B-but you hate Jane, and I ... I'm your *daughter.*"

Lady Scranford looked up at her and Isabella knew for certain that there was nothing more to say. There was nothing in her mother's eyes but contempt.

"I would be grateful if you would take yourself as far away as possible," she said, moving the knives and forks that lined her place setting with a frown. When they were straight enough to pass her own measure of perfection, she looked up again. "Perhaps, in time, I can tell everyone you died. That, at least, is something you ought to do for me."

The words were so said with such ease, such easy cruelty that Isabella gasped. She shook, an involuntary trembling of limbs she could not control as terror gripped her. The tremors racked her body and she couldn't make it stop.

"I have nowhere to go," she whispered, a breathless quality to her voice as panic held the air captive in her lungs.

"You should have considered that before you behaved like a whore." The words were emotionless, and Isabella wondered if the woman would bleed if cut. She was as cool and unmoveable as alabaster, bloodless. As nerveless as a marble bust.

Isabella watched, as numb as if she watched a distant figure in a dream as her mother rang the small silver bell beside her and her serving staff hurried in. They'd been listening for the bell, so they knew everything now. They knew her shame. They knew she was being cut out like a cancer.

"Middleton," her mother said, as Isabella watched the expressionless face remain cool and impassive. There was no pain for the surgeon of this operation. Isabella doubted her mother's ability to feel pain, to feel anything. "See she leaves."

"Very good, Lady Scranford."

Isabella's breath picked up as she looked around in alarm. Their butler moved towards her, a glint of satisfaction in his eyes as he strode forward and clasped her arm.

"No!" she exclaimed, trying in vain to tug her arm free. "No! *No!*" She screamed and struggled as a footman came to help Middleton remove her. Still a well-trained, deeply engrained sense of manners abhorred her own hysteria, yet she could not help the cries of distress and fear that tore from her throat as they dragged her from the room, sealing her fate. "Mother! Mother, please!"

The last thing Isabella saw as she left was her mother taking a sip of her wine and nodding her approval. Then the footman moved forward, the crystal decanter glinting in the candlelight as he filled her glass. The door closed.

Before she knew what was happening, Isabella stood at the gates of their estate. Despite the frosty air, cold enough to sober the most drink-addled brain, her mind felt dazed and sluggish, numb with shock. A thick pelisse and a carpet bag lay at her feet on the ice hard ground and she heard the metal clang of the gates as Middleton locked them against her.

There was no pity in his eyes, rather a superior glimmer of malicious pleasure. The staff hated her, and for good reason. This humiliating outcome would gratify them all. She had no friends in the house who would pity her. There was no one to sneak in and retrieve her more valuable possessions. She imagined them raising a glass and cheering with delight at this moment.

Don't cry. Don't cry. Don't cry.

Isabella took an uncertain breath. The trembling had become so bad she could hardly move, her legs jerky and unsteady like a marionette's. She reached out as a wave of dizziness turned her head and reached to cling to the gate before she fell. The metal burned, icy cold beneath her palm, and she snatched her hand away again.

Terror rippled over her as Isabella stared around. The countryside was dark and forbidding, unfamiliar with the unnerving absence of daylight. As a well-bred young lady, she had never ventured out at night without attendants and a carriage to protect her from the world at large. That world seemed vast and threatening now, liable to devour her in one large swallow. She gasped as an owl screeched overhead, the bird gliding through the darkness like a tiny ghost. Shivers ran over her skin, almost unnoticeable against the trembling of shock, but she saw her breath cloud in front of her face like a plume of smoke. It was so cold.

Then put the coat on, stupid creature.

Isabella cursed and reached for the pelisse, tugging it around herself and trying to force her terrified brain into finding a way out of this dreadful situation. In some dim part of her mind, she found herself unsurprised by her predicament. Life had never been kind. Her mother had been cruel and hard and impossible to please. That marriage to a vile man like Viscount Treedle had seemed like an escape spoke enough of the world she inhabited. Isabella had never expected or sought happiness; that was a state of mind confined only to books and poetry and art. She had always assumed that her life would be miserable in luxury, though.

With horror, she imagined the gossip that would begin as the servants tattled their tales and her infamy spread. Everyone would know she'd lain on her back while that repulsive man had taken her virtue. They'd know why, too, that she'd been trying to catch a title. The blush that scalded her heated her skin, at least, searing against the frigid air as it spread over her, leaving her clammy and wretched.

She had little choice left but to go to Alice Cranton's house. Alice was Isabella's only friend, though friend was perhaps not the correct choice of words. Isabella did not have friends, she had people useful to her, and Alice was at least useful. Alice only bore with Isabella for her wealth and connections to the *ton*, and because Alice was too frightened to disobey her. It was something they both knew, but never acknowledged.

It was at least five miles to Alice's house, and in the cold and the dark, it was a miserable undertaking. The knowledge she must throw herself upon Alice's mercy at the end of it did not make it any more enjoyable.

By the time she found herself at the house, Isabella was numb with cold and misery and it was all she could do to hammer the wrought iron knocker loud enough to wake the household. By now, her emotions were beyond her grasp, her body incapable of enduring more. As a startled footman opened the door, Isabella fell to the ground.

***

There was humiliation and debasement, and then there was this.

Isabella looked up at Alice's face, pinched with shock and disgust, a smug glint of pleasure showing in her eyes and betraying the insincerity of her words.

"I'm sorry, Isabella, but I'm sure you understand. I cannot risk being tarnished by association."

She looked back at Alice, knowing she wasn't sorry at all. It was the first time in Alice's life she'd held the upper hand. It looked as though she was enjoying it. No doubt she would become popular now, as she'd have the story first hand. Isabella imagined her in the coming days, the centre of attention as she recited her scandalous tale of woe. The history of a lady of quality and her fall from grace. Shame burned, but not with as much heat as anger and wounded pride. Isabella put up her chin, watching while nausea roiled in her stomach as Alice reached for her reticule.

"It's not much," Alice said, with a sorrowful little smile. "But it's all I have." She held out her hand, the metallic sound of the coins sliding against each other making Isabella grit her teeth. Alice looked at her with the benign expression of a religious icon. Virginal Mary, all charity and forgiveness. It was as superficial as paint on plaster.

Isabella got to her feet, sweeping past Alice with what remained of her dignity.

"Don't trouble yourself, Alice," she said, as the ice in the words flowed in her blood now, little spiky chips that cut at her heart. "I have no need of it."

Not allowing the girl to speak, Isabella didn't wait for the door to open for her. She left without another word. Her bones ached, her back protested, and her feet hurt from walking on the rough ground in the fine silk slippers she'd worn for dinner. How foolish it was to be walking about at this hour in such finery.

The daylight was spreading across the countryside now, a strange purplish tint to the morning. The sense of unreality rushed back to her and she could almost believe she walked in a dream. A nightmare.

Isabella looked up as tiny, icy prickles touched her skin. She gave an incredulous laugh and held out her hand as the snowflakes melted against her skin. Well, she'd sunk as far as it was possible to go. God was laughing at her for sure, retribution for all her sins crashing down upon her head with the delicacy of a fragile white flake. At least there was no one around at this hour of the morning, no one else to witness her shame. There were plenty who would enjoy it, who would say she'd got what she deserved. Perhaps they were right?

Isabella had smiled whilst delivering such pretty, little insults. She had destroyed with barbed comments wrapped up in lace and sympathetic smiles. She had never been on the receiving end of such treatment herself, though. Even her mother had been honest in her criticism, though she saved her words for the privacy of their home. She'd never bothered softening the cut with false smiles.

Well, Isabella was done with it, done with all of them. There was at least a sense of freedom in her decision. For once, *she* would choose the path her life would take. Even if it was a dead end.

Now she had made her choice. There was no way out and nothing left for her. Her pride blazed too fierce to endure the humiliation of seeing the world laugh at her. Isabella would not suffer their pity and their sneers, their enjoyment at her downfall. So, she would end this herself, now, and hope that their consciences troubled them for a day or two. She harboured no illusions it would be any longer than that.

As Isabella picked up the heavy satin skirts of her dress, the luxurious fabric caught upon the frozen ground and tore, but she trudged on, uncaring. The skies lightened overhead, a new day dawning as the sun rose, and one that would set without her. She forced her weary body onwards, resigned, as she headed towards the river.

Chapter 2

"Wherein we meet an equally unlikely hero."

"Henry." Jack waited, knowing Henry would not answer him until he had finished his breakfast. He didn't know why he bothered trying. Some stubborn sense of devilry that made him push the man's limits, perhaps? Henry shovelled the last spoonful of porridge into his mouth and set the spoon down. He placed it with care, so it didn't make a sound. The sound of metal clinking against pottery made the poor fellow twitch with anxiety. "Henry, why don't you work inside today? It's cold enough to freeze your balls off, lad."

Henry shook his head, reaching for the heavy leather coat he wore. He looked like a wild thing to Jack's eye. It was no wonder the locals called him the Bear of Barcham Wood. He was a huge man and sent fear into the hearts of those who saw him. It was a rare event for a poacher to set foot on his land. No one dared.

Jack had tried to get him to tidy up, to take care of his appearance. No matter how Jack nagged or wheedled, Henry didn't care a damn for such things. Jack had even tried bribing him into shaving his beard, but to no avail. His work was all-consuming, and time spent doing anything else was time wasted.

"Are you going down to the badger's set again?"

He got a nod this time. Henry wasn't much for conversation. Jack had worried he might not speak again after his father died. It was eighteen months ago, now, since William Barbour had gone, and Henry seemed ever more detached. His interaction with the world had always been tenuous at the best. Now he seemed not to care that he was slipping away. Poor William's last words had been to implore Jack to take care of Henry, and Jack had sworn an oath. Not that William had needed to ask. Henry was the closest thing Jack had ever had or would ever have to a son.

"Righty ho, then," Jack replied, his tone jovial in the hope of gaining a smile at least. "I'll bring you some lunch later, shall I?"

Henry didn't answer, just picking up the bag that carried his supplies and slinging it over one massive shoulder. The hulking size of him was something that worried Jack a little as he himself got older. Henry's father had been the kindest and most patient of men and the only one Henry had listened to. The lad's temper was often uneven, though, increasingly so. Jack worried that when he died and left Henry alone ... But what was the point in worrying? Jack was no spring chicken, but the reaper wasn't knocking just yet. Fifty-five wasn't so old.

Jack turned and looked at himself in the kitchen window. His reflection stared back at him against the white sky outside. His hair was black still ... well, mostly.

"You come back if it snows, you hear me?" Jack hollered, following Henry down the gloomy corridor to the back door, both men's heavy boots clumping and noisy upon the dusty marble tiles. Henry shut the door behind him with no comment and Jack sighed.

"Nice talking to you," he muttered, before heading back to the kitchen to tidy up.

Barcham Place had once been one of the grandest houses around, well, apart from the Marquess of Winterbourne's place. The marquess was one of their closest neighbours, and Longwold was something else again, a sprawling castle and centuries old. Henry's home, Barcham Place, was Jacobean, built in the early seventeenth century by Henry's ancestors. They'd been prosperous wool merchants and eager to show off their newfound status and wealth. Two hundred years later and the Barbour family had been one of the foremost names in the Cotswolds. Until Henry had arrived.

His mother had died giving birth, and his father, shattered by her loss, had put his heart and soul into Henry. It soon became clear that the boy was not like other lads, though. The boy didn't laugh and play and join in games with others. Too quiet, he would study books or pictures or draw for hours without ever speaking or making eye contact with anyone else. He couldn't abide people, either. His father and Jack were the two exceptions to that rule, though, even they seemed too much some days. If there were more than two other people in the room, Henry would become agitated until he upped and ran away.

William had cut the staff, instructing them not to enter certain rooms of the house so that his son could be left in peace. As Henry grew and grew and the staff found him increasingly odd ... they left of their own accord.

William did not see the lad as odd, however. He thought him a gift from God, and Henry had a gift. From the time he could hold a pencil, his talents had been clear and astonishing. He would draw anything, and in such perfect detail, it took your breath away.

His paintings, however, had been the final straw for many of the staff.

Jack sighed as he sunk the dirty dishes into the hot soapy water. There was only him left now. The two of them rattling around in the vast house as the dust and cobwebs settled around them. They saw no one, and no one saw them. It was how Henry liked things, but it was no way for a young man to live. Though he was twenty-nine now; it wasn't like he would ever marry. Still, there was little Jack could do. He didn't have a way with Henry like his father had done, and Jack knew no one else would ever give him a chance. He was too outwardly intimidating, too strange. No one would take the time to figure him out, to realise that the man beneath the surface was actually shy and kind and thoughtful.

So, they existed here, bound together until one of them shuffled off. Jack had even wondered about finishing the lad off himself if he felt his own time was near. Might be kinder than leaving him all alone. Some fool would discover him and put him in an asylum, and he wouldn't let that happen. Henry wasn't mad, and he wasn't a danger to anyone but himself ... on the whole.

Jack looked up to see that the snow was falling already, fine white flakes dancing on the icy air. He'd have to make a good, thick soup and see if he could get it to Henry while it was still hot. Silly sod would freeze himself to death, otherwise.

***

Isabella stared at the water, her heart beating in her throat. How strange that now, when contemplating her own death, she had never felt more alive. The river was running fast and deep after the heavy rains of the past month. That was lucky, at least. It would be quick.

She took off her pelisse and shoes and laid them down on the frosty ground, shivering as the cold and damp penetrated her stockinged feet. Was it odd that she wasn't crying? She didn't know, but she felt calm, fatalistic, perhaps. There was a sense of peace to her decision after so many weeks of fear and worry. At least it would be over. She admitted to a sense of satisfaction at doing this on her mother's doorstep. She would go out with the maximum of scandal and her mother would have to endure it. Isabella would not fade away as she'd hoped. It was a small blow, perhaps, but it was something.

The water was so icy that she cried out as she stepped into it. Her skirts clung to her, tangling at her ankles. As she forced herself to move deeper, the fabric became heavier still, pulling her shoulders down as the satin soaked up the water. The river was to her knees now, the power of it tugging at her skirts, pushing at her legs. She imagined the moment of her death and closed her eyes as fear lanced through her. Isabella took a deep breath, knowing that this was to be her last moment, meaning to step forward with her eyes shut tight ... when the baby moved.

It was a fluttering sensation followed by a sudden kick, so startling that her eyes opened with surprise. She jolted, shocked, staring down. Without even thinking about it her hand went to her stomach, covering the place she'd felt it. There was nothing more, but in that moment, everything changed.

The baby had been nothing more than a nightmare, a shadowy and unseen thing that was ruining her life and destroying any chance to escape the world she lived in. Yet despite all the evidence, it had not been real to her. It was a parasite, nothing more. She had never seen it as a living thing, as something that belonged to her. Yet now it did. This child was hers in a way nothing ever had been before. It was hers to protect and here she was, standing in the middle of an icy river and about to do away with them both.

The horror of her actions hit her hard and fast, and guilt and disgust were a weight far heavier than her shame and the world's condemnation of it. Isabella wanted to live. She wanted to see her child. She wanted more than an ignominious end to a miserable life.

Her child would live a life far different than the joyless existence she had managed. They would succeed where she had failed. Not by inheriting a title or marrying a marquess, though. Their success would come from living to the full, it would come from happiness. It would be the knowledge that they were loved and cherished as she had never been.

How she was to achieve that in her current circumstances, she could not fathom. The determination she *would* achieve it was so strong that she could taste it.

Fear bubbled up in her chest as she attempted to move and found her skirts so heavy she couldn't. She tried to turn, forcing her body to push against the current when the rushing water and slippery stones beneath her feet conspired against her. Isabella screamed as her foot slid out from under her and the shock of hitting the water knocked the air from her lungs. Flailing and kicking, she surged along with the current, fighting to keep her head above water as she was rushed along like nothing more than a fallen leaf. Terror was absolute, a scrabbling, frantic, clawing desire to live forcing her to fight the current, even though she knew it was hopeless. She had killed herself and her child, and it was by far the most wicked thing she'd ever done.

***

The spot by the badger's set was one of Henry's favourite places. He often came here at night to witness the animals in their habitat, snuffling about, searching for food and going about their daily rituals. They had become used to him as he sat still and quiet for hours at a time. That was something he was good at. But during the day this place belonged to him alone, and he enjoyed the view it gave. Here, he imagined he was the only person in the world, and that suited him fine. People were confusing, disturbing. He didn't understand them, and they certainly didn't understand him. Well, apart from his father. Father always knew the right thing to say, and the right time to say it. He knew when to keep quiet, which was even more important. He missed his father in a way he'd never missed anything before. His absence had left a dull ache that lived beneath his skin and wouldn't leave him be.

He liked Jack, too. Not as much as his father, though. Henry pushed away the strange longing that grew now, curling about his heart. That longing had threatened to undo him. He clung to his peace by his fingertips.

Once, when he was very young, his father had taken him on a trip. Henry did not know where they had gone, but it had involved a sea voyage. A storm had blown up, out of nowhere, and Henry had never been more afraid in all his life. The seas had tossed the ship back and forth, throwing Henry from one side of his cabin to the other. Unable to endure the confines of the tiny room he had fled to the deck and had been swept overboard.

Terror had been complete, the lack of control horrifying. His father said that it had been a miracle he'd been saved, yet someone had managed to get a rope about him and drag him to safety.

The nightmares of drowning, of a cruel and vicious sea, had lasted for years and sometimes resurfaced if he was upset or under pressure. He'd revisited them often in the weeks after his father had died.

There were other dreams, too, where he floated adrift, alone in a small boat. He didn't mind those so much. When he worked, when his mind was caught up and filled with enthusiasm, his dreams and the sea stayed as calm as a millpond. Things that were wrong though, sounds that jarred him, a touch of something that was odd or unfamiliar, these things made his heart pound, his chest grow tight, and the remembered fear of those vast waves would crash down upon him until he feared he might drown.

Yet if the world around him stayed the same and nothing changed, then he could breathe. He could find peace. The seas remained calm. The weight of change, though, it would press down on him like water filling his lungs, chasing the air from his chest.

Here, out in the open, with the skies wide above him and the countryside full of life but devoid of people, here his heart beat slow and even.

Henry's pencil moved with precision, the faint sound of lead on paper just discernible as the breeze rustled dead leaves, and the sound of the river rushing filled his ears. Moss and lichen were Henry's current fascinations. He had drawn the same patch over and again the past days, but he never grew bored with it. The need to record it, just as it appeared and from every angle, was undeniable, irresistible. He was driven to record it in full before he could move on with a sense of satisfaction.

The bright, sulphur yellow of the lichen entranced him, vivid and acidic on such a dull day. The colour almost dazzled under the light of a white sky, like a tiny patch of summer sunlight trapped in the winter and stuck to a rock. Beside it, a cushiony patch of moss, luxurious and soft if he touched it with a fingertip. Henry liked soft things, silks and satins and bright colours. A bright ribbon, a piece of coloured glass, sunlight shining through a crystal, these things held the power to entrance him and hold him spellbound for hours.

The scream that rent the air made him drop his pad and pencil, the air sucked from his lungs. Henry sprang to his feet, furious with whomever had disturbed his peace. This was his place, his and the badgers. Whoever it was didn't ought to be here. They had to go.

Then he looked at the river. There was someone down there, someone in the water. He caught his breath, the remembrance of being dragged down to the depths of a fathomless sea rushing to the forefront of his mind. Whoever was down there, they fought the waves, too, fighting to keep their head above water as Henry had, as he still did. The sudden sense of kinship was as strange as it was alarming.

Henry stared at the figure clinging to a broken branch, struggling to keep a hold as the torrent tried to snatch them back, dragging them down into the dark and chaos.

All at once his father's voice sounded in his head, reminding him he could not just stand and watch another creature in pain. *You must act, Henry, do not stand and observe. Take part in life.*

He ran. Knowing time grew short and that he must not fail, was exhilarating despite his fears. The desire to please his father added momentum as the figure clung to the branch. Henry heard the snap of twigs and the crunch of leaves under his boots, his breath harsh and urgent in his own ears. The water, when he reached it, forced the air from his lungs as the cold burned his skin. Henry shrugged off his heavy coat, tossing it to the bank as he strode into the water.

He could see her now, desperation in her eyes. Those eyes glinted, a sudden flash of blue, as startling and intense as a kingfisher disappearing beneath the water. His last glimpse saw them, full of pleading as her grip failed and the water dragged her down. Henry panicked, he needed to see that colour again. He lunged forward and swam after her, diving beneath the tumultuous water as his own fears seemed quiet for once. His fingers touched a billow of fabric and snatched hold, pulling her closer.

The struggle to pull her out left Henry panting and breathless as he dragged her from the current, yet he felt triumphant hauling his sodden prize to the bank. She was still and silent, and for a moment Henry feared his efforts had been too late to save her. He laid her down on the icy bank, relieved when he saw the slight movement of her chest. For a moment, he stared at her, dazzled. Her deep blue dress pleased him, the same shade as that fleeting glimpse of her eyes. Her hair was yellow, paler than the lichen, though the water darkened it now. It would be lighter once it dried. Henry reached out a tentative finger and touched her skin, sucking in a breath at the texture. So soft.

Although his hands shook with cold, his body racked by shivering and his teeth chattering so hard he had to force his jaw shut to still them, he longed for his paper and pencil. He wanted to draw her, to examine her from every angle, to study her. The desire to do so stole what little remained of his breath.

She stirred then, and he froze, a sense of exhilaration thrumming beneath his skin which was new and strange to him. He watched as she blinked and then turned on her side, coughing and coughing and retching river water. Henry held still, the same way he did when a wild thing came upon him at work. If he didn't move they would stay, they would let him study them as they went about their lives.

So, Henry held his breath and didn't move, and the girl screamed.

***

Isabella scrambled away, terrified by the man facing her. He was huge, with long, dark hair plastered about his face, a thick beard dripping water onto his sodden clothes. There was a wildness about him, an air of something untamed, of power contained by tenuous means.

"Henry!"

Both looked around as another man ran towards them, and Isabella let out a breath of relief; this man appeared harmless enough.

"Henry, whatever have you done?" the man demanded as Isabella felt relieved at being saved from his clutches. "Are you hurt?"

Isabella started, shocked that it was the brute before her who was being addressed, and that she was not the man's centre of attention as he checked the hulking fellow over with care.

"S-she was in the river."

The words from the bear-like creature were deep, his tone grudging. A rather mutinous expression settled over the wild man's features as Isabella realised that he had rescued her from drowning, and at considerable risk to himself.

Satisfied that Henry was in no imminent danger, the second man turned to Isabella. She discovered she was too relieved to be alive to feel any indignation.

"You all right, miss?" he asked, the question so ridiculous that Isabella gave an involuntary laugh. "Aye, right enough," the fellow said with chagrin. "We'd best get you both indoors before you freeze to death."

He reached down to help Isabella up and she noted a frowning show of displeasure on her rescuer's face as his friend came to her aid. Fatigue overwhelmed her as she took a step, her sodden clothes too heavy, her limbs frail, and she stumbled.

"Henry." The man turned to address the bear. "You'll have to carry her, lad."

Isabella made a mute sound of distress, clutching his arm, her eyes pleading him not to let the wild man near her, but to no avail. A moment later, she found herself swept up, the movement effortless as he carried her away. Her heart thudded with terror, wondering what on earth lay in store for her now. She would have liked to ask who they were and where they were taking her. Questions crowded her mind, but fatigue and shock and a numbing cold chased any such thoughts away. Instead, Isabella submitted her fate into their hands and succumbed to exhaustion.

Chapter 3

"Wherein introductions are made."

"Henry, get out the way, there's a good fellow." Jack came back into the room carrying a thick pile of blankets. He let them fall, and they dropped to the floor with a dull thud as dust rose in a plume.

"We'll need to get those wet clothes off her, off you, too," Jack added, tutting and shaking his head. "Go and get changed before you catch your death, you great lummox," he scolded as Henry glowered his displeasure. He folded his massive arms and Jack sighed. "You can't stay, it ain't proper."

"If you can stay, I can. I want to see," Henry objected.

Jack stared at him, taken aback. Well, that was unexpected. Henry had never shown an interest in women before, though to be fair, he'd not seen one for a good eight years. He'd never seen a pretty piece like this one in his life, that was certain. Jack frowned, wondering just how much trouble was about to rain down on them. They'd had an issue with that maid one time, and ... Well, there was no point in thinking about that now.

To his relief, the girl stirred again. Within seconds, she was sitting bolt upright in her chair and looking wide-eyed with terror. As well she might. Jack realised how this must appear to her, both staring down at her as they were. He held a hand out and took a step away.

"Don't worry, miss," he said, hoping his tone remained fatherly and reassuring. "You're quite safe, only ... only you need to get those wet things off before you freeze to death."

Her eyes widened even farther, and Jack pulled at his collar, uncomfortable with the whole situation. Damnation. Served him right for lamenting their solitary existence. This was what he got for wanting more.

Jack's eyes drifted down and for the first time, he noticed the full swell of her belly as the sodden material clung to her slender figure. Ah. That explained a lot. A wave of pity rushed over him and he crouched down at her feet.

"I'm sorry, miss, but it's just me and Henry here, see," he said with a smile. He hid it again as she looked ever more ill at ease. Clearing his throat, he carried on. "You're safe, but I got no maid to help you. You reckon you can do it by yourself?"

She gave a taut nod and Jack sighed with relief. One hurdle crossed.

"Right you are, then." He got to his feet, wondering how hard it would be to remove Henry from the room. "You wrap yourself up in those blankets and sit by the fire, I'll come back with some hot soup."

"There was a bag …" she ventured, and Jack heard the cut-glass tones of an upper-class voice with dismay as he noted the quality of her sodden gown. Damn. That was all they needed, a blasted lady to babysit. No doubt she'd have some titled father or brother out looking for blood. Jack kept such thoughts to himself, his expression impassive.

"I'll find it," he said with a nod. Turning around, he gave Henry a stern look. "Come along, Henry."

Henry shook his head.

"Henry, you can come back when she's out of those wet things," he said, his tone firm, praying Henry wouldn't dig his heels in. "Now come along. You know your father made you promise to take care of yourself, reckon he'd be pleased if you caught your death of cold, do you?"

***

Isabella watched as Henry glowered but left the room this time. Jack turned and gave her a brief nod, closing the door behind him. She let go of the breath she was holding and looked around her. The fire was blazing in the big marble hearth, at least, and she forced herself out of the chair, moving closer. The trial of removing her sodden clothes alone, and with fingers frozen to the bone, was the hardest thing she'd ever done. Knowing Henry was eager to lend her a hand added a determination to her actions, however. Knowing Jack would be back with soup gave her an extra sense of urgency.

Wrapped in several layers of warm, if itchy, blankets, Isabella pulled the chair as close to the fire as possible and sank into it. She knew she'd been lucky today. If not for the rather forbidding and peculiar Henry, she would even now be floating face down somewhere miles away. As she suppressed a shudder, she fought the urge to cry. A pitiful outburst now would get her nowhere. If she wanted to survive and give this baby the life it deserved, well, she'd need a backbone. Pragmatism had brought her this far, and she was no romantic, for sure, so she needed to consider her options. To her distress, all of them involved getting married and doing it fast.

Now the world knew her shame, and she was under no illusion that Alice hadn't shared her sorry tale by now. This meant her opportunities had narrowed to meagre proportions. Maybe a local landowner, though? There was bound to be a country squire in need of a wife? She recoiled at the idea before scolding herself. This was not for her. Her life had never been her own. Before she had lived her life at the whims of her mother, now she would do it for her child. At least this choice was hers to make.

Miserable and shivering by the fire, Isabella made a mental list of the men she might throw herself at. There were several gentlemen farmers in the region, though she used the *gentleman* part with reserve. There was Squire Booth, who beat his horses and would likely do the same to his wife, perhaps his child, too. No, he wouldn't do. Mr Goodfellow, but he drank, and his teeth were rotten. The stench of his breath was beyond anything endurable. Knowing she had to consider him all the same did not lift Isabella's spirits. John Smyth was as fat as a whale and spittle collected at the sides of his flabby mouth when he spoke, which was often and at considerable volume. She shuddered at the idea and stifled a sob.

A knock on the door sounded and Jack entered again, carrying a tray. Isabella watched as the man placed it on a nearby table and then lifted a bowl of soup. He carried it to her, placing it in her hands and handing her the spoon. It was hard to lift the spoon to her mouth without spilling it, she was shaking so, but Isabella set herself to it. Jack sat back, watching her in silence as she ate.

Isabella lifted her eyes, relieved and somewhat surprised to find no judgement in the man's eyes. She had seen him take in the evidence of her disgrace before he'd left the room. She'd not bothered trying to hide it, either, she was too exhausted to pretend any longer.

The soup was thick, bland, and the worst thing her refined palate had ever tasted. She ate every drop, grateful for the warmth as it slid down her throat.

"I'm not much of a cook, I'm afraid," the fellow said with a wry smile as he reached to take the bowl from her. "Helped take the chill off, though, eh?"

Isabella nodded, pulling the blankets tighter. They smelled of dust, the faintest tinge of mildew, but she believed the ice in her bones might melt now. The door opened again, no knock this time, and the man called Henry strode through. She caught her breath, startled again by the sheer size of him.

"It's all right," Jack said, his voice low. "Henry's a ... a bit special, but he don't mean no harm."

Isabella glanced back at Jack in horror. "He's mad?" she asked, terrified as the hulking brute moved closer.

Jack's face was full of anger in an instant, his eyes growing hard. "He ain't nothing of the sort," he growled. Isabella stiffened, realising that upsetting these two men was not in her interests.

She kept her mouth shut, deciding it was safer, and watched with confusion as Henry placed a large bag down and then pulled up another chair.

"You got *your* bag, then?" Jack demanded of him with a snort. "Don't suppose you thought to search for her things, too, eh?"

The big fellow said nothing but settled a wooden board on his lap, placed a sheet of paper on top, and then reached for a pencil.

"What's he doing?" Isabella demanded as Henry's dark eyes settled on her. His gaze was searching, intense, and she had the strangest feeling he could see right through her. She didn't want that. She felt exposed enough as it was.

"Henry's an artist."

Isabella looked around, rather astonished. The pride in Jack's voice had been unmistakable. Who were these strange people? Henry was sketching now, his pencil moving with speed across the paper, his eyes flicking from the page to her and back again as he drew her. What manner of mad house had she stumbled into, for heaven's sake?

"Does he have to do that?" she demanded, pulling the blankets tighter still. All at once, she had the distinct impression she was being studied like a curiosity, something under glass. *Come and see the bearded lady, the two-headed goat, the half-drowned, pregnant Lady Isabella.* "Make him stop!" she cried, blinking back tears. Good heavens, wasn't her humiliation comprehensive enough? She didn't need a record.

Henry jolted, a look of panic in his eyes as he glanced at Jack, who made a soothing motion with his hand. Isabella looked between them as Jack turned back to her and shook his head.

"Can't do it, miss," he said, his tone apologetic but firm. "He won't, and he'll get upset if you try to stop him, so I'd advise you to put up with it."

Isabella put her face in her hands. The desire to break down and sob her heart out was almost overwhelming, but she'd sunk low enough. Losing what little remained of her dignity in front of these two strange men was a step too far. She took an uncertain breath, trying to steady herself when a gentle touch at her hands made her glance up again.

Isabella gasped, stifling a scream as she found Henry crouched beside her, his large hands wrapped around her wrists. She stared at him in horror, her heart thudding with fear, but found only curiosity in his expression. His eyes were brown, a deep, warm colour, flecked with bronze. The impression that he was half-man, half-bear only grew at close quarters.

"I want to see," he said, his voice deep and calm as he placed her hands in her lap, one over the other. He moved away again, picking up his paper and pencil and going back to work as Isabella stared in astonishment.

"Drawing and painting, that's Henry's life, miss. Seems like you're his new project." Isabella noted the troubled light in Jack's eyes as he spoke. It didn't make her feel any better.

"Who are you?" she demanded, finding something of the imperious tone she'd been known for, that of a woman who was used to being obeyed. She needed to know whose charity she was relying upon. Isabella had thought at first glance that they were farmers, but Henry's voice, gruff as it was, was that of an educated man, one of her own class. The room she was in was not that of a farmhouse either. It was dusty and neglected, but the size, the grand marble fireplace, the quality of the furnishings … This was a grand house.

"I might ask you the same thing, miss," Jack said, a considering expression in his eyes as Isabella lifted her chin. She'd have to tell him. He'd find out soon enough. "Still, I'll go first, if you like," he added, a warm smile easing her humiliation just a little. "I'm Jack Heath and I've worked here since I was a boy."

"Where is here?" Isabella asked, racking her brain to think of all the grand houses in the area, close to the river.

"This is Barcham Place," Jack replied, his voice even as he studied her. He was looking for her reaction, she realised. "And that there is my employer, Henry Barbour."

Recognition dawned. "The bear of Barcham Wood," Isabella whispered as a shiver of fear flickered down her spine.

Jack sat forward, pointing a finger at her. "I don't want to hear that, miss," he said, his voice low, but full of anger just the same. "He ain't like most folks, I'll grant you, but he ain't mad and he don't do no one no harm that don't bother him."

Isabella jolted at the fury behind the words and gave a little nod, too disturbed and shocked to do otherwise. She glanced back at Henry, but he was immersed in his drawing. The conversation either hadn't troubled him or hadn't registered at all.

"Now," Jack said, sitting back in his chair with an air of anticipation. "Who are you?"

***

"Lady Isabella Scranford," Jack murmured for at least the tenth time as he shook his head. He'd made up a bed for her in one of the many closed off rooms in the huge building. There were plenty to choose from.

From the shadows under the young woman's eyes, she was too tired to protest about the thick layers of dust, the mismatched bedding, and the possibility of damp sheets in the unaired room. He had put a bed warmer under the covers for her and piled up the fire. That was as close to luxury as she'd get tonight. He'd shut the door on her with a sigh of relief, aware that he was only storing up trouble for tomorrow, but what else could he do? He could hardly throw a woman in her condition out of the house after all she'd been through. It would be sheer wickedness.

It was late now, and he and Henry were sitting at the kitchen table, Henry chewing his way through a heaped pile of thick, cut bread and butter.

"What the devil are we do to with her?" Jack wondered aloud, turning his mug back and forth by the handle with a distracted air.

Henry stopped chewing, a rather challenging light in his eyes that made Jack raise a hand.

"Now, Henry, lad," he protested, knowing what was coming. "She's not ours to keep. It's not like a blasted rabbit or a mouse or shrew you want to study. She's a woman, and a bloody top-lofty one at that."

Henry narrowed his eyes.

"I've heard plenty about the lady Isabella," Jack continued, knowing only too well that there would be a devil of a scene. Henry had his heart set on drawing and studying the wretched woman, and that would only spell trouble. "She's a proper bitch," he said, hissing the words as though they might be overheard. "A nasty piece of work, if ever there was one. Treats the staff like dirt." Henry was unmoved by this information, as Jack had known he would be. "And she's got one in the basket," he added, cursing himself as the unfamiliar term made Henry frown. Damnation. Too late, Jack remembered Henry's fascination last year when he'd discovered one of the stable cats was pregnant. Henry had drawn and studied the creature for weeks. The birth had been something he'd drawn in anatomical detail and had found captivating.

"What's in the basket?" Henry demanded, interest alight in his eyes now.

Jack groaned and consigned his wretched tongue to the devil. "Nothing, Henry, never mind."

"What's in the basket?" The tone was harder this time, a thread of anger beneath the question.

Jack rubbed a weary hand over his face, feeling the scratch of his beard under his fingers. It was useless. Henry would never let it go.

"She's having a baby, Henry," he said, worn out all at once. They should both be in bed and Lady bloody Isabella far from here. "That's why she was in the river, I reckon. Trying to do away with herself and her bastard." Jack frowned, shaking his head with sorrow. For all she was bound to cause them ructions, and despite what he'd heard of Lady Isabella, he couldn't help but pity her.

Henry was quiet, that unnerving stillness he sometimes found settling over him as a slight frown crinkled his eyes. He was thinking hard about something.

"She won't stay, Henry," Jack warned, feeling a prickle of anxiety as Henry's frown deepened at his words. "She needs to find someone to take her in. Some bloke to marry her and save her from ruin. Though from what she says, the story will be all over the county by now."

He shuddered as he considered her options. There weren't many men who would take another man's bastard on, but then, she was a beautiful woman. There were those who would snatch the opportunity to get their hands on a lovely young wife. He had an idea of who those old satyrs would be, too. Poor little bitch. Still, that was her problem, not theirs. Jack just needed to get her out of the house as fast as possible. The devil knew what kind of trouble she would cause otherwise.

Chapter 4

"Wherein Isabella hopes for the best and expects the worst, and Henry makes a decision."

Isabella woke, blinking in the dim light as her tired brain tried to understand where she was. The maid hadn't woken her by lighting her fire. There was no rich aroma of hot chocolate to welcome her. The light, floral scent of her favourite perfume didn't linger on the air. Panic flickered on the edges of consciousness. She sneezed, the movement jerking her awake as her nose detected dust and the odour of a room long unused.

Oh.

She pulled herself upright, looking at her surroundings with misgiving. The urge to give into the panic that rose in her chest was hard to resist.

"You're alive," she reminded herself, the words a little sharp as misery welled. "You're both alive." At this point in time, that was as much as she felt she deserved.

Her hands slid beneath the blankets to cover her stomach. As if asked to confirm her words, the baby moved, a strange, ticklish sensation that made her gasp and give a startled little laugh. Despite her predicament, despite everything, she was glad. Glad to be alive, glad to have this chance with her child, no matter how tenuous her hopes for the future might be.

With relief, Isabella noted the carpet bag she'd left by the river was by the fire. Her pelisse hung on the back of a chair to dry, the slippers placed beside it. She flushed as she imagined either Jack or Henry stealing in to place them there. She hoped it was Jack.

Henry disturbed her. He was dirty and unkempt, for starters, only increasing her impression of a wild creature kept in a cage.

The men she socialised with were pristine, pampered, and primped, their silks and finery almost as extravagant as hers. Henry looked like he could crush such a man with one hand. He was as far from a civilised man as it was possible to get. There was something raw about him, something untamed and savage that made her heart skitter in her chest. She reminded herself that it was a civilised man who had used her and thrown her away as she remembered the look in Henry's eyes as he'd studied her, a glittering intensity she'd found unnerving. Yet his touch had been gentle when he'd taken her hands from her face.

Still, mad or not, a danger or not, he was not in his right mind. That was frightening.

Isabella dressed by the fire, cursing and muttering as she'd never needed to do without a maid before. Well, she'd just have to learn and get used to it. She reached over to rub the dust off of the mirror on the dressing table and managed her hair as best she could by herself. The thick tresses tangled and knotted, as it needed washing, but she would not worry about that for the moment. There were more pressing things to think about.

Despite her exhaustion, she'd lain awake for some time, thinking over her options. To her dismay, she kept coming back to John Smythe, he of the whalelike proportions and spittle. She shuddered, but there were few choices left to her. She knew he admired her. He'd made several clumsy tries to flirt with her since she'd come out, and received several scathing set-downs for his troubles. He was bad *ton*, an oaf, repulsive to look at, and his manners were appalling. Yet he was wealthy, he would give her security, and though the image in her mind of the man touching her made her want to retch, she suspected he would not be cruel. No more than any other man.

With a resigned sigh, Isabella looked around the room they had given her. As with the glimpses she'd seen of the darkened house last night, everything was of the finest quality. That was obvious even under the thick layer of dust and neglect. This room was that of a woman of taste and refinement. Though decorated in the style of an era long gone, Isabella admired the beauty of both the colours and fabrics and the furnishings. Whoever decorated this room possessed an eye for beauty and detail.

Curiosity got the better of her.

Isabella peeked into the vast wardrobe, looked into the large chests and the many drawers about the room. With each revelation, she became more astonished. The fabrics, the colours, the sheer number of gowns and shoes and gloves and jewellery was incredible. There was a small fortune in this room alone. It told her only one thing, this family had been wealthy beyond anything she'd ever known. Whatever happened to them?

With relief, she found a lovely wool shawl, decorated with the finest embroidery of fat, golden bees and silken butterflies. It was beautiful and warm, and she put it about her shoulders with a smile. It was a luxurious piece, made for a fine lady, which she was far from being. So what? She must take pleasure in small things now. There was little else to do. With that in mind, her spirits lifted as a new thought occurred to her. She would never again have to endure another meal with her mother as long as she lived. As Isabella left her room and made her way down to the kitchen, she felt almost light-hearted at the idea.

***

Henry stared at the drawings in his hand. The wary eyes of the woman he'd pulled from the water stared back at him. The sense of excitement made him edgy, the longing to draw her again, to study her, to paint her … it was intoxicating. A new project always filled him with a sense of anticipation, a buzzing, impatient, restless feeling that prowled beneath his skin until the moment he started work. It kept him from sleep, refused to let him eat, it haunted his every moment if he didn't give into the desire.

Nothing had ever captivated him like this, though. The blue of her eyes, the mistrust in her expression, the way she tilted her head, he wanted to record it, every nuance. That she carried a child in her belly was all the more intriguing.

Henry recorded many creatures, from deer to foxes to rabbits, rats and mice. He detailed the way they hunted and fed, how they procreated, how they gave birth, how they lived, and how they died. The desire to know *how*, how things worked, the mechanics of life, gave order to a world that often overwhelmed him.

Jack said she would leave. That was unacceptable. The idea made him sick, unsettled, the restless anxiety that often plagued him making him pace with increasing speed. No. She would not leave. He would not allow it. Yet Jack said he couldn't force her to stay. His father would have been furious with him for doing such a thing. Disappointing his father made a sick, cold sensation rush over his skin, and panic rose in his throat. He had to make her stay. *He had to make her stay.*

He'd already gone down to the river to fetch her bag. There had been a coat, and dainty slippers, too. So tiny. He'd placed one next to his huge foot, intrigued by the disparity of size. He hadn't told Jack he'd brought her things. He hadn't told Jack he'd slipped into her room, either. Just for a moment. He'd not stayed, not pried, though the temptation to watch her sleeping had been hard to deny.

Henry hoped she would be pleased to have her things back. He was under no illusion that she would like him because of it. Nobody but Jack liked him, though Jack said that was their loss.

What was it Jack said? With difficulty, he forced himself to remember. Most conversations didn't hold his attention. He had no interest in them, words only muddled his mind, impeded his work. Better to do. Better to just get on and do.

Jack said she needed to marry. She needed a name and a home.

Henry stopped pacing.

He would never marry. Everyone said so. He was too strange, too …

He would never marry, they said so, Jack said so. But he *could*. He could marry her. He had a name, a good name. Father had said it was a proud name. So, he would marry her and give her his name and his home. She would stay, she would have her baby and he would see it, he would record her and the child. He would understand how they worked.

With a renewed sense of purpose and resolve, Henry rushed for the door. The woman would stay. He'd make sure.

***

Isabella reached the bottom of the impressive staircase, in no doubt that the Barbour family had once been a force to be reckoned with. She'd peeked into rooms where the furnishings hid under dusty covers, but one thing became obvious. Every corner of this vast building spoke of quality, of attention to detail, wealth of a kind even her own family could never aspire to.

She lingered on the stairs, looking up into the faces of the past generations that lined the walls. Their disdainful expressions judged her, finding her lacking. Isabella found nothing new or surprising in that. Her mother's face would fit here as if designed for the purpose. In a way, Isabella supposed it had been.

All but one portrait held the mocking superiority of the upper classes, that innate sense of self-worth Isabella had never quite convinced herself of. It was the last and most recent portrait here, and by the most skilled artist by far. Isabella touched the surface of the paint with reverence, surprised that the nap of the velvet wasn't soft beneath her fingertips, so clever was the hand of the artist. She saw Henry's eyes looking back at her, though it was the portrait of a far older man. There was a warmth in his eyes, a twinkle of amusement glimmering, though there was an air of sorrow about him, too. What had made him so sad and yet made him smile with such warmth? Isabella stared at it for a long while before a voice made her jump.

"That's William Barbour," Jack said, making Isabella cling to the bannister as she started with surprise. "Henry's father," he clarified, smiling at the portrait. He sighed, shaking his head and looking sorrowful. "No finer man ever lived, if you ask me."

"When did he die?" Isabella asked, a strange sense of disappointment filling her as she realised she would like to have met him. She didn't doubt Jack's words, either. There was kindness and understanding in the man's expression, an innate sense of goodness. Whoever had painted this had held a deep affection for the man, too, and had known him well.

Jack sighed, a wistful sound that Isabella realised was genuine. "'Bout eighteen months ago, now. Hit poor Henry hard, that did. Didn't speak a word for nigh on six months, and he weren't exactly chatty before," he added with a rueful smile. "He painted that, about eight months before the old boy passed. I'm so glad he did."

Isabella gaped at him and then stared back at the painting in awe. "H-he painted this?" she demanded, disbelieving. The notion that the hulking brute of a man who looked like he rarely washed and slept in a ditch could create work of such finesse and quality was astonishing.

"I told you he was an artist," Jack replied, amusement in his voice and something close to judgement in his eyes. "You've never seen anything like the work Henry can do. Sometimes I feel like I could step into the paint and never notice a jot of difference from the real world."

"I believe you," Isabella murmured, though Henry still struck her as an unlikely artist. She had always considered them romantic figures, and, as a girl, had harboured silly dreams of falling in love with a poet or a painter. Such nonsense. Though perhaps her fate may have been kinder if she'd done so. Isabella loved the arts, though, music and poetry and paintings. She had always found pleasure in beautiful things, but a fine painting in particular could make her heart sing. That a man like Henry had produced something of such skill and beauty … How strange.

"Come and have breakfast, then, my lady," Jack said as he turned back to the kitchen. "I've made porridge, though you may not thank me for it."

Jack's words proved true enough as Isabella forced down the glue-like texture with difficulty. She washed it down with a creamy glass of milk, refusing to remember the breakfasts at home. At least eating this … *stuff* was better than getting indigestion as her mother listed out her most recent failures and the many ways in which she was a disappointment to her.

Indigestion seemed rather inevitable as Henry shoved his way through the kitchen door, an air of restless anxiety rolling off him in waves. He loomed over the table, his presence intimidating. He met no one's eye, just stood, fists clenched as Jack shot him a wary glance.

"Sit down, Henry," he said, his tone firm as he got up and filled another bowl with the grey paste by giving the spoon a firm shake. Isabella watched, rather fascinated as the porridge hit the bowl with a dull thud. Jack glanced back to see Henry hadn't moved. "Put your backside on the chair, Henry. There's no need to make the place look untidy." He put the bowl down, pressing his hand on Henry's massive shoulder until he moved to take his place, and then sat down again. "Eat it, then," he instructed. "Before it gets cold."

Henry stared at the table for a moment, a frown on his face, before taking the spoon and digging it into his porridge.

"So then, Lady Isabella," Jack said, his eyes still on Henry, who was shovelling the porridge into his mouth with some speed. "What do you reckon you'll do now?" he asked as Isabella tore her eyes from Henry. "Not that we're throwing you out, but it's not like you can stay here."

Henry's hand stopped moving, the spoon suspended in mid-air.

"No, of course not," Isabella replied, torn between turning her attention to Jack and staring at Henry, who was fascinating and appalling and appeared to have turned to stone. "Even in my *situation*, that would be most ..." She hesitated, fighting the blush that threatened to stain her cheeks. "Irregular," she finished, deciding that staring into her bowl was safer than looking at either of them. "I ... I thought perhaps ..." Isabella stopped again, wondering why on earth she was confiding in these two peculiar men. She wouldn't even have deigned to speak with them hours ago, and now ... now they were privy to her shame and her most private, desperate thoughts.

Isabella felt no judgement from Jack, though, only a rather reserved sense of sympathy. After a lifetime of enduring Lady Scranford, that was close to receiving a benediction. It wasn't as if she was surrounded by friends and family eager to help her, either. What choice did she have?

Jack didn't prompt her to continue, there was no air of inquisitiveness or prying from him. She could tell him, or not, as she preferred. Henry was still motionless, though she had the sense he was listening with the same intensity as he had studied her last night.

Isabella cleared her throat. "I thought perhaps I would visit ... Mr Smythe." The flush came this time, along with a fear that the porridge she'd forced down would not remain where it was.

Jack's eyes grew wide with obvious horror. *"John Smythe?"* That repulsive oaf with the fat neck and a voice like thunder, he didn't say, though words to that effect were shining in his eyes. "I see," he murmured, sitting back in his chair and avoiding her eye.

"I don't have many options now," Isabella replied, unable to look at him either. She stared instead at the porridge, which was cooling fast, a thick wrinkly skin forming on the surface. She swallowed hard as her stomach turned, and then jumped as Henry stood, his chair screeching as he forced it backwards.

"No."

Isabella looked up, unsure who he was talking to.

"She's got to go, Henry," Jack said, his voice firm. "She needs to marry someone and there's few will take her now. Not with …" He trailed off, giving Isabella an apologetic shrug of his shoulders.

Henry's large hand opened and closed again, the knuckles showing white. "She'll stay here. I'll marry her."

She wasn't sure which of them was the most shocked. Jack was running her a close second. He gaped at Henry, mouth open with surprise, before pushing to his feet.

"Henry, might I have a word with you, lad?"

He walked around to stand beside Henry, tugging at his arm.

Isabella watched with shocked fascination as Henry shook his head, a slow and deliberate movement. His fist remained clenched, the other one curled around the spoon so tight she wondered if he'd crumple the metal. He looked neither of them in the eyes.

The suggestion that she could even think about marrying the strange and frightening man standing beside her was beyond horrifying. She could smell him, a mixture of earthy, woody scents and unwashed male body, that sense of barely contained power emanating from him in waves.

Then she thought about John Smythe and shuddered.

"Henry, I don't think you've thought this through, lad," Jack said, and Isabella could hear the careful tone of his voice, the way he spoke, slow and deliberate. "You don't like people around you. I know you want to paint her, but what then, eh? What about when the baby comes? It'll scream all day and all bleedin' night, too. How'll you work then? What about when it's older and runs about the house, touching your stuff, tearing up your drawings?"

Isabella watched as Henry stiffened a little, his shoulders growing tense and a mutinous set to his jaw suggesting that Jack's words hadn't gone unheard. Still, he shook his head.

"She stays."

There was a thread of anger to his voice and Isabella swallowed.

"And what if she doesn't want to?" Jack demanded, his voice growing strident now, and Isabella saw panic in his eyes. Jack thought she'd cause trouble. He gave Henry a push, shoving at his shoulder, which had no effect whatsoever. "Look at me," he said, getting no reaction. *"Look at me,"* he said again, the words louder now. He reached out and grasped Henry's chin, tugging his beard and forcing his face to him. Henry's eyes slid unwillingly around. "What do you think your father would say about this, Henry? Would he be pleased if you forced a young woman to stay here with you?"

The pain and disappointment in Henry's eyes were raw and unguarded, and Isabella's breath caught.

"Want her to stay," he mumbled, a bereft note to the words that tugged at her heart, a sense of empathy she hadn't known she possessed. No one had ever wanted her anywhere before. She didn't act the highbred lady well enough to please her mother, but she did it well enough that no one else wanted to spend time with her.

"She's *not* staying," Jack replied, his words sympathetic but hard just the same. "It'll cause you nothing but trouble, Henry." He tugged at Henry's arm, trying to move him away, but the man stayed put. With the inequality in their sizes, Jack would never move him if he didn't want to budge. He'd have more luck shifting a mountain range. "She'll want things you can't give her," Jack hissed, the words low and urgent as Isabella fought the desire to run from the table.

Her mind was turning in circles. The family had been wealthy once, perhaps they still were? Perhaps she could give her child the life it deserved here. Henry was not in a fit state to interfere in her life. Perhaps, once this desire to paint her had subsided, as Jack seemed certain it would, perhaps then she could live as she wished. She could negotiate terms.

Excitement and panic and hope collided in her heart, making her chest tight and her breath short.

"Henry," she said, rather startled when his eyes snapped to hers in an instant. "Why? Why do you want me to stay?"

He sat, pulling the chair close to her, that intense glitter in his eyes again. "I want you to stay," he said, a rather feverish tone to the words.

"Yes, but why?" she asked, wondering if he even understood the question. Was he a halfwit? Good Lord, but the humiliation when this got about, but at least the house was secluded. She could keep out of sight until her scandal died down. Henry did not socialise, that much was obvious. There would be no dinner parties or trips to the theatre.

If she married John Smythe, he'd want to parade her about the county like a prize sow. Henry didn't like people, though, Jack had told her that. She could live here in peace. She'd not have to face it. When the child was old enough, they would leave, start again somewhere else. France, perhaps? She spoke excellent French.

"Why do you want me to stay?" She wondered why it even mattered, but if he had some nefarious plan for her, she wanted to know. If he was a halfwit, he may well admit to it.

"I …" he began and then swallowed. "I want." He paused and rubbed the back of his neck. "I want to draw you, paint you, too. I want to see." He gestured to her rounded belly and Isabella gaped at him, covering the swell of her pregnancy with both hands in a protective gesture. "I want to see it born," he added, the words shocking her so much that she found it impossible to speak at all for a moment.

"No!" she exclaimed as she found her tongue, staring at him in horror as he rushed to his feet, moving away from her as fast as he could. This strange man seeing her in such a vulnerable state? It was enough to make her breath come fast, her head spinning as she fought the urge to pass out. "Never!" she added as he stood, staring at her in alarm.

He looked so puzzled by her outburst, she almost laughed.

He moved a little closer, his dark brows drawn together. "Why not?"

"Why not?" she repeated, incredulous as she turned to stare at Jack, who had been listening with obvious dismay.

"Henry, she's not a rabbit or a cat you can study, for the love of everything holy!" Jack exclaimed. "It's not done, lad."

Henry frowned, folding his arms as he scowled at the floor, his frustration clear.

"He likes to see how things work," Jack said to her, holding his hands out in a manner that asked for understanding. "He can't understand why seeing you ... why it's any different. Henry doesn't understand the rules like most folks do. He's not trying to offend you, he's just ... interested."

Isabella made a startled noise, desperately shocked. She needed to think about this in the light of her diminishing options. Henry was frightening, but he didn't *appear* dangerous, Jack had said he wasn't. Between a halfwit and a well-meaning servant, she could take control and make a place for herself here. A woman of her determination and upbringing could manage a grand house like this. It was what her mother had bred her for. Right now, she ought to be mistress of Longwold. Isabella snorted at the idea. Then she thought about all the beauty she had seen in this house. If she took it in hand, it would shine again, it would regain its beauty, its grandeur, and be everything it had once been. Isabella let out a breath as the idea took hold.

She could learn the way Henry needed handling in time. Jack would teach her. If she kept him calm and found him enough things to paint, they need never see each other.

Isabella turned to Jack. "Does he always paint the same subjects?" she asked him, irritated when the man scowled at her.

"Why not ask him?" he snapped, folding his arms.

"Because I don't know if he's capable of giving me an answer," she replied, huffing with impatience.

"He's not stupid," Jack growled, pulling his chair out and sitting down as he glowered at her. "And no. Henry will draw or paint the same thing over and again until he feels he's studied it in enough detail to record it, to understand it, then he'll move on."

Isabella nodded, turning back to Henry. He stared back at her, hope in his eyes. For such a large and strange fellow as he was, it was a rather vulnerable, soft expression.

"You'll have to wash and shave and wear clean clothes," she said, ignoring the twinge of recognition that pulled at her heart. "Often," she added, wrinkling her nose.

Henry frowned but nodded.

"This place will need cleaning and I'll need things, dresses, things for the child."

She watched as Henry shot Jack a rather panicked glance. Jack returned an *I told you so* expression that made Henry's jaw tighten.

"No people," he said, his voice deep and commanding, at odds with the anxious, uncertain man he seemed to be.

"Well, that's not going to work," Isabella retorted, folding her arms and frowning at him. "I'm not living under a foot of filth and dust, Henry."

"No people."

Isabella stared back at him, noting the stubborn glint in his eyes with misgiving. Whatever he was, the man wasn't a pushover. Still, she had time. Men could be managed, even a man like Henry, it was only a matter of discovering the knack.

"This will be a marriage in name only," she said, wondering if he had the slightest idea of what she was implying. "This child will be your heir, there will never be another."

She looked around to see Jack putting his head in his hands. "Henry, lad, you don't know what you're getting into here," he said, the words full of fury. "She'll change everything." He looked up then, staring at Isabella with deep mistrust shining in his eyes. "You'll not come and take over and bully Henry. You'll not send him away, so he ends his days in an asylum. *I won't let you.*" The words were low and threatening, full of anger. He leaned across the table, dropping his voice to a whisper. "I'd kill you first."

Isabella started, realising too late that Jack was the danger, not Henry. "I ... I wouldn't!" she objected, her heart thudding at the truth she saw in Jack's eyes. He'd do it, to save Henry. "This is his home, I can see that. He'd never survive in an asylum. I ... I'm not that cruel, I swear." She meant the words, too, though it surprised her. She'd never been the charitable kind, never given a thought to those less fortunate than herself. Now she'd sunk so low, though ... well, she belonged to the less fortunate, too.

Jack let out a breath and she hoped he'd heard her sincerity. "You'll change things, though." He folded his arms, sitting back in his chair and holding her gaze before his eyes flicked to Henry. "She will, Henry. She'll change things."

Isabella glanced between the two men, knowing she had to tread with caution. "I would like to," she said, keeping her voice soft as she looked around at Henry. "I would like to see the house clean and beautiful again. You like beautiful things, don't you, Henry?"

Henry didn't answer, his gaze on her unswerving.

"I would like us all to eat a decent meal, too," she said, looking at the cold grey porridge and wrinkling her nose. "Wouldn't that be nice?" She gave a cautious smile, turning to Jack now. "Less work for you, too," she said, but Jack just snorted, shaking his head back and forth.

Isabella frowned, wondering what tack to take. She remembered how Henry was swayed by his dead father's opinions, as delivered by Jack. "I'll bet the house didn't look like this when your father was alive," she said, the words a little sly.

Henry frowned, and Isabella held her breath, wondering if this was the way to manipulate him.

For a moment, he stood, staring at the table, deep in thought. He didn't look up or change expression when he spoke, and his gaze was clear, the words precise. "Jack will clean your room. No people."

With that, he turned and strode out of the kitchen.

Chapter 5

"Wherein chances are given and taken on both sides."

Jack chuckled, a rather mocking sound that Isabella took exception to. She turned to give him a look of frustration and he snorted at her expression.

"Henry's not a child and he's not stupid. He doesn't talk because he doesn't like to, not because he doesn't understand. He knows when he's being manipulated." Jack sat forward, giving her a hard look. "I've heard about you, my lady," he said, his voice low. "I've heard about the maids you've bullied, about that sharp and bitter tongue of yours. You treat people like dirt and you'll do just about anything to get your own way." He allowed his gaze to drift to her belly, a meaningful glance she well understood. "Well, you'll not do it here."

Isabella let out a breath and pushed the bowl containing her congealed breakfast away from her before her stomach rebelled.

"The house needs taking in hand, Jack, surely you can see that?" she said, her voice as hard as his now, hoping to sway him with reason. She couldn't deny his words, they were true enough. For the first time in her life, she felt something close to shame for that truth. "You can't enjoy living like this?"

Jack shrugged, his gaze falling on her like a weight, judging her. "Henry prefers it this way. I'm just trying to keep him safe and well and happy. I promised his father, and it's a promise I mean to keep to my last breath."

Isabella looked up at his words, surprised. There was such passion, such loyalty. Why would a servant be so dedicated to such an odd man? It made no sense. "But why?" she asked, curious now. She couldn't imagine any of her mother's staff lifting a finger for her if they weren't getting paid for it. "Why are you so devoted to him? Did you never wish to marry, to have a family?"

"Henry's my family," Jack said with a smile that softened his face.

She studied his expression, seeing the honesty in his eyes. He loved Henry, like a son.

He snorted at the surprise in her face. "You only see the surface, my lady. You think he's deranged, a half-wit; well, he ain't anything of the sort. Henry's much more than a flighty creature like you could understand, with your la-di-da ways and your *ton* and your rules and manners. He don't fit into your world, so you all reckon he's worthless. He don't talk or act like you, so you think he needs locking up." He sat forward now, his expression fierce, the words full of heat. "Well, you're wrong. More wrong that you can imagine, but he won't show you. Not unless he trusts you."

Isabella folded her arms upon the table, considering his words. Though she'd not admit as much, she was touched by Jack's defence of Henry. For a moment, she even felt a little jealous that an odd creature like Henry had found such a passionate champion when she had no one.

"Would he ever trust me?" she asked, thoughtful now and wondering why she even cared. She needed to make a home here, though, and the best method of getting her own way was to have Henry trust her.

She turned to find Jack staring at her, a considering light to his eyes. "Not if you're dishonest," he said, the flicker of a contemptuous smile at his lips. He believed her incapable. "I never knew a fellow for being able to smell a lie. If you talk to him, you must be open and honest, *completely* honest. Try to fob him off, try to manipulate him for your own ends, and he'll shut up like a clam. It might be months before he gives you another chance."

"You think me a bitch, don't you," Isabella said, staring at the table as she pondered his words. She traced the grain of the well-scrubbed wood with a finger, waiting for his reply. Though she didn't look up, she thought perhaps he shrugged.

"I know what I've heard," Jack replied, his tone dark. Isabella nodded, thinking that was it, but then he gave a sigh, and when he spoke again, his voice was softer, kinder. "But then I've heard of the Bear of Barcham Wood, too."

Isabella lifted her eyes to his, surprised by the fairness of his words. He was giving her a chance. For the first time in her life, she felt like giving something in return for that fairness, so she told the truth.

"I'm afraid the stories are quite accurate."

He nodded then, holding her gaze. "I reckoned as much."

She frowned then, wondering why his words stung her. He'd not said them with any malice, there was still no judgement visible in his gaze. He only grew angry if she spoke ill of Henry. He was a good man. His opinion mattered, she realised. It would feel good … like a kind of validation, to know that he approved of her. Why, she wondered? She'd never cared before for anyone's opinion except her mother's, and only then because she was afraid of her. Yet she'd been miserable and alone her entire life.

Perhaps if she changed, that could change?

Perhaps she could learn to be happy?

"Everything has changed," she said, hearing the tremor of a sob in her voice. She took a deep breath. No more crying. "Perhaps … perhaps if that's so … I can change, too?" There was scepticism in the words and she laughed, shaking her head. What nonsense. If she didn't believe it possible, why the hell would Jack?

"Maybe you can."

She started, staring at the man who was regarding her with a mixture of pity and curiosity, and something else she couldn't read at all. He didn't look as though he was teasing her, though. There had been sincerity in the words.

Jack leant towards her, a look in his eyes that might have been hope. "Listen here, my lady…"

"Isabella," she said, giving him a wry smile. "I don't think we need keep the formalities any longer. I'm rather less than a lady now."

He nodded, an approving look in his eyes that pleased her for reasons she couldn't understand. "Well, Isabella. I'm not as young as I was, and I worry for Henry. I often fret about what will happen to him when I'm too old to care for him, or if I'm not here at all." He paused and took a deep breath, and she knew his next words had not been spoken lightly. "Perhaps you can change that."

Isabella stared at him. This man that loved and guarded Henry like a lion with a cub and knew her to be a cold, cruel bitch, would give her a chance. Was he a fool? She stared and stared as he returned her gaze and had her answer. No. No fool. A good man.

"You'll let me stay?" she said, the words laced with astonishment. She'd been certain up until that moment that Jack meant to get her out of the house by any means necessary.

He laughed at that, shaking his head at her. "You still don't get it, do you? Henry says you're staying. I can't change his mind and I can't go against his wishes. If he's decided to marry you, he'll do it."

"B-but you accept it?" she pressed, knowing that Jack had the power to make her life hell if he chose to do so.

A harder light entered his eyes at that and Isabella shivered a little. "I'll give you a chance, is what I'll do," Jack said, though his voice held little warmth now. He sighed and sat back in his chair again, observing her with that curious glimmer in his eyes. "Truth is, I'd like to believe you could change things, make life better for him. I'm not getting anywhere alone, that's for certain. Henry's going down, if I'm honest." Jack rubbed a weary hand over his

One benefit of pregnancy was that there was little point in worrying over her figure. Isabella's mother had watched everything she'd eaten like a greedy hawk, waiting to snatch it from her if she thought she was over indulging. She wasn't to eat anything that might put weight onto her slender bones, and Isabella often fought pangs of hunger and dizziness. It only added to her irritation and bad temper. The food at Barcham Place might leave a deal to be desired, but it was plentiful.

After three cups of tea and as many slices of crusty bread spread thick with butter, they cut the cake. Isabella had protested that they should wait for Henry, but Jack had just laughed and said he wouldn't care a jot so long as they didn't eat it all.

In fact, that was harder to do than she might have imagined. As Jack had bought and not made the cake, it was good. Isabella eyed a third slice with chagrin.

"Go on, lass," Jack chuckled, catching her longing expression. "Put some meat on your bones."

Isabella snorted and reached for it with a sigh. "That seems to be taking care of itself, I assure you," she replied, the words tart but holding no heat. She smoothed a hand over her stomach as she chewed on her third slice. Today she'd given her child a name and a home and she need not fear that she'd be made destitute. Perhaps the world was gossiping about her, but hidden away here, she need not know about it. Her life was drastically different from what she had hoped for, but she was free of her mother's vitriolic presence and she was too pleased to be alive to find fault.

They both looked up as Henry came in. There were bits of twig in his hair and he was a little rumpled now, but he was still astonishingly attractive. If she had ever been fanciful enough to dream about being swept off her feet by a handsome prince, he would have looked like Henry. Isabella stared at him, the piece of cake suspended before her mouth. She wished that she could paint like he could. Beauty like that deserved recording.

face and Isabella could see the strain and the worry around his eyes. He looked up at her and his fears were etched on his face. "He's talking less, interacting less. It's like he gets locked in his own head and he can't get out."

He paused, staring into space for a long while, and when he turned back to her, she could see anguish in his expression. "I'd like to think you could reach him, if you tried. I'd like to think his interest in you could bring him back into the world like his father did."

"But you don't think I will." Isabella put no accusation into the words. That this man loved and worried for Henry was clear enough. That he should mistrust her was only natural. She could find no blame or resentment towards him for that.

"I don't trust you, no," he said, holding her gaze. "But I'd dearly love you to prove me wrong."

Isabella let out a breath, something between shock and laughter. "Then ... you'll give me a chance?"

Jack nodded, though he didn't look happy about it. "I'll give you a chance. Not like I have a choice," he muttered, glowering a little now.

"Thank you," she said, still unsettled that a man who distrusted her would allow her such a chance, when in his position, she would be doing her utmost to get her out the house. Confused but relieved, she went to get to her feet, but Jack's hand shot out, pinning her wrist to the table. The movement was so sudden, she almost screamed, but the sound died in her throat as she registered the expression in his eyes. Fear prickled down her back at what she saw there.

"You'd best heed my words, though," he said, the words soft, but so menacing. "I'll not let you make him miserable, and there's plenty of places to hide a body in Barcham Woods."

Isabella swallowed and gave a taut nod of understanding. He meant it. He really did.

***

The first challenge to face Isabella was the wedding itself.

Jack had bought a common licence, which meant they need not wait for the banns to be read. They would, however, need to marry in a church, with witnesses. Jack would serve as one, but the priest and the other witness made a crowd of vast proportions to Henry's way of thinking. That this idea was a challenge for him appeared to be an understatement.

"Then don't marry her, lad. Suits me," Jack said, folding his arms as they watched Henry pacing the length of the kitchen and back with increasing speed. His fingers clenched in his hair, which Isabella noted still looked matted and filthy. He'd made no effort to wash or shave in the past twenty-four hours. She would *not* marry him looking like that.

He stopped all at once, his huge chest heaving as his eyes slid to Isabella.

"No other way?" There was pleading and panic in his eyes and it seemed odd to see a man of his size quaking at the idea of having to leave his home and stand before a few people who were new to him.

She shook her head in response to his question, holding his gaze and wishing she knew how to chase the fear from his deep, brown eyes. They seemed to be looking to her to do just that, but she didn't know how.

"We can't get a special licence, Henry. We don't have contacts high up enough in the church and it would take too long." Not that Isabella thought they'd help such an odd couple if it were possible. "Even if we did, there would still be a priest, and another witness," she added, realising it would change nothing but the location. "If we are to marry, you must endure that."

He stared at her, breathing hard.

"Jack will be there," she said, casting around for ways to reassure him. "And then I'll stay."

"You'll stay," he repeated, as Isabella forced herself to take a step closer to him.

She pushed away thoughts of France and a new life. That would not be for some time, when the child was old enough to travel with her without too much difficulty. For the next year or two, her life would be here. She accepted that.

"Yes, Henry," she said, holding his gaze. "I'll stay."

He let out a breath and then swallowed. "Tomorrow?"

"Tomorrow," she agreed, watching a new expression creep into his eyes, determination.

Henry nodded.

"Tomorrow."

He left, closing the door behind him, and they didn't see him again for the rest of the day.

***

There had been little packed for her in the carpet bag Middleton had thrown at her feet. A simple day dress would serve to get married in, though. It wasn't as though she wanted anyone to see her. The material was growing tight across her expanding waistline and her pelisse would no longer fasten.

"You'll need new things," Jack observed, scowling a little as he noticed her stomach pushing through her pelisse.

Isabella nodded. "Can he afford such expenditure?" That her curiosity burned to know about the financial state of the place was obvious. She hadn't dared ask just yet, but she wanted to know she wasn't marrying into penury.

Jack snorted, returning a scathing expression. "He'll manage it," he said, a knowing look in his eyes that made Isabella flush to her toes. "But don't get any ideas. His father gave me the power to manage his money and the estate, and a marriage won't change that. You can count on the fact I checked. You'll not get a penny 'less I say so."

Staring at the man in shock, Isabella discovered she was less surprised by his words, which were only natural, and far more so by Jack himself. His clothes appeared good quality, but showed signs of wear, as did his boots. They ate simple, frugal fare, and she'd observed no signs that the man drank. He was not using Henry's money for his own ends, then. Was the man a saint, or was it a brilliant act? Surely he dipped into the funds a little? She'd never known a servant that hadn't … though, thinking about it, that was her mother speaking. Isabella's personal staff had never stolen from her. They wouldn't dare.

Any further conversation on the matter halted as footsteps sounded on the stairs and Isabella turned to see Henry coming down. She caught her breath. It couldn't be the same man.

It was impossible.

She had never seen such a handsome man in all her days. If he attended a ball, he'd have women throwing themselves at his feet so fast he wouldn't have been able to move. Until they realised he wasn't right in the head, at least. That did not detract from the beauty of him, though.

He moved down the stairs with slow, steady steps. The suit was of the finest quality and cut to perfection to show massive shoulders and powerful arms. The sight of the material that clung to his thick, muscular thighs made Isabella suck in another breath, though she would need to exhale soon. He looked like a duke, like a warrior, until you looked into his eyes.

He glanced at Jack, anxious and seeking reassurance, and the man nodded at him.

"You look right fine, Henry," Jack said, patting him on the shoulder. "Your father would be proud of you."

His eyes slid to Isabella next, such an uncertain, vulnerable tint to the brown that her heart ached for him. What a man he might have been.

"You look very handsome, Henry," she said, smiling at him. There was a flicker of pleasure in his eyes that surprised her, but it disappeared as fast as it had appeared when Jack moved to the front door.

Henry stiffened, his broad shoulders taut, his breathing growing faster.

"You sure you want to do this, lad?" Jack asked, giving Henry a narrow-eyed look that suggested he'd be overjoyed if they cancelled the whole affair.

For a moment, Henry stood still, frozen, and Isabella thought perhaps he would bolt. His eyes found hers again, though, and whatever he saw there seemed to make his mind up. He took a deep breath and walked out of the front door.

The carriage ride to the church was brief, thank heavens, as Henry seemed to sink deeper into himself the further they went from his home. At least with no banns being read, no one would know about the marriage. They'd not be before an audience. Isabella watched, concerned as Henry pressed himself into the corner of the carriage. He seemed to be trying to make himself as small and inconspicuous as possible. Needless to say, it wasn't working. He stared, his gaze intent, at a thin piece of blue ribbon, which he turned and twisted around his fingers in a series of elaborate moves. Isabella watched him covertly, noting that the moves were not random, but a series of complicated turns and twists repeated over and again. Once he finished, he would smooth the silky fabric between his fingers and start over.

"It's a lovely colour," Isabella said, making him start as she spoke to him. "The ribbon," she added, wishing she'd kept her mouth shut as his intense gaze focused on her instead. He said nothing for a moment but watched her. It was unnerving.

"Kingfisher blue," he said, his stare unwavering. "Ultramarine, azurite, smalt, Egyptian blue … cobalt." He stared at her a moment longer and she felt once more she was being studied. "They're in your eyes." Henry turned his attention back to the ribbon, leaving Isabella feeling a little off kilter. Strange as the fellow was, it was the most wonderful compliment she'd ever heard.

Getting Henry to set foot in the church was the next hurdle, and one that Isabella doubted they'd get over. He paced before the big oak doors, agitated and sweating despite the freezing temperature, while the priest gawped at him with growing misgiving. The stony-faced fellow cast dubious glances between him and Isabella, who had been trying to hide the swell of her stomach.

Jack was doing his best to talk Henry into a state of calm and giving him every opportunity to change his mind. Taking him home seemed to be at the top of Jack's list right now. Isabella couldn't blame him. Whatever it was Henry was enduring, it was upsetting them both and she could not help but feel compassion for such a tortured soul. She turned to the priest, furious that a man of God could not feel such empathy for a fellow creature in pain. Instead, the man looked disgusted and even rather afraid.

Despite her condition and her shame, Isabella put her chin up and remembered who she was.

"My fiancé just needs a moment to himself," she said, her voice dripping contempt. "I suggest you take yourself inside and leave him in peace. *At once,"* she added, her tone giving him no doubt he'd regret it if he didn't move. She received a look of equal revulsion as the priest sneered at her belly, but he left them alone.

Isabella snorted, she and Henry were in the same boat now, both outcasts. She turned back to find Henry and Jack both staring at her. It occurred to her then that only his father and Jack had ever defended Henry before. He looked calmer now, his eyes fixed on hers. There was no time to lose, and Isabella walked towards him, determined to get this done. She took his hand.

"Come along then, Henry. If you want to marry me, we must repeat the words to the priest."

Henry stared down at his large hand engulfing her far smaller one, the long fingers curled around hers. He took a breath, loosening and tightening his fingers around hers, as if to assure himself it was real. He looked up at her, warmth and trust in his eyes. Her touch had captivated him, given him confidence, and Isabella experienced a strange sensation at the sight. She felt suddenly protective of him, which was outrageous in the circumstances. It must result from her pregnancy, perhaps? She'd heard it did odd things to a woman's emotions. She held his hand tighter anyway, giving him a little tug of encouragement. Henry continued to stare at her and followed her inside.

Chapter 6

"Wherein Mr and Mrs Barbour are an odd couple."

The wedding breakfast was not what Isabella had imagined for herself.

By the time they returned to Barcham Place, Henry was a sweating, shaking heap. He disappeared, leaping from the carriage before it had even stopped and running into the woodland like the devil himself snapped at his heels.

Isabella looked for Jack, who jumped down from the driver's seat and gave her a grim smile.

"He'll be back soon. Just needs to calm his head. Bit of an ordeal for him, that was."

She nodded and accepted Jack's hand as he helped her down. "I could tell. Why, though? What is it he's so frightened of?"

Jack shook his head. "Not sure frightened is the right word. I think …" He paused, taking off his hat and running his hand through his hair, frowning. "I don't know what goes on with the lad, truth be told, but…" He stopped again and looked at her and Isabella realised he was wondering whether to let her into his and Henry's confidence. She was surprised and gratified when he continued. "You saw that painting of his father, right?"

She nodded, wondering where this was going, but kept her mouth shut, eager to hear more.

"Look at it again," he said, his voice becoming rather awed. "Really look at it and study the detail. See the different flecks of colour in his eyes, his every eyelash defined, the folds of his cravat, the texture of silk and embroidery on his waistcoat. You can even sense what William was feeling, can't you?"

Isabella smiled, though it was a sad expression as she remembered the warmth and amusement in the man's eyes, and the overwhelming sense of sorrow. "He loved his son, and he knew he was dying."

Jack nodded, his expression stark now. "The detail is staggering," he said, sounding so full of wonder that Isabella's throat tightened. "You've not seen some of his big canvases, but when you do, you'll understand better because I think it's how Henry sees the world," he said, the words simple but giving Isabella a glimpse of what Henry experienced. "There's so much detail, so much to take in, it overwhelms him. You add a couple more people to the mix, too much noise, too many emotions, and he can't endure it."

"I didn't realise," Isabella said, wondering why she was apologising, but accepted the sense of guilt.

Jack shrugged and moved back towards the horses. "No one ever does. His father and me are the only ones who ever saw his genius. His father reckoned he was too good for this world, that he needed protecting." He gave her a narrow-eyed glance and Isabella nodded, knowing she was being warned.

"You do a fine job, Jack," she said, her voice quiet, the words sincere.

Jack paused, glancing at her, and she knew he was wondering if she was as sincere as she sounded.

"Put the kettle on, then," he muttered over his shoulder. "I'll see to the horses and then we'll celebrate. I ... I bought a fruit cake," he said, the words a little grudging as he gave her an awkward smile. It was rather endearing.

"Thank you," Isabella replied, walking through the elegant doors of the grand building that had once been the finest in the county. Her home.

***

His gaze flicked between them and then he sat down, looking a bit awkward and staring at the cake, and then back and forth between her and Jack.

"It's all right, we're peaceful. Enjoying a cuppa and this fine cake." Jack's voice was soothing, and Henry's shoulders relaxed.

"Would you like cake, Henry?" Isabella asked, and the air left her lungs in a rush as the man shot her a pleased smile. Good Lord. She had never seen him smile before. It was a devastating expression that stole her breath. The man had the talent of a genius, the face of an angel, and the emotional capacity of ... of she didn't know what. A child? An imbecile? She didn't know. For the first time, she found herself curious, though, wanting to know the answer to the enigma that was Henry Barbour, her husband. The realisation that he really was her husband hit her hard and she almost dropped the plate she was passing him. He took it, smiling and lowering his eyes to the cake she'd given him. His eyelashes were thick and long, hiding those warm brown eyes.

"That carpet bag," Jack said, startling Isabella, who was watching her beautiful husband with rapt concentration. "That all the stuff you left with?"

Isabella turned back to him and gave Jack a twisted smile. "I didn't leave, I was ejected, and that thrown at my feet."

Jack frowned, a dark expression that surprised her. "They really turned you out of doors in your condition, in the middle of the night? In this weather?"

"They did no such thing," Isabella replied, amused and touched by his indignation. "My mother did it, they just obeyed her."

"No wonder you grew up to be such a little bitch," Jack said, shaking his head as Isabella choked on her cake. "Not like you had a chance to be anything else, I reckon."

She stared at him, the furious retort that was hovering on the tip of her tongue losing its impetus as she considered his words.

There had been no malice in his tone. Isabella reached for her tea, her hand shaking a little as she took a sip. Her anger at Jack slid away, replaced with something far hotter that burned with fury as she thought of her mother and the life she'd endured. She had never been given affection, never played with, never told she'd done well or she looked pretty or that her mother was proud of her. Emotion built in her chest, making her heart pound and her eyes prickle.

"No. I didn't have a chance," she said, the words angry as she put the teacup down with a clatter. Henry jumped out of his skin. "Sorry!" she exclaimed, reaching out to place her hand on his before he could bolt, or she had even thought about her actions.

Henry stilled, eyes wide and staring at her hand, and then letting out a breath. Isabella flushed a little, withdrawing her touch as Henry returned his attention to the cake. She let out a breath of her own, relieved, and then turned back to find Jack staring at her in astonishment.

"Well, I'm buggered," he murmured.

***

The deal that Henry would marry her, and in return he could draw her as much as he wanted, began the next morning.

Isabella woke and stretched, luxurious beneath the covers. She had plans to set Jack to work on her room today, but felt toasty warm snuggled under the blankets, the fire still blazing. That someone must have come into the room to keep it going was disturbing, but probably not as much as it ought to have been. Her priorities were changing.

She'd gone to sleep late, half afraid that Henry might appear and demand his rights as her husband, but he'd never come. She wondered if he even knew what happened between men and women? Was he a virgin still? That intriguing thought was still in her head as she opened her eyes and came face to face with the man himself.

She screamed.

Henry leapt from the bed, dropping his drawing-board, paper, and pencil, and backed off, looking so much more terrified and appalled than Isabella herself that she forced herself to calm down.

"Henry!" she exclaimed, trying her best to moderate her voice as she drew the bedcovers up to her neck. "What are you doing in my room at this hour?"

He gave her a wary look before sending a longing glance at the paper and pencil he'd dropped.

"I married you. You must stay now, and I can draw you. You said I could," he added, a defiant glint in his eyes.

Isabella looked back at him, somewhat surprised. It was the longest sentence she'd heard him speak.

"Yes, I did," she agreed, wondering if she ought to feel afraid or threatened by this large man in her bedroom, even if he was her husband. "But you can't just come in and draw me while I'm sleeping."

"I can," he objected, gesturing to the paper as he inched closer to it. "I did."

Isabella snorted, amused despite herself. "That doesn't mean you ought to," she replied, her tone dry.

Henry shrugged his huge shoulders, unimpressed. "I didn't wake you. I was quiet, so you could sleep."

"That's true," Isabella allowed, trying to be fair to him. Jack had said he didn't understand the rules like most people, so she would have to teach him. "But I cannot have you coming in and out of my room as you please. It's not right."

Henry moved to pick up his paper and pencil and the wooden board he leaned on to draw. "It is," he replied, the words firm. "I married you."

Isabella quailed a little, wondering if he was implying his rights extended further than that, but he settled himself back on the bed and showed no interest in anything further than drawing her.

"Henry!" she exclaimed as he put a new piece of paper out and began once more. "I won't let you draw me." Isabella scowled, folding her arms over the bedcovers in fury.

"Can't stop me," Henry said, his tone placid. "I'm bigger than you," he added, which might have been alarming if there hadn't been the slightest glimmer of amusement in his eyes.

Isabella scowled harder and wondered just how much he understood.

"Go away!" she insisted, feeling irater than ever as he ignored her. She may as well have been a statue for all the good it did her. Henry sketched with the single-minded concentration of a man absorbed. Sitting back against her pillows with a flounce and a huff of fury, Isabella ignored him and hoped he went away.

A good forty minutes later, her stomach growled, and Henry was still sketching.

"At least show me what you've done," she snapped, reaching for one of the growing pile of sketches on the bed. Henry's hand slammed down on the papers and Isabella jumped. "They're of me," she objected, refusing to be cowed by him. He might be the size of a prize bull, but he wasn't exactly bright. She could handle him.

"They're my work," he countered, tugging the papers further from her.

"Show me," she insisted, frustrated by his obstinacy.

To her surprise, Henry paused, staring at the papers and then looked up at her, a smile at his face that made her breath catch. Good heavens, she hoped she could get used to that smile, it was disarming in the worst way. "Say please," he said, grinning at her now.

"Why should I?" she demanded, more out of curiosity than any unwillingness to do so.

"Because you must ask permission to touch," Henry replied, a note to his voice which made her skin prickle with awareness. He was staring at her now with that intensity burning in his eyes that made her doubt he was the half-wit she'd believed him to be.

"Please, Henry," she said, the words grudging as she didn't want him to feel he could manoeuvre her. Not him.

Henry pulled the drawings up the bed where she could reach them, and Isabella turned them to face her. One by one she sifted through them, and her heart grew cold as she saw the image of an angry, hard-faced young woman staring back at her. Her throat ached, and she couldn't swallow.

"Is that what you see, when you look at me?" she asked, hearing misery in the words.

Henry shook his head, his expression a little puzzled as he gazed at her. "It's what you showed me. It's the mask you wear. Everyone has one," he added as she stared back at him, bewildered by his words.

"What do you mean?" she asked, though she knew what he meant well enough.

"This is how I see you," he said, picking the drawing up that had fallen to the floor. He handed it to her and Isabella felt tears prickle at her eyes. She had received lavish compliments in her time, told she was a beauty, a diamond, the embodiment of perfection, yet she had never felt it. The men were always flattering her for their own ends and her own eye was too critical. She'd been well trained to pick out the flaws by her mother, who was only too ready to point them out to her. Her hair was too yellow, a common shade. The heart shape of her face was attractive enough, but her nose too narrow, her cheekbones not high enough. Her mouth was a perfect little cupid's bow, but too small.

None of this showed in Henry's drawing.

The sketch revealed a sensuous image, a beautiful woman lost in dreams. Her hair spilled over the pillow in luxuriant waves, serenely content in her repose, the faintest trace of a smile at her lips.

Isabella felt a tear gather and fall and slid the picture back to Henry, afraid to damage it by crying over the paper. Once more, her emotions seemed to push at her chest, threatening to overwhelm her. Henry got to his feet, his expression one of confusion and alarm.

"Why are you crying?" he demanded, a thread of panic in his voice.

Isabella wiped the tear away with the back of her hand. "I'm not," she said, aware that he looked anxious again and not wanting to upset him further.

"Don't lie," he shouted, making her jump. "I saw … I …"

She gasped, about to explain, but before she could say another word, he'd slammed the bedroom door behind him. It opened again a moment later, a furious-looking Jack stalked in.

"Good heavens!" Isabella cried, snatching the bedcovers to her neck once more. "Am I on public display?"

"What'd you do to Henry?" he demanded with no preamble. "He just went past me in a right passion."

"Nothing!" she retorted. "I woke up to find him sitting on my bed, drawing me!" The words were indignant, and Jack hesitated, knowing as well as she did that this was pushing the limits of their agreement. He looked at the bed, though, and the half dozen sketches of a bad-tempered young woman. "Looks like you didn't throw him out right away," he observed, his tone insinuating.

"As if I could!" Isabella shot back, furious and horrified, especially as she'd noted what a handsome man Henry was. Jack wasn't to know how appalling her one encounter with a man had been. She had no desire to repeat the experience, no matter how handsome he was. Not with a man who was touched in the head. What an idea! Good Lord, what if she was to have a child like him?

"All right," Jack said, relenting a little. "I'll have a word with him, though I doubt it'll stop him," he added. "And don't bother trying to find the key to the door. You'll only make him angry, and then you'll get woken up, all right." There was a warning note to his voice which, made Isabella stare with alarm.

"You mean to say I can't lock my own door?" She stared at him in horror.

Jack shook his head. "No. I'm saying it's not a good idea. Henry don't like locked doors. He worries what's behind them. He'll get upset and likely break it down."

"Am I to have no privacy at all?" That both men had waltzed into her room without a 'by your leave' seemed to answer the question, but she asked it anyway, furious by now.

She watched as Jack scratched his head, his expression thoughtful. "I'll speak to him," he said, nodding. "But you remember," he added, his tone accusing. *"You* wanted to stay."

There wasn't much she could say to that, so she glowered at him.

"Well, then," he asked, astonishing her as he returned to his first question. "How'd you upset him?"

Isabella threw herself back against the cushions with a flounce, rolling her eyes at him. The impropriety of Jack conversing with her while she remained in bed was staggering, but really, what was the point? "It was that," she said, gesturing to the lovely drawing on her lap. "It ..." She paused, her tone softening as she looked at it again. "It's so lovely. I ... I don't know," she said, throwing up her hands. "It touched me. I've never seen myself look so beautiful and it made me feel rather weepy, I suppose."

"Oh, Lord," Jack said, shaking his head. "Don't tell me you turned into a watering pot?"

"No!" Isabella sat up a little straighter, indignant at the accusation. "One tear!" she objected. "And I wiped it away when I saw he was bothered by it."

"So," Jack said, watching her. "He asked why you was crying and you said …"

Isabella hesitated, remembering now that Jack had advised her to be honest, always. "I… I said I wasn't," she replied, feeling foolish now, though heaven knew why.

Jack shook his head at her, his expression resigned. "He'll think you lied to him. You *did* lie to him."

"I know!" Isabella snapped, frustrated now. "I just didn't want to upset him further …"

"He's not a child," Jack said, the words irritated now. "Don't treat him like one. Why not tell him the picture was beautiful, and it moved you? He'd have understood that. It would have pleased him."

Isabella bit her lip, wondering the same thing. It would have been easy enough to confide her feelings to him, and she felt certain he would have understood, just as Jack said. So why not? She would have seen him smile, too, seen that happy warmth bloom in his trusting brown eyes. Yes. *That* was why she hadn't.

Chapter 7

"Wherein Henry plans for the future."

"Henry, I'm telling you, it isn't decent. I won't do it." Jack gave Henry his list back and folded his arms, aware of Henry's determined gaze watching him. "No." Henry stared, silent, but displeased. Jack huffed and shook his head. "You can't expect me to ask for such things," Jack wheedled, knowing he would not win this. Henry had made his mind up, and he'd not let it go now.

Henry slid the piece of paper with the lists of items he wanted from town back across the table and Jack groaned. Going into a book shop was bad enough, the snooty devil that ran it always treated him like dirt. Having to order every available medical text on pregnancy and childbirth was the outside of enough. There was no way around it, though. Henry would get back at him if he didn't do as he asked. As he was showing signs of joining the world again, Jack couldn't risk sending him into a month of silence as he fumed at being thwarted. It gave him an opportunity, though.

Jack let out a breath and sat back in his chair, regarding Henry now, eyes narrowed.

"I tell you what, Henry. If I do this for you, you give something in return."

Henry's shoulders stiffened, a wary expression clouding his face.

"Isabella is a lady," Jack began, wondering how best to proceed. "Life here is very different for her, difficult, too. You're her husband now, and it's your duty to make her happy. You remember, when your father spoke about your mother, about their life together?"

Henry nodded, a slight frown at his brow as he considered Jack's words.

"She won't want to live like we do, Henry."

Henry's frown deepened. He shifted in his chair and stared down at his hands on the table-top, avoiding Jack's eyes now. To be honest, Jack wasn't sure why he was interceding on Isabella's behalf except ... he hoped. He still didn't trust her an inch. That she was plotting to run away the minute a better opportunity presented itself was more than likely. Yet the way she'd acted with Henry a time or two, instinctively, and with no fear, it made him wonder. If Jack could make things comfortable for her, more like what she was used to, and if she could see the man Henry really was ...

"I think you need to start by giving her some of the things she wants," Jack said, praying that the woman wouldn't prove him a fool. "Let her have her room decorated, and the parlour, too. Give her a place that's clean and pretty, where she can be comfortable."

Henry's hands clenched as he shook his head. "No people."

Jack sighed. "Look, you're usually out all day anyway, they could come and work while you're not here. You'd be none the wiser. I'd make sure they're gone before you get home."

Henry shook his head, still avoiding Jack's eye.

"Don't you want her to be happy, Henry? Don't you want her to stay?"

Henry looked up then, fear in his eyes, such anxiety visible that Jack worried all the more. "I married her, she has to stay now."

Jack shrugged, hoping he was doing the right thing. If he upset the man too much, there'd be hell to pay. "She might not," he said, his voice cautious. "If she's unhappy. Women can leave, even married ones, they can run away, especially if their husbands don't treat them well."

Jack watched the play of emotions across Henry's face. It was strange how some days he was so shuttered up, and others he'd give himself away, his heart an open book. He stared at the table, at his big fists clenched one beside the other.

"While I'm not here?" he asked, the words careful. He glanced up at Jack, who gave him an encouraging smile.

"You wouldn't see them. I'll make sure."

Henry chewed at his lip, mulling this over. "I want to draw her," he muttered, and Jack realised what he was getting at. Their conversations were often a kind of short-hand, with Jack filling in the gaps as best he could. Knowing Henry like he did, he usually understood.

"Yes, that's a problem," Jack replied, rubbing his chin as he considered. "She'll not be able to stay out all day like you do, even if she goes with you. Not in her condition." Jack pondered the problem. "Well, we'll get the decorators to work short days. It'll likely cost twice as much, but that hardly matters to you, does it?" He wondered if Isabella had guessed just how wealthy Henry was. He certainly wasn't going to volunteer the information. "You'll have to make sure she keeps warm, though. Look after her, make sure she rests. Take blankets and light a fire for her, eh?"

Jack watched as Henry nodded, his face grave. "I'll look after her, and the baby," he said, the words serious.

"Good lad," Jack said, giving a sigh of relief. "One more thing, though," he added, remembering his conversation with Isabella. "You didn't ought to let yourself into her room whenever you like."

Henry's expression turned mutinous in a second and he folded his massive arms. "We're married." The words were succinct, and Jack shot him an anxious glance. "That's true," he said, treading this dangerous path with care. "But you wouldn't like it if she disturbed you while you were working."

To his astonishment, Henry frowned at that and then shook his head. "Wouldn't mind."

Jack gaped. He knew exactly how much Henry minded being interrupted while he worked. He stared, bewildered, so much so that Henry shifted, uncomfortable under his astonished scrutiny.

"I like her," Henry added, sounding defiant as he sat up straighter, folding his arms tighter still.

"Well!" Jack said, rather indignant. "I like that. And what about me?"

Henry looked startled by the tone of Jack's voice, not understanding his annoyance at being usurped. "I like you, too, Jack," he said, giving Jack the impression he'd bolt from the room if he didn't moderate his tone. "But I like to look at her. She's pretty."

Jack stared for a moment and then burst out laughing, finding himself laughing harder at the relief in Henry's face.

"Well, I can't fault you there, lad," he admitted, amused now. "She's easier on the eye than my ugly mug, I grant you that."

Henry looked puzzled and then got to his feet. He paused and then turned back to Jack. "Not ugly at all, Jack," he said, shaking his head and looking perplexed. "You have a good face. Honest and strong. Kind. It shows in your eyes."

Jack felt a lump in his throat as Henry left, and laughed a little more quietly. The fellow was disarming without even trying. He wondered if Isabella could resist the real Henry if he allowed her to see the man he really was.

***

Isabella was unimpressed at the thought of spending hours of the next day outside.

The weather had improved, and the sun shone, at least, but it was still frosty and cold. By nightfall, they huddled around the fire as the temperature plummeted. She stared into the flames, now, and spending the whole of tomorrow freezing while Henry studied her did not appeal.

Still, Jack had no doubt had to work to get Henry to agree to have the decorators in, and Isabella was excited about it. She'd enjoyed choosing from the paper samples and material swatches they had supplied for her, spending days poring over them, and the catalogues of furniture that Jack had brought for her from Bath.

Her mother had never allowed her to choose things for herself before. Lady Scranford had always ruled the house, its décor, and Isabella's wardrobe. Not that she'd been badly dressed. Her mother had a good eye for fashion, but her choices were always rather severe of cut, and the colours muted. Isabella had longed for something with a splash of bright colour, something that caught the eye. The deep blue dress she'd been wearing the night her mother had thrown her out had been the only one she'd ever got her own way on. Her mother had never allowed her to wear it out of the house before, though. Ironic, really.

All the time she had pondered and made lists of her choices, Henry had studied her.

She looked up now as she made her choices for the parlour they sat in, finding his dark eyes upon her as they flicked back and forth between her and his paper. The muted scratch of the pencil was as constant as the clock ticking on the mantle and Jack's soft snoring from his chair by the fire.

Henry sat, cross-legged at her feet, silent and still other than the movement of his hand and his eyes. He'd not spoken a word to her since her reaction to his drawing the week before and she knew he was punishing her. Though she'd tried to speak to him, he refused to answer, and he wouldn't show her his work.

Isabella vacillated between frustration, anger, and, to her own surprise, sadness. She became ever more curious about him as the days passed, and his stubborn silence vexed her.

He'd held to his word and kept himself clean and shaved and well-dressed, something she was regretting demanding of him. It was far easier to think of him as dim-witted and peculiar when he looked like half-man, half-bear. Sitting at her feet and looking like a fallen angel in the fire-light, his eyes so full of softness and warmth, it became hard to remember just how strange he was.

She pushed the furniture catalogue away and looked back at the fashion plates Jack had supplied her. The list of her choices sat by her elbow, her only decision remaining the fabrics to choose. The swatches scattered the table and Isabella stared at the brighter fabrics with something like longing. There was an emerald green, a bright sunny yellow, and a fiery vivid orange. They called to her from a sea of pastel pinks and safe muted colours. There were plenty of blues this season, at least, and she'd chosen several gowns in various shades. She refused to acknowledge that Henry's compliment to her eyes had anything to do with her choices.

On hearing the rustle of paper, she looked around to find Henry pulling another clean sheet from the pile on the floor beside him. Suddenly she found she wanted to speak to him. Jack had said he would likely cut her off for weeks, months, even, as punishment for lying to him. Why that bothered her so, she didn't know, but it did.

"Henry."

He stilled for a fraction of a second, but then carried on as though she'd not spoken.

"Henry, I'm sorry." The words hung in the air and Isabella realised she'd never apologised before. Never apologise, never explain. That was one of her mother's many rules of life. Well, Isabella didn't have to abide by those rules now. In fact, she felt determined to break as many of them as possible. "I am," she added as he still didn't react. "I was crying," she admitted, feeling foolish talking when he was ignoring her, but determined to get a reaction. "I denied it because you looked upset and I worried about making you feel worse." Henry picked up his pencil, moving it to the paper, though she believed he was paying attention now. "The truth is, your drawing made me cry. It was so beautiful, Henry, and … and I couldn't believe anyone could see me like that."

He looked up and Isabella's breath caught. There was an expectant look in his eyes, watchful, waiting, and she knew if she wanted forgiveness, she needed to continue.

"I'm not a very nice person, you see, and … and you made me look so lovely, I …" Isabella swallowed, sucking in a breath to steady her emotions. "I'd like to be like the woman you drew. She looked … she looked like a good person. She looked happy."

Henry frowned, puzzlement in his eyes. "I drew you," he said.

Isabella laughed and shook her head. "You drew me sleeping." He frowned harder, and she smiled at him, her expression rueful. "I suspect I'm easier to like when I'm asleep."

He didn't laugh at her joke, but looked troubled instead. "I like you now, and you're not asleep." He put his paper aside, moving to sit up on his knees beside her. "Are … are you unhappy?" he asked, such concern in his voice that Isabella felt quite taken aback. Why should he care if she was happy or not?

She shrugged, unsure of how to answer such a question as a lump formed in her throat. Isabella turned away from the apprehension in his eyes, staring down at the table, scattered with patterns and fabrics. His hand taking hers made her jump.

Henry snatched his own hand away, startled by her reaction, and she smiled at him, shaking her head. "I'm sorry. You startled me," she said, wondering why she was apologising. It wasn't like she wanted to encourage him to touch her.

He reached out again, and she allowed him to take her hand. There was pleasure and curiosity in his eyes as he placed her hand against his, palm on palm. He traced the outline, each of her fingers, so much smaller than his large hand. "I'll make you happy," he said, his voice low and filled with sincerity. Isabella felt her breath catch at the expression in his eyes as he looked up. "I'd like to," he added, that dazzling smile adding force to his words.

Before she could think of an appropriate reply, if such a thing existed in the circumstances, he had moved away, returning to his work. Isabella stared at him, bewildered and unsettled, but he was absorbed now. He didn't speak another word for the rest of the evening.

Chapter 8

"Wherein Isabella sees Henry for the first time."

The decorators were due to arrive to prepare the rooms, emptying them of furniture. Isabella found herself torn between excitement at seeing her vision come to life and dismay at having to spend a large part of the day outside.

Her breath clouded before her, little white puffs on the icy air as she stamped her feet. Wrapped up warm with as many layers as she could fit over her, she still felt chilly. Henry picked up his heavy bag, full of drawing supplies and a picnic, and slung it over his shoulder. She noted with surprise he carried a blanket and a cushion tucked under his arm, too. Had Jack given him those, she wondered, or had he thought to bring them himself?

Jack would take her order to the dressmaker tomorrow when he returned to Bath. For now, she'd had to make do with the clothes and items still in her room. An old pair of lady's boots discovered in the back of a wardrobe had helped. Of finely tooled leather, the workmanship was exquisite, if old-fashioned, but a little too big. Her feet were already cold though, and she huffed with irritation as Henry strode off down the garden, towards the woodland. He clearly expected her to keep up.

She did her best for the first half an hour, but the woodland made walking far more difficult, and Isabella rested, leaning against a tree and puffing hard. Henry didn't appear to have noticed, but she was indignant now and lowered herself to sit on a fallen trunk. She'd go back home if he didn't turn and wait for her. Her back ached, now, and as she sat, the baby gave her a swift kick.

"Don't you start," she muttered, smiling as she smoothed her hands over her stomach.

As she looked up, she noticed Henry turn, having realised she was no longer following. He dropped the bag and the blanket, his face filled with alarm as he ran back to her and knelt at her feet.

"What?" he demanded, eyes full of concern. "What's wrong?"

"Nothing's wrong," she said, her voice tart. "But I can't keep up with you when you stride off like that. I'm carrying a baby, remember. It's tiring."

With remorse shining in his eyes, Henry reached out, placing his large hand on her stomach. Isabella yelped with surprise at the intimacy of it and shoved his hand away.

"Don't do that," she said, breathless and shocked.

Henry folded his arms, his hands tucked under his armpits, looking mortified. "It's all right?"

Isabella's heart softened at the fear she saw in his eyes as she realised he'd been acting out of concern, not taking liberties. "Yes," she said, feeling rather awful now. "Yes, Henry. It wasn't your fault. I'm afraid you must go a lot slower, though, and not too far."

He nodded and settled himself down, crossing his legs. He had taken her at her word. Isabella laughed, amused.

"I can go further than this," she said, smiling at him. "I just needed to rest for a moment. I'm fine now."

She watched as he frowned, giving her a searching look, followed by a tentative smile. "Sure?"

"I'm sure."

They continued at a much slower pace, and Isabella was struck by how attentive he was now. He helped her over difficult patches and ensured they stopped if she seemed breathless. It seemed he didn't always understand what she needed, but if she pointed it out, he was willing to bend for her. Up to a point, at least.

At last they arrived at their destination, and despite the cold, Isabella discovered she was glad she'd come.

It was a beautiful spot with far-reaching views across the countryside. The only downside was the clear view it gave of the river. Isabella shuddered as she remembered, and then started as Henry took her hand, giving her fingers a squeeze.

"We won't go down there," Henry said, releasing her fingers again and gesturing to the river with concern in his eyes. "It's calm here, though. Quiet," he added. "No waves."

Isabella frowned, not understanding what waves he was referring to, but realising that he'd read her distress with perfect accuracy, without her saying a word.

"Thank you," she replied, watching as he set about collecting wood for a fire and ringing it with stones before he reached for the tinder box. He was most efficient, quite at home in his surroundings, and within a short time, a merry fire was blazing. He arranged the blanket with care and placed the cushion against a tree to support her back. Isabella settled down, quite comfortable, bearing in mind they were in the heart of the woodland.

She watched him arrange his own supplies before picking up his pencil and staring at her, tilting his head as he looked at her with that penetrating gaze.

"Don't you ever get bored with drawing the same thing, over and over?" Isabella asked him, wondering how long he'd keep this up for. Not that she minded now. She was becoming rather used to being observed. It was actually quite flattering.

"Not the same thing," he replied, puzzled by her words, going on his expression. "Changes all the time."

Isabella laughed, shaking her head. "But I don't change that much. You draw me dozens of times in a day. Perhaps my position changes, but nothing else."

Henry looked up from his drawing, frowning and shaking his head. "That's wrong," he said, staring at her. He looked up at the sky and pointed at the sun. "Your hair is gold in this light, like ripe barley. Last night it was darker, the firelight changed it. It was … it was bronze and gold, with hints of copper. Not the same at all."

She stared at him, refusing to acknowledge the pleasure his words gave her. "But, Henry, you are drawing with a grey pencil. The pictures are all grey." She felt a little smug, like she'd caught him out, but Henry snorted and shook his head. He gave her a pitying look.

"These are just my preparation drawings," he said, rolling his eyes now as she raised her eyebrows at him. "I can remember the colour, just as if I were looking at it." Then he smirked and pulled out a large wooden box from his bag, opening the lid to show an array of water colour brushes and paints. "I will make paint sketches, too, though."

"Oh," she replied, chastened and a little amused to get a set down from him.

She sighed and sat back, closing her eyes. The fire burned fierce and hot now, thawing out her frozen toes, and a faint brush of warmth from the sun touched her face. It was rather pleasant.

Isabella dozed as Henry worked. He never seemed to mind how she looked, or ask that she pose for him, just drawing her as she was. As the morning stretched to midday, her stomach gave a growl of protest, however, and she stretched and yawned.

"I'm hungry. Would you get the picnic, please?"

Henry ignored her reaching for a new sheet of paper as she'd changed position.

"Henry," she said again, her tone a little louder now. "Please, would you stop, I'm hungry."

She sighed as he remained unresponsive and got up to fetch it herself. Let him try to draw an empty space. Just as she began to move the baby kicked and she sucked in a breath, clutching at her stomach. That had been the strongest one yet.

Isabella heard the clatter of a pencil falling and Henry was beside her, wide-eyed.

"What is it?"

Isabella let out a rather breathless little laugh. "The baby kicked. It was so strong it took me by surprise." She exclaimed as the child repeated the action and she laughed again. "My, it's lively today," she exclaimed, grinning at him.

Henry moved his hand, as if he might touch her again, but then his face fell, and he tucked his hands under his arms. Isabella watched him, seeing his desire to feel the child moving reflected in his eyes. Jack had said he wanted to understand everything, he wasn't trying to overstep a mark. From the innocent curiosity in his expression, she believed it.

"Would …" She hesitated, not quite believing she was inviting him herself. "Would you like to feel the baby move?"

The smile that broke over his face was magical, pure delight, and Isabella could not help but return it.

"Give me your hand," she instructed. Isabella focused on that, trying not to look at his face. It would make the moment too intimate, too … too something. She didn't know what, only that she didn't trust it.

His hand was rough, calloused, and as she guided him beneath her pelisse, the sensation of his large, warm palm pressing against her stomach was enough to make her cheeks flush. He waited, his expression rapt, and Isabella thought perhaps the baby would not perform for him. A moment later, it proved her wrong as it kicked again. Henry's eyes widened, staring at her with wonder. He laughed then, delighted, and Isabella felt a rush of warmth for him.

Jack was right. Henry needed protecting. No one could react in such a way, with such artless joy, if there was an ounce of malice in them.

"Do you think it's a boy or a girl?" he asked, his brown eyes sparkling with interest.

"I don't know," Isabella replied, watching his face. My word, but he was handsome. "A boy, perhaps, the way it kicks."

He grinned at her, shaking his head. "No. A girl. I would like a girl," he said, looking down at her stomach, awed by the prospect. "She'll be beautiful, like her mother." Isabella felt her heart kick this time, a strange, fluttering, unnerving sensation. "With hair the colour of ripe barley," he added. He looked up then, removing his hand from her stomach, and reaching out instead to touch her hair. He coiled a lock around his finger as Isabella held her breath. She didn't dare move, unsure of what she wanted from the moment. Fear kicked in and she decided she wanted him to stop, but she said nothing, not wanting to hurt his feelings despite her misgivings. "So soft," he whispered. "Like a yellow ribbon."

He looked back at her, then, and perhaps saw something in her eyes, as he dropped his hand, his expression becoming a little guarded.

"Could we have something to eat now, please?" Isabella asked, her tone gentle, experiencing a sudden sense of regret that he'd withdrawn from her, which was ridiculous. He wasn't a man in the full sense of the word, despite his beauty. He could never be a real husband. "I think the baby is hungry," she added with a smile. "It's hoping Jack put some cake in."

His eyes flicked to hers, returning her smile, though it was shy now and a little reserved.

They ate their picnic in silence, though it wasn't uncomfortable. Isabella watched, amused at the volume of food Henry could devour in a short space of time. No wonder his bag had been so heavy.

After lunch, Henry was gracious enough to allow her to stretch her legs before he returned to work. This time, Isabella lay down on the thick rug, and tucked the cushion beneath her stomach.

"I never realised being with child was so exhausting," she said, smothering a yawn. Despite having dozed on and off for most of the morning, she felt sleepy. With the fire warming her face and the winter sun at her back, she sighed and settled herself for a nap.

What seemed to her moments later, she awoke to find Henry crouching over her.

"Time to go home," he said as she blinked in surprise.

"It is?" Henry helped her to sit up and she noticed the sun had moved around, the air a little chillier than before.

"It will get colder now," he said, and she realised he'd already packed up his work and the remnants of their lunch. "Need to get you home. Mustn't catch a chill," he said, his voice serious.

Isabella nodded, touched by his concern, and allowed him to escort her home.

Chapter 9

"Wherein hasty words bring pain and the beauty of art stirs an anxious heart."

Isabella stared at the fabric swatches in her hand. Although Jack had remained tight-lipped about the state of Henry's financial affairs, he said they'd get whatever she needed. According to Jack, Henry wanted her to have whatever she wanted, and she wasn't to worry about the cost.

The trouble was she didn't know if he was just being generous and she was pushing his finances, or if this was a drop in the ocean. She'd written a list of things she couldn't do without, but … the bright emerald fabric called to her. It was hardly appropriate, to be wearing such bold colours after her fall from grace, however, and it wasn't as if she was going anywhere.

It was late now, the fire in the parlour burning low. The decorators would move in here once her bedroom was done, but for now it was peaceful. Jack was pretending to read some sporting journal, though his eyes were closed, and Henry was drawing her.

He'd left his clean paper on the table, and got up to reach for another sheet, when his attention fell upon the fabric swatches. She watched as he reached for them, his thumb testing each piece of material. He picked up the green one and his eyes lifted to hers, considering. He set that swatch aside and smiled as he picked up a vibrant orange one she would never dare wear.

"Get this one," he said, a note of command in his voice she'd only heard once or twice before.

"I can't wear that, Henry," she protested. "In my condition, and after everything …" She paused and shook her head. "I've no wish to draw attention to myself. Though I love the green," she added with a wistful note.

Henry picked up both the orange and the green, considering them for a moment.

"Get this one," he repeated, his tone brooking no argument.

Isabella sighed with dismay as he placed the orange one in front of her.

"I want to paint you wearing it," he added, that intense look he got sometimes glittering in his eyes. "You'll look like the goddess of summer."

Isabella blinked, the green gown forgotten in the light of such fulsome praise.

"Very well," she said, her voice faint as she dipped her head to hide a blush. She picked up her pen, dipping it in the inkwell and added the orange fabric to the list of materials for her gowns. Henry's large hand appeared in front of her eyes, as he set the green swatch down on her list.

"Get this one, too," he added, his words soft. "Because you like it."

***

As the men decorating the rooms only worked short days, it seemed to take forever to complete the job.

Isabella kept her word and spent her days outside with Henry as he worked on various poses. It appeared he was working towards a specific painting now, though he would not tell her what he had in mind.

Some days he was easy to be with, like the first day she had accompanied him. On those days, she could almost forget his odd ways and feel affection for him. Others, he seemed quiet and tense, for no reason she could fathom. Those days were hard, as he would not speak with her and his concentration was absolute.

Isabella had tried various means to get through to him. Keeping up a constant stream of chatter, wheedling and pleading for a response, shouting at him, and walking off in a huff. None of them had worked. In fact, this last attempt had not pleased him at all. She'd relented, noting his agitation, and returned to sit for him. It changed nothing, though, he'd shut down and not spoken a word all week.

She could only feel grateful that the decorating was all done.

Isabella stood in the middle of her bedroom, a rather strange sensation blooming in her chest. Pride was a part of it. She had never had free range to decorate as she pleased before, never had a choice to makeover colours or textures. Though she'd been excited to see the results, she'd been equally terrified. What if she'd chosen badly? What if it looked dreadful and she'd wasted all that money? The idea had kept her awake at night. She hadn't dared even peek, too frightened to discover it was a horrible mistake. Instead. she'd walked past the door and straight on to the bedroom she'd been given for the duration.

Now, though … She clapped her hands together, wanting to squeal with pleasure. Instead, she ran downstairs to the kitchen to where Jack was preparing something dubious for dinner. The familiar scent of burning lingered on the air.

"Jack, where's Henry?"

Jack looked up from the pot he'd been staring at with a quizzical expression and jerked his head.

"In the library," he said as she turned and ran out again without another word.

"Henry, Henry," she said, running into the library. She discovered Henry's dark head bent over the desk, studying a heavy text book. He didn't look up. "Oh, Henry, please come. I want to show you something."

He didn't budge, and the surge of disappointment that flooded her was startling. She really had wanted to show him.

"Please," she said again, her voice low now, and rather sad, as she expected him to continue ignoring her. To her surprise, he looked up, a wary expression in his eyes. Sensing weakness, she ran to the desk and took his hand, tugging at him. It was akin to tugging at a mountain, but after a moment, he relented and got to his feet. "Thank you," she said, beaming at him. "I know I'm not an artist like you but ... Oh, do come," she said, impatient now as she towed him behind her.

She felt rather nervous as she opened the door and pulled him through. After all, Henry was a genius as far as his art was concerned, and ... If he didn't like it, she'd be rather crushed.

Henry stared, turning in a circle. For a long time, he looked and looked, a surprised expression in his eyes as Isabella almost bounced with impatience.

"Well?" she demanded. *"Well?"*

He took his time, as ever, moving to run his fingers over the paper on the walls, to touch the curtains and inspect the furnishings. He even knelt, sinking his fingers into thick rugs that covered the floor.

"You're wrong," he said at length, making Isabella's heart drop. "You are an artist."

Isabella gave a crow of triumph, delighted by his words. Why his opinion mattered so much, she didn't know, but it did, and she took pleasure in his approval.

"I like this," he said, stretching out on the rug before the fire. He lay on his side, one large hand stroking the pile of the carpet with a rapt expression. Henry looked up at her, his eyes warm. "Come and see."

Isabella hesitated, but Henry held his hand out to her. With difficulty under the growing bulk of the baby, she got to the floor.

"I hope you can get me up again," she muttered, feeling awkward now and wishing she'd stayed standing.

"Of course," he said, grinning at her. "Though you must stay here until I let you go."

Isabella looked away from him, troubled by their sudden intimacy. She reminded herself of his behaviour outside the church, of the blue ribbon, and a dozen other peculiarities that marked him as odd, not right ... not normal.

"We must go down for dinner soon," she said, hoping Jack would call them.

Henry sighed and lay down on his back, his hands resting on his chest. "I know," he said, a thread of amusement in his voice. "I smelt burning."

Isabella snorted, as he turned his head to grin at her. She wondered if this might be a good opportunity to broach a tricky subject, as he seemed relaxed.

"If we got a cook, we wouldn't have to eat burnt food, you know," she said, keeping the words light and unconcerned. "And it would make life much easier for poor Jack."

The change was instant. Henry's face closed off and he sat up, turning away from her. "No."

A sudden rush of anger with him, for his stupid fears, made her lash out for no reason she could understand.

"It's just one person, for heaven's sake," she snapped. "How can a man of your size be frightened of a cook? It's ridiculous."

He was on his feet in a moment, and before she could take the words back, the door had slammed hard.

Isabella cursed herself. To her dismay, she discovered she didn't care about the blasted cook as much as she did that she'd hurt him. That made her angry, too, though, and frightened. She mustn't care so much for what Henry thought, for what he wanted. It wasn't as if she was staying. That reminder made something like fear and regret twist in her chest. As soon as she could, she would leave. She repeated the words to herself with greater emphasis.

Hopefully Jack would be pleased for things to go back to normal and they'd give her an allowance, so she could live a decent life and raise her child.

For now, though, Henry was unhappy, and she realised she regretted that fact. She must make it up to him.

***

Isabella could do nothing to make amends, as Henry disappeared from their lives. They knew where he was, locked in the room he'd taken as his studio.

According to Jack, he was painting now, and she disturbed him at her peril.

Jack had a key and would enter to take him food, most of which came out again untouched. He said Henry became obsessive during these periods, not sleeping or eating for days. That Jack worried for him was clear.

Isabella found her regret over her harsh words only grew as the days passed. With nothing much to occupy her mind, she dwelt upon them, remembering how peaceful and happy he'd been until she'd opened her mouth. She wondered if he would have locked himself away if she'd said nothing, though Jack assured her it was normal behaviour for him. That Isabella's definition of normal was shifting was something that both worried and confused her. As the days continued into weeks, with no sight of Henry, the realisation she missed him only made her even more unsettled.

Her restlessness and guilt had one, positive outcome.

"What the devil are you doing?" Jack demanded as he came into the kitchen to discover her up to her arms in flour.

Isabella turned, pushing an irritating lock of hair from her eyes with her arm, as her hands were sticky. "I'm not sure I know," she admitted, blowing at the lock now as it fell back before her eyes. "I'm just sick of being bored and if Henry doesn't want a cook ..." She shrugged, turning back to stare at the incomprehensible instructions in the cookery book she'd found. Jack knew how terrible she felt over that conversation, as she'd admitted it to him. So, he'd know, too, that she was doing it to make amends. The fact made her feel vulnerable, exposed.

Jack came to stand beside her and peered into the mixing bowl.

"Is it supposed to look like that?" he asked, looking at the clumpy mixture with misgiving.

Isabella chewed at her lip for a moment. "I don't know." She nodded at the recipe. "Do you think it needs more eggs?"

"How many in now?" Jack frowned at the pages, squinting a little.

"Six, but ... *should* it look like that?"

Jack scratched the back of his neck and read out the list of ingredients as Isabella confirmed that she'd added them.

"Here, how much butter d'you put in?" he asked, frowning at her.

Isabella shrugged. She hadn't known how to measure the ingredients, so she'd guessed. "That much," she said, holding out her finger and thumb.

Jack treated her to a snort of amusement as he rolled his eyes at her. "It says a pound of butter, you dozy creature."

Isabella gaped at him, about to give him a nasty set down for speaking to her so, when she recognised the teasing note of his words. No one had ever teased her before or spoken to her in such an informal, friendly manner.

"I ... I didn't know how to measure it," she said, unfamiliar with the rather sheepish tone to her voice.

"You do surprise me," Jack said, winking at her. "Come on then, lass. If you're going to make yourself useful, I'll show you how to do it right."

***

The cakes were burnt when they came out. They were also heavy enough to use as a paperweight. Jack could see that the young woman was ridiculously pleased with herself, all the same. It was rather touching.

She'd wanted to take them to Henry at once, but Jack had forced her to rethink.

"I'm not trying to punish you," he said, registering her disappointment with hope lifting his spirits. "Truth is, I get in and out as fast as I can. He's liable to lose his temper if I disturb his concentration."

"What happens?" Isabella asked, falling quiet as fear flickered in her eyes. "What happens when he loses his temper?"

Jack realised what she was thinking and hurried to reassure her. "Oh, he'd never hurt me, if that's what you're thinking. No. I'm afraid he'll hurt himself." He shook his head, giving her a rueful smile. "Worst one was a couple of years ago. I was frightened he would make himself ill, he'd eaten so little. The weight was dropping off him, see. So, I tried to get him to look at me ... you know how he avoids your eye sometimes?"

Isabella nodded, understanding and concern in her expression. Jack tried to squash his hopes. He didn't want to be disappointed. Henry's feelings would be hard enough to bear.

"Well, it didn't go down well," Jack said, thinking that was the understatement of the century. "He lost his temper good and proper, throwing things about. Ended up cutting his hand on a broken bottle. Frightened me bad, it did," he admitted, remembering the fear that Henry would bleed to death before he'd calm down and let Jack bind it. He let out a breath. "So, I tread real careful now."

Isabella sighed. "Yes, I see what you mean," she said, the regret in her voice obvious. "Well, you take them into him for me, then, please."

Jack nodded and took the plate of rather blackened cakes from her and placed them on the tray beside the bowl of stew he was taking in for Henry's dinner.

"Will do, lass, don't fret. I'll tell him you made them for him, too," he added with a wink.

Hours later, long after midnight, Jack crept into the ballroom. This was the room Henry used as his studio. It was light and bright during daylight hours as glass doors ran the length of the vast room. Jack had forced Henry to bring a bed in here, but to his dismay he discovered it empty and Henry still at work.

He was all ablaze, lit up by dozens and dozens of candles that surrounded the canvas he worked on.

Jack stared, as astonished as always by the genius that was Henry Barbour. The subject matter unsettled Jack's heart, though. Henry often painted things that troubled his mind, as much as intrigued him, things he was trying to understand. This time, it was different. The painting was beautiful, serene, intimate.

Isabella asleep on the forest floor.

It was autumn in the painting, and her golden hair tumbled over the fallen leaves. Her body rounded with pregnancy, the burgeoning swell of her stomach echoed by the scattering of glossy, mahogany chestnuts and conkers. Henry was working on her hands now, and Jack wondered at the God-given talent behind such work. One hand cradled her stomach, a reassuring, protective pose which made a lump rise in Jack's throat. The other lay half-open, resting on the floor beside her head, a silky blue ribbon curled around her fingers.

Jack prayed. He'd never been much of a man for believing in God, or much of a church-goer, not before Henry. Henry had made him believe there was some greater plan, something beyond the basic human instinct to survive, to procreate, to live.

The beauty in the painting before him was easy enough to appreciate. The detail exquisite. Golden leaves lay crisp and thick, the folds of material that covered the sleeping figure falling in soft drapes he could almost see flickering in an autumn breeze. Isabella's hair was glossy, silky, and her eyelashes thick as they rested against her warm skin. He'd captured every nuance with such startling realism. Jack had never seen the like. Even by Henry's standards, this was something extraordinary

What struck him most, however, what made his heart fill with both hope and fear, was the tenderness of the image. Henry had painted it with such delicacy that his emotions shone through.

If Isabella left now, it would destroy him.

With as much stealth as he could manage, Jack moved away to gather the tray with the dinner things on it. With a sigh, he smiled as he noticed the stew remained untouched, but Isabella's burnt cakes were all gone.

Isabella stared down at the tray of cakes and beamed. The tops were golden, the buttery scent filling the kitchen. With growing excitement, she reached for one, pulling it in half even though it was hot still and burned her fingers. Light as a summer cloud, the cake broke in two with a fragrant burst of steam, and Isabella gave a little crow of delight. She couldn't wait to send them into Henry.

She'd not seen him for three weeks now, but he had at least eaten every cake she'd sent in for him, via Jack. Some of them had been near to inedible, but even when he touched nothing else, he always ate her cakes. Did that mean he'd forgiven her? She wanted to know. With frustration, she realised that it would be hours before Jack returned from town. With a huff which was part exhaustion and part irritation, she sat herself down at the kitchen table and ate the cake she'd examined, and sighed with pleasure. It was delicious.

She was approaching her eighth month now and felt fat and heavy, not to mention unattractive. Doing her hair without looking in the mirror was something she'd become adept at. The plump face that looked back at her seemed foreign and made her wonder if she would lose her looks and her figure now. Such punishment as she felt her body to be enduring would leave scars, damage. She had never felt unattractive when Henry looked at her, though. He found such joy and wonder in the child she carried that it made her feel rather special. The yearning to see that warmth and wonder in his eyes again only made her feel more alone.

April was here, and the weather full of spring promise, the landscape as fecund and full of life as Isabella. She found an odd kinship with the ewes and their newborn lambs who gambolled over the lush green fields, full of the joy of living. From her position at the table, Isabella could see blue skies and bright white clouds scudding in a crisp breeze. A sudden longing to be out in the woods with Henry hit her square in the chest and she cursed herself for a fool. Her emotions were all off kilter, no doubt the nearness of her due date turning her into a watering pot.

She wondered if Henry would have eaten the breakfast Jack had taken in before he left, and knew the answer. Which meant Henry would eat nothing before dinnertime when Jack returned. The thought troubled her. That she could creep into the room, set down the tray of cakes, and then leave with Henry none the wiser, seemed a distinct possibility. She would be careful not to make a sound and not try to speak to him. Seeing him and reassuring herself that he was well was hard to resist.

Isabella hauled herself to her feet and arranged a pile of the little cakes onto a china plate before hurrying from the kitchen.

Her nerve almost failed her as she wondered if Henry might notice her and lose his temper. Jack would be furious with her, and the idea Henry might be angry with her was enough to make her quail. Some stubborn sense of determination would not quit, however, and so she reached for the door handle, turning it with care so as not to make a sound.

Once inside the door, Isabella held her breath. Henry was standing at a large canvas, and though he moved little, there was a sense of urgency, of intense activity that blazed around him. From here she could not see the canvas, and as curious as she was, she didn't dare move to take a peek. Instead she looked about for the breakfast tray, and then forgot about it at once. The contents of the room took her gaze.

That this had once been a grand ballroom was obvious, the sheer scale and opulence of the space, the marble pillars and gilded plaster mouldings quite breath taking. Yet nothing could hold a candle to the hundreds of canvases stacked about the room.

As she moved, her elbow touched the edge of a small canvas, balanced against a jug full of brushes, and it clattered to the floor.

Isabella froze, her heart leaping to her throat as she held her breath. Horrified, she turned, daring to look, to find Henry had turned to stare at her.

He was silent, blinking at her as though he'd just woken from a deep sleep. He looked exhausted, dark circles under his eyes, his beard grown thick once more.

Henry said nothing, just stared at her. Isabella found herself torn between apologising and running from the room without a word. She was too afraid to do either, and so the two of them stood frozen. She watched as Henry frowned and then rubbed a hand over his face. He looked back at her, a little surprised, but not displeased.

"Hello."

As her heart was beating in her throat, it took Isabella several tries to reply to him.

"H-Hello, Henry," she stammered. She licked her lips and then gestured to the plate she'd brought. "Jack's gone to town and I ... I thought you might be hungry, so I b-brought you some cakes. I didn't mean to disturb you," she added in a rush. Her palms were sweaty, and she wiped them on the front of her dress, watching him for any signs of distress or anger.

Henry smiled.

"I like your cakes," he said.

"Oh." Isabella let out a breath of relief, pleased by his words. She watched as he set down his palette and brush and walked towards her to inspect her offering

"I'm so glad," she said, and then hesitated, wondering if this was just the calm before the storm. "Henry," she began, unsure of whether this was a good time. "I'm ... I'm sorry I upset you."

Henry paused, his hand hovering over the cakes. He didn't look up at her, but shrugged, a guarded, rather troubled expression crossing his face.

"It's true," he said, his voice soft.

Isabella frowned, wondering what he meant, but wanting to take the sadness from his face. Henry ought to never be sad. The thought came from nowhere, but the truth of it settled in her heart.

"What's true, Henry?" she asked, her voice soft as she moved closer to him. He took the plate of cakes and moved away from her. There was a bed, she noticed now, pushed against one wall. He settled himself there to eat the cakes, and she knew he wouldn't answer unless she pressed him.

With a mixture of trepidation and determination, Isabella followed him, sitting at his side. At first, the impropriety of the situation alarmed her until she remembered they were married. That thought was both alarming and reassuring at once, and she wasn't sure which bothered her most. Henry, however, was unhappy, and the sight of it tugged at her heart.

"Henry," she said, getting no reaction from him. Taking a breath and her courage in her hands, she reached out as she'd seen Jack do, and put her hand to his face. His beard was soft beneath her touch as she forced him to turn to her.

"What's true?" she asked again, keeping the words gentle.

Henry glanced at her, such sorrow in his eyes that her heart ached now. He looked down, unwilling to hold her gaze. "I ..." he began, and then faltered. "I am ridiculous."

Isabella had given out many insults in her days, some of them designed to cut to the quick. She spoke without care for the results, without bothering to consider the effect of her barbed comments. That she had said such a thing to Henry, though ... She wanted to cut out her own tongue.

"Oh, Henry," she said, blinking back tears now. "It isn't true. Not at all. That was a wicked and terrible thing to say, and I've regretted it every second since."

He looked up at her then, doubt shining in his eyes, and she placed her other hand upon his cheek, cradling his face between them both.

"Look at me," she said, needing him to see the truth in her words. "I didn't mean it. I was cross because I'm spoilt, and I wanted my own way. It's me that's ridiculous, Henry. Not you."

She watched him, watched the worry leave his eyes, a tentative smile at his lips.

"You're lovely, Isabella," he said, his voice quiet. "I like you, very much."

Isabella's breath snagged in her throat, her emotions torn as her heart sang and her mind told her she was being idiotic. This could lead to no good, for either of them. Henry didn't know what he was saying. Not in the way a husband would say it. She was a fool to believe otherwise.

"I like you, too, Henry."

He beamed at her, such pleasure in his eyes she could not help but laugh.

"Now eat your cakes," she said, a scolding tone to her voice as she tried to break the intimacy of the moment. "You must eat, you know. Jack and I have been so worried for you."

He popped one whole cake into his mouth and turned to give her a quizzical look whilst he chewed.

"You have?" he asked, once he had devoured the cake.

"Of course," she said, tutting at him. "You lock yourself in here for weeks on end, not seeing a soul, not sleeping, not eating. It's bad for you. You'll make yourself ill."

He took another cake and chewed it. "These are good," he mumbled with his mouth full before reaching for another. "It's not been weeks," he added, shaking his head as Isabella frowned at him.

"How long do you think it's been, then?" she demanded, curious now.

He shrugged. "A few days," he said, before popping another cake in his mouth and chewing with a contented expression.

"Henry!" Isabella exclaimed. "You've been shut in here for nineteen days."

Henry turned to look at her, his expression wary. "I have?"

"You have," she agreed, her voice stern as she reached out and tugged at his beard. "And you've not washed or shaved like you promised."

Anxiety glittered in his eyes and Isabella was contrite at once. "Oh, it doesn't matter," she said, stroking his cheek until the fear left his expression. "I'm just worried for you, that's all. I didn't mean to scold you."

Henry raised his hand, covering hers as he turned his face into her palm, closing his eyes.

Isabella tried to squash the feeling that rose in her chest at the sight of her big, handsome, troubled husband, leaning into her caress. "You're tired, Henry," she whispered, wishing she could persuade him to rest. He looked grey with exhaustion. "Won't you sleep for a while, please?"

He opened his eyes, glancing back at his painting and frowning.

"For me," she added, wondering if that would mean anything to him.

His eyes flew back to hers, a considering look in his eyes.

"If you stay," he said.

Isabella sat back, trying to remove her hand from his cheek, but Henry wouldn't let her go. He lowered it from his face, but held it still, his thumb caressing her palm now.

"Stay while I sleep … please," he said.

Isabella opened her mouth to refuse him, but the look in his eyes was irresistible. My word, even unshaven and unwashed, he was beautiful.

"Lie down, then," she instructed, her tone business-like. There was no harm in watching over him whilst he slept if it would make him rest.

Henry stuffed the last cake in his mouth and set the plate down before reaching to pull off his boots. Isabella watched as he crawled up the bed and collapsed against the pillow with a sigh. She suspected he'd only just realised how tired he was. For a moment, she thought he'd fallen asleep the moment his head had touched the pillow, but then those dark eyes opened again, and he patted the spot beside him.

"Stay with me. You promised," he added.

"I did not promise," she retorted, amused that he would put words in her mouth.

"You're going to stay, you said …" he began, sitting up again.

"All right, all right," Isabella assured him, wondering what on earth she was doing. "But you stay on your side."

Henry huffed a little, but appeared too tired to argue. "Be here when I wake up," he mumbled, the words slurring as his eyes closed again.

Isabella settled herself beside him, feeling a smile curve over her mouth. "I promise."

He gave a contented sigh and fell asleep in seconds.

She watched him for a long time, staring at him, listening to the steady sound of his breathing, watching the rise and fall of his broad chest. His hair, dirty and unkempt as it was, still showed a rich dark brown. His eyelashes, too, so thick he'd be the envy of every woman who would give their right arm for such luxuriant lashes. He looked peaceful in sleep, contented, his heavy limbs relaxed, one hand reaching across the bed, as if he held it out to her.

    Isabella didn't know what motivated her, why she did it, but she took his hand, entwining her fingers with his, and slept at his side.

Chapter 11

"Wherein a taste of happiness."

Jack worried when he returned to find no sign of Isabella. That she'd left them already was a thought he found burrowed into his heart and wouldn't let go. How ever would he break the news to Henry?

Yet it made no sense to him. Isabella was just weeks away from having her baby, she wouldn't leave now. He'd believed her happy here, contented, at least. He didn't doubt she wished life had dealt her a different hand, but in the circumstances, she didn't seem miserable.

Then he discovered the cakes. These were perfect golden queen cakes. Well, well, the girl had taught herself how to cook. Jack felt a sudden rush of pride for her. She'd not given up, like he might have believed of a hoity-toity girl of her class. He took one and bit into it, savouring the delicate flavour of rose water and almonds, the juicy burst of the currants against the fluffy sponge. Heaven.

All at once, he knew where she'd gone. Oh, good Lord.

It was quiet outside Henry's studio. Jack didn't know if that was a good thing or not. He might find the whole place wrecked and Henry gone. With a deal of trepidation, he opened the door, and eased his way in.

It was dark, the evening having set in. The fires had long since burned out, as no one had attended them, but as far as he could see, nothing was out of place. There were no smashed bottles or canvases flung hither and yon.

With no expectation of finding him, Jack turned towards the bed and froze. Henry was there all right, and so was Isabella. Torn between curiosity and mortification, Jack moved a little closer. They were sleeping side by side, chaste as nuns, but Jack noted their hands linked, the fingers curled around each other.

"Well, I'm blowed," he murmured, shaking his head and not knowing quite what to make of it. That Henry had feelings for the girl was clear enough, though Jack wondered if he understood what they meant. Not that Henry was too stupid to understand, only that he'd missed the period where young men found out about the fairer sex, isolated as he was. He was naïve in matters of the heart. Though he knew well enough, the mechanics of what happened between men and women. You couldn't be that interested in nature and animals and not pick up a few clues.

He wondered if Isabella understood what she was playing with. If she thought to treat Henry like a child, or a brother, Jack suspected she'd be in for a shock.

Either way, there was little he could do about it. This hand would have to play out, and Jack would have to pick up the pieces if things didn't turn out as he hoped.

***

Isabella woke to the flickering of candlelight and blinked, disorientated. Her nose cold, the air chill, though the rest of her felt warm under a thick layer of blankets. She smothered a yawn and hauled her heavy body upright. With a start, she realised she was sleeping in Henry's bed, and as it was now dark out, she'd been there for hours. He must have put the blankets over her when he'd woken up.

Henry was painting again. The canvas blocked her view of him, but she could see his shadow cast from the blaze of candles around him. The desire to look at his work was tantalising, but she wouldn't. Not until he invited her. She'd learned her lesson there. What was he painting, though? He'd sketched her with such fascination for so long, she'd assumed he was painting her, but for all she knew, it could be another of the disturbing pictures of dead things, or a still life. She had no idea. There was also the lingering sense of anxiety she might not like what she saw. The first drawings he'd done of her had showed her a side of herself she'd not liked at all. She wanted to leave that girl behind. At least that would be one good thing to come of her fall from grace.

As she considered her words, she wondered what she was thinking. There was more than one good thing to come out of her disgrace. She smoothed her hands over her stomach, still startled by just how large she'd grown. Jack had arranged a doctor to come and see her whilst Henry had shut himself away, and he'd assured her that it was a normal, healthy pregnancy. His manner, however, had been unpleasant. She knew he must know all the gossip about her, must know her circumstances. A man like that attending her during the birth filled her with horror and fear. She didn't trust him. Jack said he was the best accoucheur in the area, though, and the nearest to them here. There weren't a lot of choices open to her.

Isabella tugged one blanket from the bed and wrapped it around her shoulders. The fires had been lit, but the heat hadn't touched the cavernous space. With a surge of embarrassment, she realised that Jack had been in here, as Henry would never have thought to have lit them once he'd begun work again.

Emboldened by the fact he hadn't lost his temper on discovering her in his studio, Isabella crept closer to the canvas. She peaked around the side, careful only to look at Henry, and not at his work. To her surprise, she found that he wasn't painting, only staring at the picture with a critical eye. It took a moment for him to realise she was there, but when he did, the pleased smile he gave her stole her breath.

"You stayed," he said, the words infused with such genuine happiness that Isabella experienced the strangest sense of belonging. No one had ever been so happy to have her company, just for the pleasure of being with her.

"I promised," she said, and then caught her breath as her stomach tightened. For a moment it was like her body had turned to rock, the sensation frightening and painful.
Isabella cried out, reaching out to grasp for something to steady her and finding Henry, his strong arms supporting her.

She looked up, finding him watching her, quiet and calm, no sense of concern or fear in his eyes. It gave her courage.

"It will pass," he said, the words so certain and reassuring that Isabella didn't doubt him. Sure enough, the pain receded, and her stomach relaxed.

"How did you know?" she asked, staring at him, clutching at his arm even though the pain had gone. "How do you know it isn't starting now?" The terror of that thought had her gasping for breath again.

"I've been reading about it," he said, looking a little guarded now. "And I've watched animals, cats and mice, horses, they often seem to have pains long before the birth. It's normal. Like practising."

Isabella stared at him, unsure how she felt at being compared to a horse, but he was serious, sincere. She'd seen how single-minded he was first-hand, the intensity with which he studied. If Henry said this was normal, then she believed him.

"Do you feel better now?" he asked, concern in his eyes, such warmth that Isabella could only stare at him for a moment before she found her tongue again.

"Yes," she said, only now realising how intimate was their position. One hand grasped his arm, the muscle hard and heavy beneath her fingers, the other rested on his chest. The steady beat of his heart thudded beneath her palm, the heat of him fierce through his shirt. It was only now she realised he'd washed and shaved, the clean scent of soap lingering. There was no sickly cologne, which she often found cloying and overpowering. He smelled clean, with a faint touch of linseed oil and paint, a familiar combination she now recognised as distinctly him.

Henry held her gaze for a moment, and then he knelt before her, reaching out a hand to her stomach. He paused, his hand suspended before she smiled at him and nodded her permission. Isabella fought the rising tide of emotion that swelled inside her at the sight of him, knelt before her, his touch so gentle.

"Hello," he said, and Isabella choked back something between a laugh and a sob. She tried to think of a single other man of her acquaintance who would have gone to his knees and spoken to her unborn child. She couldn't think of one. That she might have missed this by refusing Henry's offer for one of those she'd had in mind for potential husbands made her feel ill.

He moved closer and rested his head against her stomach, both hands holding the child. Isabella smiled as the baby responded, stretching out in its increasingly confined surroundings, pushing at Henry's hands.

Henry looked up at her, his eyes sparkling with delight. "She's saying hello."

Isabella swallowed hard, emotion pushing at her chest, filling her heart.

"It might be a boy," she replied, the words rather thick now, though she was smiling still.

Henry gave her a look filled with mischief and put his head back to her stomach. "No," he said a moment later, his tone serious. "She says she's a girl."

Isabella laughed. It filled her with joy and wonder, and hope, and as the sound echoed around the grand space that had once been a ballroom, a new and incredible thought occurred to her.

She was happy.

The thought stopped her in her tracks, her laughter dying, though the sense of peace and contentment remained. She looked down to find Henry watching her, his eyes filled with adoration. It was humbling, to be on the receiving end of that look, and she knew she must treat him with care.

Before she could consider what to do about it, Henry got to his feet.

"Close your eyes," he demanded, sounding excited and nervous at the same time. Isabella went to ask why, but he seemed to grow anxious now, and so she did as he asked, not wanting to upset him. She felt his hand take hers, the other hand at her waist as he guided her where he wanted her. "You can open them now," he whispered.

Isabella opened her eyes, about to laugh and demand what game he was playing, but the painting was before her and she could not find the words.

The emotions that had seemed to fill her chest just moments before seemed too powerful to contain now. She gasped, her hand going to her mouth as she tried to take it in. Tears gathered and spilled over and she sensed rather than felt Henry's distress as he noticed. She reached out, taking his hand and bringing it to her lips.

"Oh, Henry," she said, laughing and crying now. "I … I don't know what to say, how to thank you … I'm overwhelmed."

Henry hesitated, his expression still anxious. "You … you like it?" he queried, and she realised her laughter and tears were confusing him. He couldn't read what she was feeling.

"I love it," she said, holding his hand between both of hers, holding him tight so he didn't run away from her in his confusion. "It's so beautiful."

He relaxed then, reaching out with his free hand and wiping her tears away. "I don't like to see you cry," he said, his voice rough.

"People sometimes cry when they're happy," she said, smiling at him now as he took a step closer. As she said the words, Isabella realised it was true, but she had never done it herself before.

"You're happy?" The intensity of his expression told her how much her answer meant to him.

Isabella nodded, holding his gaze so he could see the truth. "I am. You made me happy."

The smile that broke over his face was devastating, crumbling any remaining defences she had erected against this strange and wonderful man. He glanced at the painting before turning back to her.

"You think it's beautiful?"

Isabella nodded, finding her throat growing tight. "The most beautiful thing I've ever seen in my life."

Henry's smile was the most disarming she'd ever known, and when he moved closer and whispered in her ear, "That's because you're the most beautiful thing I've ever seen," Isabella knew she was lost.

Chapter 12

"Wherein hearts and confidences are shared."

The days that followed were the happiest Isabella had ever known. Now that Henry had completed his painting, he returned to them. He sat in the kitchen, drawing whilst Isabella tested her skills with a variety of recipes. She got more adventurous, under Henry and Jack's extravagant praise, her confidence growing, even though one in three results were disastrous. They never minded, commiserating and eating the stodgy puddings and leaden cakes with no complaints. Jack said she'd eaten enough of his burnt offerings, it was only fair.

In the afternoon, Isabella would pack up cakes or whatever she had baked, assuming it was edible, and she would go out with Henry. They didn't go far now; her growing bulk tired her and made her cumbersome. The gardens around the great estate were worth investigating, though. It must have been beautiful once, and still was, though nature was taking over, many of the paths inaccessible and the lovely lawns more like meadows. There was a peaceful spot overlooking an ornamental pond that Isabella liked.

They had been there for an hour, Isabella lying on the blanket, the late spring sun hot on her face.

"Aren't you tired of drawing me yet, Henry?" she asked, turning to smile at him and squinting into the sun.

"I could never get bored drawing you," he said, the words quiet and thoughtful, not the throwaway comment that slipped from a glib tongue. "You're more beautiful every time I look."

Isabella sighed, shaking her head. "It will make me impossibly conceited if you keep saying such things. You make me feel like I'm something special."

"You are," he replied, the words honest and simple, and Isabella knew he meant them.

She sat up then, wanting to return the compliment. Henry was special. Jack had told her he was, and she hadn't believed it, hadn't understood. She could see it now, though, in a way she never believed she would understand, but Henry didn't know it. Isabella looked at him, wondering at the man before her. It was hot for early May and he'd stripped off his jacket and waistcoat, leaving only his shirt, rolling up his sleeves to expose powerful arms.

"Can I have paper and a pencil, please?" she asked, struck with sudden inspiration.

Henry gave her a quizzical look, but handed the items over to her.

"I'll need your drawing board, too," she added, crooking her fingers with a rather imperious air.

"I'm using it," he objected, frowning now.

"Well, you can't." He blinked at her, his expression doubtful and a little confused. "Please," she added, realising she was troubling him. "I would like to draw, too, or at least try to."

His expression cleared in an instant and he grinned at her, putting his own drawing aside and placing a clean sheet in its place.

"What are you going to draw?" he asked, eager now as he gave her the board and shifted closer.

"Well," Isabella said, struggling to balance the drawing board as her stomach got in the way. "I'm going to draw something special."

"What?" he demanded, curiosity sparkling in his eyes.

"You might not recognise it," Isabella warned him, as the large white sheet now looked rather intimidating. "I'm not very good, I'm afraid. Not like you."

Henry sat back on his heels, his expression a little puzzled. "Shall I draw it for you?" he asked as Isabella laughed and shook her head.

"No!" she exclaimed, trying to sketch out the shape of his face. She paused, biting her lip as she concentrated.

Henry stared at the page, ever more perplexed by the odd form appearing on the paper. "Well, what is it?" he demanded again.

Isabella frowned, staring at the shape she'd drawn with consternation. His jawline was much stronger than that.

"Guess," she replied, distracted as she stared at her terrible drawing.

"Can you see it?" he asked, perhaps wondering why she didn't look up from the paper, but she didn't want to give the answer away. It was clear he wouldn't guess by looking at it.

"Yes."

She glanced up to see him frowning as he looked around them, noting the square line of his chin, and the shape of his lips. His lips were full, they looked soft. With difficulty she dragged her gaze back to the paper.

"Is it pretty?" he asked, still puzzled as he stared about them. Isabella stifled a laugh.

"Not pretty," she replied, trying not to smile too much. "Beautiful."

Henry scratched his chin, turning around to look behind them and then moving back with a sigh. "Is it the lake?"

"No. Much warmer and more interesting than the lake."

Isabella glanced up, trying to draw the shape of his eyes, glad he wasn't looking at the drawing. They were large, wide eyes, guileless and full of honesty. They turned their attention back to her, and she tilted the board, so he couldn't see. With a frown she stared at the paper and her dismal effort.

"Is it an animal?" He sounded fed up now, annoyed that she wouldn't tell him. "Or a bird?"

"No," Isabella replied, frowning as she realised she'd drawn one eye higher than the other. "Much bigger and far more special than any animal or bird."

Henry huffed, frustrated. "Why are you drawing it?" he demanded, startling Isabella with the question.

She looked up then. "As a present for someone."

"Who?" The word was a little suspicious, anxiety in his eyes, and she sighed, realising she'd worried him.

"For you, Henry."

The way his face cleared was almost comical, delight replacing a wary expression that might have been something akin to jealousy.

"For me?" He moved around, trying to look at the paper, and Isabella turned so he couldn't see it.

"I've not finished yet!" she exclaimed, laughing as he reached for the drawing board. "No, Henry, stop it."

Henry wasn't to be denied, though, and wrested the board and the paper from her grasp. He sat staring at it and Isabella moved to kneel behind him, staring at her poor effort with a sigh.

"Oh dear, it really isn't very good. I've made you cross-eyed."

Henry was silent, staring at the page, and Isabella rested one hand on his broad shoulder.

"You're far more handsome than my pitiful skills can capture," she said with regret. "I wish I could paint you like you did me."

He looked up at her then, his eyes searching hers. "Why?"

Isabella hesitated, wanting to explain how she felt, so he understood. "Because you're a wonderful man," she said, stroking his soft hair, warmed by the sun. "Because I want you to see yourself as I see you. Like how you made me feel when you showed me your painting. You made me feel special, beautiful in a way I've never felt before." She frowned at the rather childish drawing, disappointed. "I'm afraid I've failed terribly," she said with chagrin.

He put the picture down and reached for her hand, holding it to his face, and it was only now that she saw he was struggling to keep his composure.

"Henry!" she said, horrified that she'd upset him. "Henry, I'm sorry … I didn't mean…"

Henry laughed, a choked sound as he shook his head. "You're were right, Isabella," he said, the words thick. "You can cry when you're happy."

Isabella laughed too, the sound quavering a little now. "I know," she said, blinking hard. "I know."

He put his arms around her, his head on her chest and Isabella hesitated for a moment before lying back down on the blanket, taking him with her. With any other man she would have expected him to make a move, to take advantage, but Henry seemed content to lie with his head on her chest as she stroked his hair.

The sun had moved around now and the shade they'd been sitting under almost gone.

"It's hot," he said, the words a sleepy murmur.

Isabella nodded, too lazy to reply as the heat sapped her energy.

"Let's go for a swim," he said with a sudden burst of enthusiasm. He sat up, grinning at her. "The lake's lovely and cool."

"Ugh." Isabella stared at the dark water with misgiving, shaking her head. "The water will be freezing, and muddy, and … no, thank you." She shuddered, remembering the water of the river dragging her down. Henry reached over and touched a finger to her cheek.

"I'll look after you," he said, understanding at once.

Isabella didn't bother to fight the swell of emotion that rose at his words, not anymore. He was sincere, and he wasn't just talking about going for a swim.

"I know you will, Henry, thank you, but I'd rather not."

He looked a little crestfallen and Isabella laughed. "You can if you want to, though. I'll watch."

A few moments later and Isabella wondered if she ought to have been so hasty as Henry stripped off. Her mouth grew dry at the sight of him, her breath catching at a display of masculine beauty to rival that of any marble interpretation of such perfection. Somewhat to her relief, he kept his smallclothes on before flashing her a grin and running into the water.

Once the water was up to his hips he dived forward, sleek as a seal, disappearing beneath the surface and reappearing farther into the lake, shaking his head like a dog.

Isabella laughed, waving at him and wondering at how her life had changed. She had been so close to making a terrible mistake that day at the river, yet somehow her life had turned around. It wasn't what she'd expected, and it was perhaps a narrow existence, the three of them hidden from the world as they were, but it contained more happiness than she'd hoped for or deserved.

She squealed, broken from her thoughts as Henry strode from the water, dripping icy droplets over her as he stood shivering.

"It is cold," he said, teeth chattering.

Isabella tried not to stare, but he was impossible to turn away from. He lay down beside her in the sun, pushing wet hair from his eyes as Isabella tried not to notice what little he still wore was all but transparent. He closed his eyes, laying an arm over them to block out the sun, and Isabella sat up a little, free to look her fill.

She'd become used to the fact that he was a large man, his presence so gentle, he'd long since ceased to cause her any anxiety. Seeing him like this, however, only illustrated that fact. Huge shoulders, a muscular chest and arms, powerful thighs ... he could so easily intimidate. Her gaze lingered on his chest, the coarse hair there was intriguing to her and the urge to reach out and touch hard to resist. She wondered what he would do if she did.

Her greedy eyes travelled over him, a little unnerved by her train of thought. She'd accepted Henry for what he was, accepted her feelings for him, but that he might be a husband to her in every sense of the word was something she'd not allowed herself to consider ... Her breath caught.

Too late, she realised she was being watched. His dark eyes rested on hers.

"Have you ever been kissed?" The words tumbled out before she could think them through, and she regretted them at once as a troubled look entered his eyes.

He nodded, but didn't answer, and she sensed that whatever had happened hadn't been a happy experience. Jealousy rose in her chest all the same and she wondered who it had been.

"A girl worked here," he said, frowning now, turning onto his side to face her. "A long time ago. There were more people here then." He huffed out a breath, rubbing his face with his hand. "She was pretty ..."

Isabella swallowed, unsure if she wanted to hear more.

"But only on the outside. Not like you." The look in his eyes melted her from the inside out and Isabella reached out, pushing his wet hair from his eyes again as it fell forward.

"What happened?" she asked, though she suspected she knew. Henry was so handsome; a man that women would desire and might wish to seduce.

He shrugged, lying on his back and wrapping his arms about himself, such a defensive gesture that Isabella felt a surge of fury at whoever the girl was.

"Did she kiss you?"

Henry glanced at her and nodded. "I didn't like it. She ... she ..." He looked agitated and Isabella put her hand to his face.

"It's all right, just tell me."

"She said I ... I forced myself on her. She said I should be locked up." He sat up then, hugging his knees to his chest. "But I didn't. The girl did it. She was hard and bony and she didn't smell good, she pushed and said things and ... and when I said no ..."

"Henry." Isabella held his face between her hands, forcing him to look at her. "She wasn't very nice. Not the sort of girl you want to kiss."

"No," he said, sounding a little calmer now. "Father sent her away. He said she was a ... a devious baggage."

Isabella smiled despite herself, thinking she would have liked his father a good deal.

"He was right," she said, her voice firm.

He sighed, the tension leaving him, his eyes growing warm as the light of curiosity glittered now. She knew what he was thinking. It was all she could think about herself. Isabella caught her breath as he reached out and touched her mouth with a fingertip.

"Would ... would you like me to kiss you?" she asked, wondering if he would like it with her. Did he even feel that way about her? That she was asking him seemed incredible. After her horrific encounter with Viscount Treedle, ever allowing a man near her was abhorrent. She had promised herself it would never happen again, but Henry wasn't like any other man. He was gentle and kind and loving and ...

He nodded, his gaze falling to her lips.

"Close your eyes," she said in a rush, courage failing her at the last moment. She couldn't do it if he watched her. He did as she asked, holding himself still.

Isabella's heart felt like it would beat itself out of the cage of her ribs, it thudded so, but she placed her palm against his cheek and leaned in. His lips were every bit as soft as she'd imagined, and it was tempting to linger, but she pulled away to see his reaction. She had no desire to upset him or … or to encourage him too far. In her condition, she really must be out of her mind, she scolded herself, but then she saw his eyes.

She smiled, a little laugh escaping her lips as she saw the wonder with which he stared at her.

"Do it again, Isabella," he said, the words little more than a whisper.

A strange, fluttering sensation filled her chest, anticipation as she leaned towards him again. She pressed her lips against his, a little firmer, for a moment longer, before moving away again. She heard him sigh as she lay down again. The baby made sitting up awkward and she lay against the pillow Henry had brought for her with relief.

He stared down at her, the desire to continue this new delight shining in his eyes.

"Kiss me again." There was a rougher note to his voice now that Isabella couldn't ignore. She was playing with fire and she knew it. Denying him was impossible, though, she wanted to kiss him. Isabella shook her head, a teasing smile at her lips.

"No, Henry," she said, seeing the disappointment cloud his eyes. "You kiss me this time."

The smile that curved over his lips was new to her, a masculine smile, just a little smug. He leaned forward, and Isabella squealed as icy drops of water fell from his hair.

"Ugh, not until you're dry," she said, rubbing her bare arms as she shivered.

Henry huffed, impatient now, and grabbed his shirt, rubbing it over his hair with vigour as Isabella snorted at his haste. She turned on her side to watch him, moving the pillow to rest under her stomach. When he was dry, he came to her, lying at her side. She half expected him to grab for her, to act on the excitement she saw in his eyes, but he didn't. Instead, he reached out, touching her face with his hand, tracing the line of her jaw, stroking her cheek.

"You make my heart hurt," he said, his eyes serious.

Isabella frowned, her mouth opening in shock, not understanding what he meant. "Why?" she asked, worried that she'd done something wrong.

Henry shook his head, looking puzzled. "I don't know," he said, a crooked smile at his lips. "But when I'm with you, I … I want to touch you, I want … I want to always be with you and the feeling fills me up. It's like I …"

Isabella's breath caught as she blinked away tears. She couldn't hear any more for fear of crying. "Kiss me," she said.

He leaned in, pressing his lips to hers. Isabella closed her eyes and he didn't move away, but continued to brush his lips against hers, light, caressing kisses that lit a desire for him a woman in her condition had no right to. The hated memory of Viscount Treedle forcing his tongue into her mouth came back to her and she stiffened for a moment. Henry retreated at once, concern in his eyes.

"Don't stop," she whispered, needing him to push back the horrid picture in her mind and replace it with something new, something rare and wonderful. Isabella reached out, daring to place her hand on his chest. His skin felt warm now, silky beneath her touch, and the urge to explore him became hard to resist. Her palms moved over taut muscle, the ridges of his abdomen, her fingers tangling in the coarse hair at his chest which had so intrigued her. Henry's eyes were dark, but still they shone with warmth, with love for her.

That he loved her was something she could not think about yet. It was too overwhelming, too frightening. Instead, Isabella gave herself up to the moment. She opened her mouth a little and Henry hesitated for a moment before she felt the tentative touch of his tongue against her lips. She sighed, pressing her lips against his again, encouraging him. Their tongues met, the touch making her shiver with longing, and Henry grew bolder. His tongue tangled with hers, warm silk, caressing and gentle. The difference between his touch, so full of care for her, and that of the cruel viscount could not have been more different.

He drew back, studying her, and Isabella blinked back tears.

"I wish the baby was yours, Henry," she said, the words broken as the truth hit her. The idea would have horrified her once, but now she could think of nothing she wished for more. He deserved more than this, a ruined woman and a bastard child. A tear slid down her cheek and she looked away from him, but Henry took her face in his hands, forcing her to look at him as she'd done to him before now.

He wiped the tear away with his thumb. "It is mine, Isabella. You're both mine now."

She gave a sob and Henry moved towards her, his arms pulling her closer, and she rested her head on his chest, hearing the reassuring thud of his heart. They stayed like that for a long time, with Henry stroking her hair, comforting her as no one had ever done before. She could not remember being held with such care, being petted and kissed with such tender affection, not even as a child.

"What was it like?"

Isabella stilled, hoping she'd misunderstood his question.

"What was what like?" she asked, praying he'd say something else.

He shifted onto his side, moving her so that her head rested on his arm now and he could see her eyes.

"When …" He hesitated and laid his large hand upon her stomach. "When you made the baby. What was it like?"

Isabella closed her eyes against the memories that rose again. Treedle with his impatience and his ugly words, hands that grabbed and grasped and pinched. She shook her head, swallowing hard as her emotions threatened to spiral out of control.

Henry held her tighter, steadying her, and she dared to look at him, finding nothing but concern in his eyes.

"You didn't like it?"

She shook her head, swallowing hard to stop the tears that threatened.

"He … he wasn't kind to you?" There was a darker thread to his voice now, though she could see it wasn't aimed at her.

Isabella took a deep breath and shook her head. "No. He wasn't like you," she said, almost laughing at the understatement in the words. "He wasn't kind like you. I didn't like it at all."

"Then why …" He began and then closed his mouth, his jaw taut. Leaning in, he kissed her again and lay his head down.

"Because I felt I had to," Isabella replied to his unspoken question. It touched her that he hadn't asked, but she needed him to know. "My mother told me my only purpose in life was to marry well, to take the family into the higher reaches of the *ton*. My mother groomed me my whole life to marry the Marquess of Winterbourne."

Henry's head came up then, his dark eyes flashing with anger. "Was it …"

"No!" she exclaimed, shaking her head. "No, it isn't his child. He married someone else, you see." Isabella sighed, reaching out and stroking his face. The urge to touch him seemed to grow stronger with each moment. "She was so angry with me," she said, the words resigned now. It was like talking about a nightmare. One that had frightened her and would always linger in her mind, but that was no longer real life. "Mother said the only way to make amends was to ensure I caught Vi ... another title," she amended. She'd seen the fury in Henry's eyes, there was no need to give him a name to focus it on. "She said I had to do whatever it took to get him to marry me."

Isabella blinked, trying to stop the tears that gathered as she remembered her mother's rants. Isabella was useless, worthless, ugly, and pathetic. It was little wonder no man of worth wanted her.

"He said he would marry me if ... if ..."

She broke down, then, and Henry held her while she wept, letting go of all the pain and the hurt and the hatred, the humiliation. Once the tumult of her emotions subsided, she looked up, wondering what to expect. Would he be disgusted that she'd given herself to a man she didn't even like, let alone love?

There was no judgement in his eyes, only sadness for her.

"You don't need to hear her words anymore," he said, his voice as strong as the arms that held her, reassuring. "I married you, you belong here, with me." He stroked her hair, her face, his touch gentle. "She didn't understand what was true. A woman like that lives for lies, she wears masks and lives on the surface. There is nothing beneath the façade, Isabella." He moved closer, pressing his lips to hers, stealing her breath and her heart. "When she dies, no one will mourn her, she'll leave no mark on this world because there was no weight to her, no depth to her heart. Not like you."

Isabella stared at him, astonished. Henry rarely spoke, and certainly not at any length, but when he did, he was far wiser than anyone she had ever known. She wrapped her arms about his neck and held him tight, and he held her as close as she needed him to.

Chapter 13

"Wherein Isabella discovers an unlikely ally."

The next morning, Jack hurried into Isabella's parlour, his face one of shock.

"Whatever is the matter?" she demanded, casting her book aside as fear clutched at her heart. "Where's Henry?"

Jack held his hand out to calm her. "Henry's fine, Isabella, he's gone out to paint like he told you."

Isabella let go of the breath she was holding. It was the first time Henry had been out without her in months, but she hadn't slept well and had woken late. When she'd come downstairs, her limbs felt too weary to walk the gardens. Making it to the parlour had seemed a monumental effort. Henry had been unhappy about leaving her behind and would have stayed. He was preparing for a new drawing, though, and she knew he was excited to begin, so had persuaded him to go out alone. She'd spent the last hour regretting it, however, as she now felt restless, and she missed Henry more than she cared to admit.

"The Marchioness Winterbourne is here."

Isabella gaped at Jack and then gave a startled laugh. "Don't be silly," she retorted, thinking such a thing so unlikely that it had to be wrong.

"I'm not being silly in the least," he hissed, looking like he might be sick, he was so nervous. "I've left the blasted woman waiting on the doorstep."

"Oh, Jack!" Isabella exclaimed in horror. She could just imagine the gossip that would get around now after such impolite treatment. No doubt the woman wanted what gossip she could garner about the scandalous Lady Isabella and her marriage to the Bear of Barcham Wood. Isabella took a deep breath, furious now. She'd give them something to damn well talk about, and Belinda Winterbourne was a fine one to pass judgement. Everyone knew she'd trapped the marquess into marriage.

Isabella sailed out of the parlour, chin up, ready to battle and face down anyone who would sneer at either her or Henry. "You'd best make tea and bring the cakes I made yesterday," she called over her shoulder.

Opening the door, Lady Winterbourne confronted her. The woman she'd met when she'd stayed at Longwold one Christmas. Isabella's mother had rejoiced at the invitation. It was her daughter's chance to snare the Marquess of Winterbourne. It seemed a lifetime ago.

The woman on the doorstep was older than Isabella, blonde and blue-eyed. Once upon a time, Isabella had sneered and believed herself far more beautiful. Then Belinda had captured the marquess where Isabella had failed. That she had trapped him was common knowledge. That the man now adored her was hard to miss if you'd ever seen them together.

"Good Morning, Lady Isabella," the woman said, smiling at her. "I hope you will forgive me calling unannounced?"

Isabella gave a taut nod. "Of course," she replied, standing back to allow the woman entry. She longed to slam the door in her face, but she knew well enough how to endure half an hour of barbed comments and slights. Isabella was the queen of the set-down, after all. If Belinda thought she'd sit and receive insults with a resigned smile, she'd find herself mistaken.

They exchanged polite nothings until Jack came in with the tea tray, casting Isabella a wide-eyed look of alarm that she ignored.

Isabella poured the tea and served Belinda, offering her a cake.

The woman took a bite and then gave a little sigh. "Oh, that's delicious," she said, with what sounded like genuine pleasure.

Isabella smiled, and then decided she may as well give the woman something to talk about, as that's what she'd come for. "I made them myself."

As expected, the woman's eyes grew round.

"We don't have a cook, or any servants other than Jack, though he's more a friend than a servant." The words dared the woman to judge her. *Make of it what you will,* Isabella thought, her expression hard. "My husband is an artist, a brilliant one," she added, the pride she took in saying that unmistakable. "But he doesn't like people. We live quietly, Lady Winterbourne, so there will be little gossip to take back to your friends other than what I've just told you."

Belinda flushed a little but took a breath, not so discomposed as Isabella had expected. Hoping to do so with a second volley, Isabella stood.

"I assume you've got what you came for," she said, the sneer behind the words hard to miss.

"No," Belinda said, looking a little awkward but holding her ground. She reached for a small parcel that Isabella hadn't noticed her carrying. "I came to give you this."

Isabella hesitated, wrong-footed, as she hadn't expected a gift. As she took the parcel from her, she noted the yellow silk ribbon and the care with which it had been wrapped. She sat down again, and her hands were unsteady as she pulled the parcel open to reveal a little lace-trimmed cap and gown, perfect for a newborn. It was the finest Indian muslin and must have cost a pretty penny. Isabella looked up to see warmth in the woman's eyes, not the judgement and salacious desire for gossip and scandal she'd expected.

She burst into tears.

"Oh, my dear!"

Belinda hurried over, kneeling on the floor at Isabella's side, unheeding that she was crushing the skirts of her lovely dress. She took Isabella's hand, holding it tight and murmuring reassurances.

"There now, you have a good cry," she said, her voice soothing. "I turned into the most dreadful watering pot in the last months. Drove poor Edward to distraction, he worried for me so, but half the time I didn't even have the slightest idea what I was crying about."

Isabella gave a strangled laugh, recognising the description only too well. The motherly concern given so freely by a stranger, however, and one who had no reason to think well of her, was too much to take. Isabella cried harder as Belinda stood, moving to sit beside her. Before she could do so, the door burst open.

"Leave her alone!"

Both women jumped, the vehemence of the words startling them. Belinda gave a frightened gasp and staggered back, and Isabella paused in her crying long enough to look up and stare at Henry.

He was glaring at Belinda, an air of fury rolling off him in waves. He moved to stand in front of Isabella, the protective stance touching her heart even though he was terrifying her poor guest.

"Henry." Isabella wiped her eyes and got to her feet, fighting to calm herself as she recognised Henry's distress. His chest was heaving, his fists clenching and unclenching. "Henry, I'm fine. It wasn't Lady Winterbourne's fault."

"Winterbourne?" he repeated, something dark flashing in his eyes.

"Yes, Henry," she said, keeping her voice steady and soothing. "She came to bring a present for the baby."

Henry stared at her, breathing hard. He paced away from her and then back again, pointing at Belinda who was standing stock-still. Isabella suspected she was holding her breath. "She made you cry. Not happy tears. I heard. I *heard* you," he said, accusation in his tone, his eyes darting between her and Belinda with confusion.

"Yes, Henry, that's true." The admission made him suck in a breath, one large fist pressing against his temple as he shot a sideways glance at Lady Winterbourne. "But it was my fault. I assumed she was gloating, that she'd come to … to laugh at me. I was wrong." Isabella walked closer to him, aware that Belinda was watching the exchange with fear in her eyes, but there was nothing she could do about that. She needed to calm Henry down. As she placed a hand on his arm, the tension sang beneath his skin, the muscles taut and hard. "I didn't think there was anyone who would be my friend. Anyone who would give me a chance. Her kindness overwhelmed me, and that's why I was crying."

Alarm filled his expression now, and he avoided her gaze.

"I'm your friend," he said, panic beneath the breathless words. The fear she might not need him, that she might leave him, showing bright and feverish in his eyes.

Isabella smiled and reached up, turning his face to hers. Standing on tip-toe she leaned in, kissing his mouth. "You're much more than a friend, Henry," she whispered, stroking his cheek now. His gaze slid to hers, staring at her, searching her expression for the truth, and his breathing steadied. She remained, stroking his cheek, speaking quiet words to him, uncaring that Belinda watched them.

"I won't leave, Henry," she said, wishing her guest were not here so she could hold him close. "I'm not unhappy. The baby and I belong to you, remember?" Henry leaned into her, resting his head against hers.

"Sorry," he whispered. "I'm sorry."

Isabella shook her head, her heart aching for him. "There's nothing to be sorry for. You weren't to know."

She watched Henry as he stood, head bowed, casting sideways glances at Belinda. He looked awkward now, ill at ease, and she knew he wanted to leave.

"Will you come and say hello?" Isabella asked, watching the panic grow in his eyes with dismay. He shook his head. "Please, Henry. For me."

She could almost see the mental struggle, the desire to please her set against the fear of someone new.

He shook his head again, his hand finding hers, holding her tight. "She thinks I'm mad," he whispered, not looking at her.

"She does *not* think you mad, Henry." Isabella said the words loud and clear, sending Belinda a challenging look that dared her to disagree. To be fair, although the woman had plastered herself to the far wall and hadn't moved a muscle, Belinda forced a smile to her lips and took a breath.

"Indeed, I don't," Belinda said, inching away from the wall to illustrate her words. "It is a pleasure to meet you, Mr Barbour." She held out her gloved hand and Henry stepped closer to Isabella, shaking his head.

Belinda faltered, her hand suspended in mid-air.

"Your wife was telling me what a talented artist you are," Belinda said, and Isabella could have hugged the woman as Henry's gaze slid back to her. He gave Isabella a doubtful look, and she smiled at him.

"I did," she said, adding with sudden inspiration, "In fact, I was wondering if I might show her the beautiful painting you did for me?"

Henry frowned, glancing back at Belinda, who had the good sense to keep her mouth shut. He gave a taut nod. "You show her," he muttered, rather ungraciously, though Isabella saw it for the gift it was.

"Thank you, Henry," she said, kissing his cheek.

He nodded, his expression still rather gruff. He went to let go of her hand, but Isabella held onto him. "Where are you going?" she asked, worried that he might disappear now. She didn't want him running into the woods or locking himself in his studio for days.

He rubbed the back of his neck, his desire to be gone plain. "Upstairs."

She smiled with relief and kissed his cheek. "All right, then, I'll see you later."

He nodded, casting Belinda one last, mistrustful look, before heading for the stairs.

Isabella let out a breath. She turned back to Belinda, wondering what she'd made of it, and decided she'd not ask. "Come with me," she instructed. If anything could explain Henry, it wasn't her words, it was his work.

They had ordered a frame for the painting, so for now it still stood on the easel in Henry's studio. She heard Belinda's intake of breath as she saw the hundreds of canvases stacked around the huge room, but she knew nothing would prepare her for this.

"Oh!"

Isabella studied her guest instead of the painting as Belinda took in the work Henry had done of her, asleep on the forest floor. The woman covered her mouth with her hand, tears glittering at her eyes.

"My husband doesn't find people easy to deal with, Lady Winterbourne, but he is very far from mad."

"Oh, my dear," Belinda said, the words sounding rather choked. "I believe you, and it's clear from his concern, and from this …" She gestured to the painting, wonder in her eyes. "He adores you."

Isabella smiled, looking back at the painting as a lump rose in her own throat. "Yes, he does. Heaven alone knows why," she added, the words rather choked. "God knows I don't deserve it, or him."

To her surprise, Belinda shook her head and threaded her arm through Isabella's. "Everyone deserves a second chance at happiness. Circumstances make people say and do things they would not if life wasn't so hard."

"Why are you being so kind?" Isabella demanded as the likelihood of crying again became inevitable. "I was beastly to you, and your sister."

Belinda shrugged, the kindness in her eyes showing what the marquess had fallen in love with. According to gossip, the bad-tempered, violent, and unpredictable man had become meek as a lamb under his wife's gentle hand.

"I understand, you know." Belinda's voice was low, confiding as she turned to Isabella. "Edward, he … he suffered in the war. Scars that aren't visible but that are still raw, even now. It has never left him, and sometimes …" She paused, staring at the painting and taking a breath. "Sometimes the world, and the people in it, they get too much. So, he lashes out in anger, upsetting those who would help him, or … he runs away." She reached out and grasped Isabella's hand. "If you ever need a friend, you may depend on me."

Isabella's throat ached with the effort of not crying, but she managed a smile and gripped the woman's fingers.

"Thank you, Lady Winterbourne."

The woman shook her head. "My name is Belle."

"Belle," Isabella repeated, wondering at what she'd done to deserve such a visit. She'd treated Belle and her sister like the enemy when they'd first met, but then, she'd seen her as a rival. Rightly, as it turned out.

"I do hope you're not a Bella," Belle said, laughing. "We shall get in a muddle." Her new friend grinned and stared about at

Henry's work. "May I see the rest?" she asked, eyes alight with pleasure. "And … do you think Henry would ever do a formal portrait?"

Chapter 14

"Wherein bravery, fear, and joy visit Barcham Place."

Isabella stretched under the covers of her bed and sighed. Exhaustion tugged at her eyelids, her eyes gritty and dry. Stomach cramps which had woken her at odd intervals had disturbed her sleep. She still had at least two weeks to endure, though. She was the size of a whale and the effort of carrying the baby about more than she could bear. From the light brightening behind her bedroom curtains, she could tell it was long since time she ought to be up. Her stomach rumbled, clamouring for food as the baby shifted, perhaps agreeing with the sentiment. *Not if it involves moving,* she thought with a groan.

For a moment, she dreamed she could smell food, and hot chocolate. Her mouth watered, but she didn't move until a weight upon the bed startled her. She turned to find Henry stretched out at her side.

"Henry," she said, pleased to see him. He'd kept his word after Jack's talk to him and hadn't barged into her room unannounced again, until now. This time, she found she didn't mind.

"I brought you breakfast," he said, gesturing to the tray on the table beside her and the source of the pleasant scent of chocolate, perfuming the air.

"Oh, how lovely," she said, struggling to sit up.

Henry got up and opened the curtains and a window, allowing a sultry breeze to filter in. The air was heavy, that strange taut stillness that often preceded thunder an almost tangible presence.

"It's stormy." He leaned outside, staring up at the skies, which were sombre, the purplish colour of a bruised plum.

"Will you still go out?" she asked, watching as he nodded.

"Yes, I don't mind getting wet."

Isabella patted the bed, and he returned to sit beside her. "Your paper will," she said, smiling at him and offering him a bite of bread and jam.

He took it from her fingers, chewing with content as he shrugged. "Doesn't matter."

The baby kicked, upsetting the tray she'd balanced on her stomach, and Henry laughed, righting the lid on the sugar bowl. To her relief, Isabella held the cup of chocolate in her hands.

"Little devil," she muttered, allowing Henry to take her cup from her and smoothing her hands over her stomach. "Oh, Lord, I'm so fat," she groaned, wondering if she'd ever be able to see her toes again. What her body would look like when all this was done, she didn't even dare to consider.

"Not fat," Henry said, shaking his head. He pulled back the covers, despite her gasps of shock, and kissed her stomach through the cotton of her nightgown. "Beautiful," he said, staring up at her, the sincerity in his eyes undoing her composure in an instant.

"Oh, stop it," Isabella, protested, waving her hand at him. "You know it will make me cry, and it isn't even true. I do have a mirror, you know."

"It is true," he said, the words firm as he moved up the bed to kiss her lips, her nose, her eyes, before returning to her lips. "So beautiful." The word and the look in his eyes were insistent and Isabella sighed, resigned to be his muse, his flawless beauty. There were worse fates. She gave a hopeless sigh, allowing him his romantic view of her.

"You can't argue with me, I'm an artist," he said, his voice grave now, knowing she didn't believe it was true, but just his idealistic vision of her. "I know these things."

Despite herself, she laughed, and Henry grinned at her as he got up.

"Don't get too wet," she called after him as he left. Henry paused at the door and turned to blow her a kiss.

"Goodbye, beautiful Isabella."

She watched the door close and then lingered in bed, finishing her breakfast and wishing she'd asked him to stay. He would have done. He'd like it if she insisted, pleased to be wanted, but she knew he got restless if he stayed indoors for too long. Henry was like a big friendly dog, knocking over ornaments and stepping on toes if he couldn't get out and burn off his energy.

Once washed and dressed, which seemed like a marathon effort of late, Isabella made her way down to the kitchen. She felt restless today, tired but unable to sit, bored but unable to concentrate. A half hour passed as she flicked through a recipe book before she resolved to stop being so indolent and make a cake.

Outside, thunder rumbled overhead, the trees whipping back and forth as the storm that had threatened all morning drew closer. The first fat drops of rain pattered against the window panes and Isabella wished that Henry hadn't gone out. They needed a storm, though, the air was hot and weighty, the atmosphere oppressive with a sticky heat that made her skin prickle. She sighed, wondering if he'd seek shelter or hurry home, hoping for the latter as the rain began.

Jack bustled into the kitchen where the sweet scent of cinnamon filled the air, and Isabella reached down to pull the cake from the oven. As she moved to straighten, her stomach tightened, a contraction slicing through her that stole her breath. The cake almost tumbled to the floor, but she slid it onto the table top as Jack hurried to stand beside her.

"Oh dear," she said, the words breathless as the patter of liquid on tiles announced that her waters had just broken. She clutched the back of a chair, staring at Jack, who'd gone a remarkable shade of white.

"That's never, it's not ... it can't b-be," he stammered, wide-eyed with alarm. He looked horrified.

Isabella drew in a deep breath, feeling remarkably calm in the circumstances. "Well, I'm afraid it is, Jack. It is about time, I suppose."

"You said two more weeks!" Jack threw back at her, pointing at her as though not keeping to the schedule had been her idea. The poor man sounded so terrified that Isabella bit back the retort brewing on her tongue and smiled instead.

"So I did," she remarked, heading for the door. She needed to get out of her wet skirts and prepare herself.

"I'll ... I'll ..." Jack followed her out into the hallway, at a loss for what it was he needed to do. "I'll fetch the doctor," he said with sudden inspiration.

"No." Isabella paused with her foot on the stair as the realisation hit her. She didn't want that obnoxious man and his sneers and his insinuations. The thought of having his judgemental presence when she was in such a vulnerable state made her feel ill. Yet then she'd be all by herself. A thrill of fear rolled down her back at having no one to attend her until she realised she didn't have to be alone. "I don't want the doctor, Jack," she said, turning back to him.

"B-but, Isabella!" Jack spluttered, outraged now. "You've got to have someone, a doctor ... *You have to!*"

Isabella started as thunder exploded overhead, rumbling through the great building.

"The doctor won't come out in this, anyway," she said, feeling sanguine about the whole thing now. She felt certain that God would not have sent Henry to save her from drowning if he meant only to take her away again in childbirth. Whether that was true, she had no idea, women died all the time giving birth. She wasn't special. Yet her conviction remained. She turned back to Jack. "No doctor, Jack. I don't like him, and I don't want him. I want Henry."

Jack gaped at her. "Henry?"

Isabella rolled her eyes and wondered why Jack had to choose this particular moment to turn into such a ninnyhammer.

"Yes, Jack. Henry. My husband. Fetch him for me. *At once!*" she added, as Jack still stood staring at her in shock. He moved then, like someone had lit a fire under him, and Isabella sighed with relief and made her way up the stairs.

***

"Henry!"

Jack's voice bellowed through the woodland, drowned out by the sound of the rain and wind and the glittering crackle of lightning as it lanced across an angry sky.

"The devil take you, man, where are you!" Jack leaned against a tree, fighting for breath. He'd been searching for hours now. Exhausted, his throat hoarse from shouting, and his unease at leaving Isabella alone for so long growing by the moment, Jack realised he ought to have ignored her and gone for the doctor. She didn't know what she was saying, though she was likely right about the blasted fellow not coming out in this. The wretched dandy-prat had been full of his own importance and Jack hadn't liked him one bit. No wonder the poor girl didn't want the old fool at such a moment. The fact remained, however, he was a doctor and right now the girl was all alone.

Jack pushed on, remembering Henry mentioning a rough, woodsman's shelter he'd found down by the river a year back. He's said it was in bad condition, but any shelter was better than none in this weather. Jack decided that if he didn't find him there, he'd have to go back alone and prayed his instincts were right.

The walk to the river was tortuous, fighting the wind and the rain that lashed at him, but at last he made it. The water rushed past him, swollen, surging and violent, and Jack kept calling.

"Henry! *Henry!*"

Jack had gone as far as he dared and was about to turn back when a familiar voice hailed him.

"Jack?"

In the dim light of the storm, Jack saw the dark shape of an uncertain structure leaning against a tree.

"Henry, thank God," he said, staggering through the trees. "I've been searching everywhere for you."

"What is it?" he demanded, as Jack reached forward and grasped his lapels, shaking him as guilt and terror stole his composure.

"It's Isabella! The baby's coming. She won't have that fool doctor and she sent me to look for you."

"Isabella?" Henry repeated, fear in his eyes. "She's all alone?"

"Yes!" Jack shouted, guilt rolling over him once more, the weight of it sickening. "She's been alone for bloody hours now. For the love of everything holy, get yourself back to the house."

Jack discovered he talked to thin air as Henry had already turned, running back towards the house as fast as it was possible for a man to move. Jack let out a breath of relief and then groaned as he turned himself back to follow with as much haste as he could.

***

Isabella knelt on the bed, clutching the bedpost, panting as the pain ripped through her. Curses, swear words, obscenities she wasn't even aware she knew, seemed to spill from her mouth, but the pain was nothing she'd ever experienced or had expected. She was of the firm opinion that pain of this sort would be fatal under any other circumstances. Before she could rain down another curse on whoever decided women ought to be the ones to have babies, the pain came again. Her scream rent the air, a primal, animalistic sound that echoed around the room.

The pain receded, giving her time to breathe, and she collapsed on the pillows she'd piled up to support her stomach. The contractions were coming faster and stronger now. Isabella whimpered, her earlier calm and stoicism fleeing as she realised she would have this baby alone and she didn't have a clue what she was doing. To be fair, her body appeared to be managing things perfectly well with little thought from her, but the longing for Henry was an ache in her heart.

The pain rolled over her again and she inhaled, readying herself for the onslaught. Thunder rumbled overhead, drowning out her cries as Isabella bore down, knowing at least this would be over, one way or another, before very much longer.

Isabella breathed deep, dazed with exhaustion, blinking in the light of the candles she had lit, to see the most beautiful sight in the world.

Henry.

She cried out, reaching for him, uncaring of the state she was in, the indignity. He was here and that was all she cared about. Relief overwhelmed her, her previous certainty she would be all right returning to her as he climbed onto the bed.

"It's all right," he said, his voice calm and certain as he leaned in to kiss her, stroking her hair.

"You're freezing," she said as his cold lips left hers.

"It's raining."

He grinned at her, the sight so wonderful and reassuring she no longer felt afraid. Henry would take care of her.

Henry stripped off his wet things, but this time she didn't have the time or the energy to appreciate the view. Another contraction gripped her, holding her stomach in a vice as the pain overwhelmed everything else. As she came back to herself, she noted Henry moving about the room. He'd covered the floor with pillows, covering them with a thick layer of sheets and towels and arranged a chair. What the devil was he doing?

As he came to her on the bed, he smiled, taking her hands. "Time to get up," he said, as Isabella glared at him, astonished.

"I'm a little busy, Henry," she said, her tone irritated now, despite having longed for him to be here.

"I know, love, but it'll be easier for you over here."

She narrowed her eyes at him. "You're not confusing me with a horse or a rabbit, now are you?"

Henry's mouth twitched, but his face remained placid. "I promise," he said, the words solemn.

Walking to the chair was the most exhausting thing she'd ever done, and that was with Henry practically carrying her. She felt dazed, outside of herself, when at last she sat and realised she wasn't sitting on the chair at all, but that Henry sat behind her, supporting her.

She leaned back, reassured by the sturdiness of him, by the large hands that gripped hers.

"Come along then, my beautiful Isabella," he whispered in her ear. "Time to meet our daughter."

"It's a boy," she grumbled, with the certain belief only the male of the species could cause her this much pain and trouble.

"Whatever you say, love," Henry chuckled, kissing her forehead as the next contraction pulled her body tight. "Now push."

Chapter 15

"Wherein a new beginning."

Henry stared at his wife and child. Isabella slept now, her beautiful face flushed still, her eyes shadowed with exhaustion. She was still perfect to his eye. The most wonderful sight Henry had ever had the privilege to look upon. Apart, that was, from his daughter.

It didn't matter to Henry that another man had sown the seed for the child. They were his now. The sad and unpleasant circumstances in which they had created his little girl tugged at his heart, both for the baby and Isabella. Though the thought of another man touching his wife was enough to make jealousy rage, stealing the breath from his lungs, he'd rather they had made her with love. It didn't matter now, though. He had love enough for them both, to make up for whatever had gone before. The emotion surged in his chest, threatening to overwhelm him, to tip him over into the strange place that made him run away from life, that made him want to hide, or to smash the world around him to pieces in fear and fury. Not today, though. Today he would not run.

The desire to reach out and touch the downy hair on the baby's head was an ache beneath his skin, but he didn't dare. Short of lifting the newborn into the arms of her mother, he'd not touched her, too afraid to do so. She was so perfect, so fragile, and he so big and clumsy. Terror filled his heart at all the things that might befall her if he failed to protect her.

His lovely Isabella had endured a life without love, without kindness or understanding, and he would never allow either of them to be hurt ever again. Possessiveness was a living thing beneath his skin, the desire to protect his family and keep them safe something that prowled with sharp claws and sharper teeth.

He let out a shaky breath, unsettled by such powerful emotions, torn between laughter and tears as he gazed upon them.

He wanted to paint them, the urge almost overwhelming, though he forced himself to keep still, to stand watch over them. Instead he pictured the image in his mind, Isabella as his Madonna. Instead of the blue cloak about her shoulders, she would lie beneath a wide lapis lazuli sky, full of hope and joy and promise for the future.

A soft knock at the door broke into his thoughts and he moved to open it, finding Jack on the other side. His familiar face was full of anxiety and hope, and on seeing the proud smile that Henry could not keep from his face, the man let out a breath of relief.

"Thank God," he said, the words heartfelt. "She's well?"

Henry nodded and opened the door a little, allowing Jack a privileged glimpse of his sleeping family. Jack swallowed hard, dashing his hand over his eyes.

"Girl or boy?" he asked, his voice rather thick.

"A girl, of course," Henry replied, though the words were still full of awe at the fact.

Jack held his hand out, grinning. "Congratulations."

Henry beamed at him and pulled him into a fierce hug. You didn't shake hands with family, to his way of thinking.

"Can't breathe, Henry," Jack muttered as Henry let him go. "Right, well, I'll leave you to it," he said, once he'd caught his breath. Jack waved a hand at him and Henry nodded, closing the door and turning back to his wife.

With as much care as was possible for a man of his size, he crawled onto the bed beside them, laying down on his side so he could look his fill. The baby stirred, giving a soft huff as her rosebud lips parted and settled back into a contented little pout. Henry swallowed hard, and as exhausted as he was, he stayed awake, watching over them.

***

A strange and unfamiliar sound tugged at Isabella's tired brain and she jolted awake. With a peculiar mix of astonishment and acceptance, she blinked as her daughter came into view. The baby was crying, a fretful mewling sound that made her womb tighten and her breasts prickle.

"She's hungry."

Isabella looked over, unsurprised to find Henry at her side. That he had guided her safely last night, that he hadn't run away or demanded a doctor take over ... the knowledge settled inside her, a warm weight. Henry would never let her down. It was an unfamiliar feeling, to have someone she could always rely upon, come what may, but she clung to it.

Feeling a little shy, which was rather ridiculous after the events of last night, Isabella undid the tie that closed her nightgown and guided the baby to her breast. As she latched on, Isabella's breath caught as her stomach contracted, pain lancing through her. Well, she hoped that didn't last for long. She let out a breath as the pain lessened and the baby suckled, her tiny fists pressing against Isabella's breast, her face peaceful and content now.

Isabella sighed, resting her weary head back against the pillows and looking to Henry. Her heart expanded as she saw the wonder in his eyes.

"You were right, of course," she said. "It's a girl."

Henry nodded, and she understood that he couldn't talk to her, his emotions too overwhelming. They sat together, silent except for the greedy noises the child made until she fell asleep. She released Isabella's breast as her mouth grew slack, a contented breath puffing over her mother's skin as she drifted back to sleep.

Isabella blinked back tears and grinned at Henry. "Do you want to hold her?"

To her surprise, Henry scrambled off the bed, shaking his head. He tucked his large hands under his arms, his head bent, though his gaze remained on the baby.

"Henry," Isabella said, her voice soft. "Don't run away, come and sit with me and your daughter."

Henry shook his head, though she could see longing in his eyes. He was afraid, fear of doing harm an anxious glint in his eyes. Isabella smiled at him, knowing this wasn't the time to push.

"Well, if you won't hold your daughter, come and hold me. I need to feel your arms around me. Please, Henry." She hid her smile this time, knowing Henry couldn't refuse such an entreaty. He settled beside her, opening his arms to her as Isabella lay back against his chest with a sigh of pleasure. Henry rested his head on her shoulder, watching the sleeping baby, and Isabella turned her head, kissing his cheek.

"I love you, Henry," she whispered as her husband turned to her, eyes wide and incredulous. He opened his mouth, and there was a sharp inhalation of breath but no other sounds. She leaned in again, pressing her mouth to the corner of his lips. "I know, my love. You need not say anything. Just hold us both."

Henry swallowed hard and nodded, his hold tightening just a fraction as they both gazed at their new arrival with wonder.

***

Isabella stared at the painting. If she lived to be a hundred, she would never cease to be amazed by the talent contained within the man beside her. He paced, impatient for a reaction, but Isabella was dumbstruck.

"Look what your father did for us, Marine," she whispered once she'd found her voice. The baby's blue eyes blinked up at her, the cause for her naming. Henry had insisted both her and the baby had eyes the colour of ultramarine. Though Isabella had assured him their daughter's eyes could change yet, Henry was adamant, so Marine it was. They shortened it to Marie, and it pleased Isabella, as everything in life pleased her now. "You make me look like an angel, Henry," she said, turning to him now. "I can't believe you still see me this way." Not after sleepless nights that could make her fractious and short-tempered, but Henry never reproached her.

"It's the way you are," he insisted, his voice a little stubborn now.

Isabella laughed, shaking her head at him. "How you can still say that after the abominable things I said to you last night." He'd come to her room in the early hours, called by Marine's full-throated wailing, and received little thanks for his efforts.

Henry snorted, rubbing the back of his neck. "You were tired."

"It's you that's the angel, here," she whispered, leaning into him. He looked down at her, such warmth in his eyes that her heart seemed to turn in her chest. The fleeting press of his lips against hers only intensified the sensation. It wasn't enough. In the weeks following the birth, it had relieved her to find her spirits, and her body, returning to normal. Her feelings for Henry only seemed to grow stronger, though, and having him so near was tantalising. She had fantasised about seducing him, her own husband. The idea made her smile even though she knew she must tread with care. He still hadn't held Marine, too afraid of her tiny size and frailty, though she knew he wanted to more than anything. She wouldn't push him into something he wasn't sure about.

Isabella looked back at his painting, her holding Marine, their eyes as blue as the skies above them. There was a worshipful, almost religious feel to the work she knew people might disapprove of, citing it as blasphemous, perhaps. Isabella saw it for what it was, though, an expression of love for her, for their daughter. No matter that the child had another father. Isabella would never allow herself to think on that again. In the first days after the birth, she had watched the child, afraid she might glimpse something in the baby's eyes of the cruel man who'd created her. Now, though, she accepted the truth. Marine was born in innocence, to parents that loved her, and that was the only truth that mattered.

"Let's have a picnic," she said, turning to Henry now. The weather had grown hotter with each day as it moved through the month of June, but under the shade of the apple trees in the orchard it would be cool enough. Without giving Henry time to comment, she hurried off to prepare what they needed.

***

Isabella congratulated herself on her idea as she lay back on the rug with a sigh of content. Marie slept in the little wicker basket under the shade of an apple tree. Her daughter was a greedy little madam and had drunk her fill, and Isabella watched Henry with lazy contentment, his dark head bent over his drawing as ever.

"Henry," she said, her voice low as a sense of anticipation tightened her body, her heart picking up a beat.

"Hmmm." He didn't look up, too focused on whatever part of the drawing was holding his attention.

"Come and kiss me, Henry."

He looked up then, and Isabella smiled as his eyes grew dark. She held out a hand to him. "You've drawn me enough for one day." The words were soft but firm, and she saw him take a breath, perhaps knowing she wanted more than a kiss today. "Come and see if I taste of strawberries." She smiled as he had teased her for the amount she'd eaten, but had shared his with her with obvious pleasure.

He set aside his pencil and the drawing, and Isabella's breath quickened as he lay down beside her.

"Do you want to kiss me?" The sound of her own voice was seductive, sultry in a way she'd never heard before, never believed herself capable of.

"I always want to kiss you," he said, the words simple but honest as he looked back at her.

Isabella reached out a fingertip, tracing the outline of his lips. "Then why don't you?"

He lowered his eyes, a slight frown gathering his eyebrows together. "Because I'm not sure if you always want to be kissed."

Isabella moved closer to him, so that their bodies almost touched, his breath fluttering warm against her mouth. "I'll tell you a secret, then," she said, leaning over to whisper in his ear. "I always want you to kiss me, Henry."

He swallowed, but reached for her, his hand settling on her waist as he leaned in, pressing his lips to hers. It was the sweetest of kisses, but a fire had been lit beneath Isabella's skin now and she wanted more as he drew back.

"You do taste of strawberries," he said, amusement in his voice.

"Are you sure?" she asked, turning onto her back now. "I think you should try again, just to be certain."

He didn't need asking again. The kiss was deeper this time, slow and lingering as Isabella ran her hands over his back. She tugged his shirt loose, sliding her hands under the material and across his broad back, hearing his breath catch.

"Do you like that?" she asked, one hand skimming his side and coming up to rest over his heart. Henry nodded, and she smiled, tugging at the shirt with one hand. "Take it off then."

Her breath snagged in her throat as she watched him, desire a living, breathing thing inside her. She wanted him, needed him, to touch him and be close to him. It made her skin ache with longing, her body clamour as that need echoed in a hollow space inside her reserved for him.

As he moved back to her, she pulled him down, not wanting him to be so careful now. His hand remained at her waist, though, and she knew he would not move beyond this position unless she invited him.

"Touch me," she whispered against his mouth, urgency in the words. "I want you to."

He paused, staring down at her, his eyes dark with desire, though something held him immobile.

"Please, Henry." There was something close to desperation behind the demand now and she sighed as his hand moved up, over her ribcage, cupping her breast through the fine fabric of the muslin. Her body had changed after Marine, her figure less angular, softer and more rounded, fuller, and she revelled in the feel of Henry exploring those curves. His mouth returned to hers and she sensed the anticipation in him now, the growing desire as his kisses grew fiercer, deeper. It wasn't enough, not nearly enough, and they both knew it.

She pushed at his chest and he stopped at once, drawing back with doubt in his eyes.

"Help me take this dress off, please." The look in his eyes made her smile, somewhere between shock and relief. He moved away so she could sit up, and busied himself undoing the ties. His usually sure fingers seemed to fumble each fastening and Isabella bit her lip, struggling not to laugh as happiness and anticipation mingled.

At last she was free, and she stripped off each layer, sending up a silent prayer that Marine should sleep for a while longer yet. She turned back then, shy all at once as she met Henry's eyes for the first time.

He stared, his breathing rapid. "Isabella," he said, the word reverent, making her feel worshipped in the same way the portrait had. "Isabella, you're so beautiful. I want to paint you this way."

Isabella's eyebrows hit her hairline. "Certainly not!" she exclaimed in horror. "Imagine if Jack saw or …" She didn't get to say another word as he tumbled her onto her back, his mouth covering hers. Isabella sighed and wrapped her arms around his neck as his lips left hers and kissed her jawline, her neck, along her collar bone.

Henry paused, drawing back, a question in his eyes. She reached up and touched his mouth, smiling her assurance. "Don't stop and don't ask. If you want to, I want to. I trust you."

His chest expanded as he caught his breath, anxiety lingering. "But Isabella, I ... I've never ..."

"Neither have I, Henry, not like this," she said. She wasn't a virgin now, but this still felt like the first time, the first time that mattered to her. "I want you." She reached for the fall of his trousers, undoing the buttons and sliding her hand beneath. They both caught their breath as she found what she sought and curled her fingers around the hard length of him.

He groaned, his head falling forward as he closed his eyes and Isabella quailed a little. Henry was everywhere in proportion, and as she remembered the pain of her first time, she felt a tremor of doubt. She could not help but touch him, though, astonished by the silk of his skin as she caressed him.

"Isabella," he whispered, the word aching with desire. "I ... I want ..."

She nodded, releasing him and pushing the trousers down his hips, tugging him closer to her. They both gasped as he slid against the slick heat between her legs.

"I don't want to hurt you," he said, the words breathless as he moved against her skin.

The desire for him, the ache to feel him inside her, chased away any fears or doubts. "You won't," she said, guiding him to where he needed to be. "I know you won't."

He moved slowly, the tension in him growing with the wonder in his eyes. As he eased inside her, Isabella relaxed, realising there would be no pain, and no regrets, not this time. She slid her hands over his shoulders, pulling at his neck, tugging his mouth back to hers. This was all for him, her pleasure secondary to wanting to love him, to show him what he meant to her. Yet the helpless sounds he made, the way his breath caught and held, exhaled on a heavy sigh, all of it built her own desires into a fire that only burned hotter. Soon she was clinging to him, teetering on the edge of a precipice she'd not known existed.

They clung to each other, clumsy kisses and grasping hands that neither minded, expressive only of need and love and inexperienced desire. "Henry," Isabella murmured, clutching at him, watching the stunned delight in his eyes before her own closed and the world fell away in a shower of bright lights. Pleasure rippled over her, stealing any coherent thought and leaving her boneless and astonished. Only the sound of Henry finding his release, holding her so tight, had the power to bring her to her senses. They clung together, breathless and sweaty and surprised in the shade of an apple tree.

She watched as Henry drew back a little, bracing on his arms to look at her. "Isabella?" he said, struggling to catch his breath. "You … you liked it?"

Isabella couldn't help herself. A sudden bark of laughter burst from her, startling in the peace of a languid afternoon. Marine wailed, her little lungs illustrating her fury at being woken, but Isabella only laughed harder.

"Oh, H-Henry," she said, wiping her eyes. "Yes. Yes, my love, very much."

"Good," he replied, grinning at her, a rather smug glint in his eyes. "Because I want to do it again."

***

Henry stared, still disbelieving. Isabella lay beside him, asleep on the rug he'd laid out, her skin dappled by the shade of the apple tree. The play of light and shadow would be enough to hold him spellbound in any other circumstance, but Isabella, loving her, touching her again, was all he could think of.

That she had given herself to him in such a way had changed him. He'd accepted the fact he would never marry. He was too strange, too out of step with the world to find someone who could understand him, let alone love him. That Isabella had agreed to marry him had been revelation enough. That she cared for him had stolen his breath and filled his heart. This, though, this was something he had no words for, something his heart could barely contain.

He moved closer, watching as she slept. The artist in him itched with the desire to pick up his pencil and paper and sketch her, but he realised that would be a betrayal of trust. She would let him, one day, because Isabella was everything that was kindness and generosity and she would deny him nothing, not even herself. How she could ever have believed herself cruel and unkind, he did not understand. She had been nothing more than a wild thing kept in a cage, snarling to protect herself. It had taken little time to discover the real woman hiding beneath that frightened façade.

Henry reached out a fingertip, trailing it along her collarbone, and then down, between the valley of her breasts. His breath caught as desire burned and he allowed it. Until Isabella had kissed him that day, he'd thought he had squashed such feelings, buried them down deep where they'd not torment him. The day the hard-faced woman who had worked here had tricked him into a quiet corner and tried to use him had made him afraid of such feelings. He'd wanted to touch her as she'd invited him to, just to see what she felt like. A mixture of curiosity and fear and excitement had struck him, but the woman's greedy reaction, the way she'd grabbed and demanded and the crude things she'd said had unnerved him. The taunts when he'd refused to do as she'd asked had been worse.

Now, though, with Isabella, everything was different. She welcomed him with love and trust, and that changed everything. He dipped his head, pressing a kiss to her lips as she sighed, waking under his touch. His lips explored a little further, tentative as she blinked, her sleepy sigh fluttering against his skin as he feathered kisses along her jaw and neck. Her hands found his neck, stroking his hair, and he knew she didn't mind him touching her in this way.

So, his questing lips continued their exploration, brushing the skin of her breasts with wonder. "So soft," he murmured, then found the peak of her nipple stiff and touched it with his tongue. Her breath caught and Henry looked up, startled.

"Don't stop," she said, giving him a lazy smile. He sighed with relief and did as she asked, exploring with lips and tongue, his hands sliding over her hips and stomach. The little thatch of curls at the apex of her thighs was fascinating too and he sat up, noting her breathing hitch once more as his fingers discovered the hidden terrain beneath the curls. He touched the tiny nub of flesh he discovered there and then dipped lower, finding her slick beneath his fingertip. Isabella arched, her eyes growing dark as he watched. A smile curved over his mouth as he returned to the soft little bud and discovered the source of her pleasure, moving his fingers over her with gentle, caressing touches.

He stared, bewitched by the sight of his wife, her skin growing rosy as she murmured, increasingly restless as he touched her.

"Henry," she said, holding her arms out to him. "Henry, please."

He moved over her, knowing what she was asking for despite the incoherence of her plea, as his body was clamouring, too, desperate to find his place within her. His breath snagged in his throat as their bodies joined, the moment so perfect, so irresistible, it was almost too much to comprehend. This place was the only one he had ever found where he didn't feel awkward, or different, but where he belonged.

She wrapped her arms around him, her legs about his hips, urging him on, whispering words of love to him that were miraculous to one who had believed he would never know what love would be like.

"Isabella," he whispered against her skin, the word a prayer of thanks to a God who was perhaps not so cruel as he'd supposed. "Isabella, my love."

Chapter 16

"Wherein fate is cruel and kind in turn."

"You look happy."

Isabella looked across at Belle and blushed a little, caught as she'd been daydreaming about Henry. Yesterday was still fresh in her mind. Henry had been as good as his word and loved her again in the orchard. They'd dressed in reluctance, forced back to the house by the lateness of the hour and the fact little Marine needed changing. A fact she'd impressed upon them with some force. But later, in the comfort of Isabella's bedroom, Henry had come to her again, and he'd stayed. Waking to find him beside her, albeit at an hour of the morning only a six-week-old baby could find reasonable, well, it had been one of the most wonderful moments of her life. It hadn't taken her long to realise every wonderful moment she'd ever had revolved around Henry.

"I am," Isabella said, the smile at her lips confirming that fact.

Belle returned her smile, though there was caution in her eyes. "I was wondering," she began, giving Isabella a rather anxious look now. "If you might like to go shopping with me?"

Isabella started, a panicky, fluttering feeling growing in her chest. She opened her mouth to refuse, but Belle held up a hand. "You don't have to tell me now, Isabella, just think about it; only … are you going to live the rest of your days confined within these walls?"

"I like it here," Isabella retorted, setting her teacup down with something of a clatter.

"I know that," Belle replied, her tone kind and soothing. It was impossible to be cross with someone so good-hearted, although Isabella wanted to usher her out the door right now for allowing the real world to intrude. "But do you want your daughter to grow up in isolation, with no friends?"

Isabella frowned. She wanted everything good in life for her daughter, for her to know what it was to be loved and happy. For that to happen, the child would need to see more of the world than these four walls. That Henry would not share in those experiences was a pain in her heart, but she knew he would not want the girl to miss out either.

Belle got up, moving to sit beside Isabella, and clasped her hand. "My family are not immune to scandal, you know."

Isabella nodded, knowing what the woman referred to. Her sister, Lucretia, had run away with the terrifying figure of Lord Gabriel DeMorte. The world knew DeMorte as a murderer, a dark and sinister man with a reputation for cruelty. That the lovely Crecy had returned with a babe in her belly and DeMorte's ring on her finger had not stopped the gossipmongers from tattling their tales. Isabella burned with shame as she remembered that she'd been one. How different things looked on the other side of the story.

"How is your sister?" Isabella asked, avoiding Belle's eyes for fear she'd see the guilt that dwelt there. She promised herself that she would never think or repeat another ill word about another human being so long as she lived. Cruelty had lost any appeal after witnessing the way life could be with someone as open and generous as Henry.

"Blissfully happy," Belle replied with a smile that held a little reserve. "And far braver than I. I was all for her hiding away at home, you see. Living quietly and not giving the gossips any more fuel for their tales … but not Crecy."

Belle gave a wry grin which Isabella could tell was full of pride.

"Crecy took herself and the baby out and about and spat in their eyes, metaphorically," Belle added with haste. "I thought she was out of her mind," she admitted with a sigh. "But she had the right of it. Once the world saw how nauseatingly happy she was, they grew bored with talking about her and moved on."

"To me," Isabella said with a snort.

Belle shrugged and patted her hand. "For now, yes, but eventually there will be another unfortunate young lady to carry the burden of their censure. Until then, however ..."

Isabella gave her a dark look. "I should face them and spit in their eyes?"

"Quite so."

She watched as Belle reached for another cake, her expression placid. The woman would not push her, she knew that much. She also knew she was right. Little did she want to admit it.

"Marine needs christening," she murmured, worrying at her lip with her teeth.

Belle nodded. "Yes," she replied, taking another bite of her cake. "You said that at least two weeks ago."

Isabella huffed. "It's not that easy," she said, reaching for her teacup and setting it down again with a grimace as she realised the tea had gone cold. "It's so hard on Henry. When we got married, it ... Well, it's difficult for him."

"But he did it." Belle held up her hands in a peaceable gesture as Isabella glared at her. "I am not making light of the problem, I assure you. But in my experience, if a man wants to do something enough, he'll do it. Does Henry want his daughter christened?"

"Yes, of course," Isabella said, feeling a little irritated by Belle's placid voice when her own heart was beating in her throat. "More than anything. I think it troubles him she's not."

"Well, then," Belle said, as if that settled everything. "There you have it."

Isabella glowered at her feet, wishing the next words were not about to leave her mouth. "She'll need a christening gown."

Belle grinned at her, a rather devious smile that made Isabella wonder if she'd not just been manoeuvred about like a gaming counter. "Well, do you know, Isabella, I know just the place."

***

Isabella plucked at the pretty swathes of muslin, casting an anxious look out of the window of the shop towards the park.

"They're fine," Belle said, her voice soothing. "Believe me, if Rachel can cope with my son, your daughter will *not* be a challenge."

Isabella nodded, knowing she was fretting for nothing. They'd only been apart five minutes. "I know, she looked accomplished and capable," she said, trying to concentrate. "I've just never left her before."

Belle grinned at her. "I know. Enjoy it while you can," she instructed, her voice tart.

She snorted, rolling her eyes at Belle. "Yes, Lady Winterbourne."

"Oh dear, am I being bossy? I promised myself I wouldn't." Isabella laughed this time and took Belle's arm as they walked farther down the aisle of the shop.

"No, you are being a dear friend and I'm grateful. I shall stop being such a goosecap, I swear."

"Are you sure it's only Marine you're worrying about?" Belle teased her.

Isabella gave a wistful smile and shrugged. She wasn't worried about Henry, exactly. It was more that she knew he worried about her. Having her out of his sight in a world he thought cruel and incomprehensible had not put him in the best of humours. That he'd supported her despite his misgivings had been just one more reason she was so keen to return to the safety of their little idyll.

It took the best part of an hour, but they bought the christening gown, along with some new gloves for Isabella and a length of bronze-coloured ribbon.

"What's the ribbon for?" Belle asked, and Isabella demurred, murmuring about trimming a hat. That she'd bought it for Henry was not something she would tell Belle.

The little market town was bustling today, but at least it was the locals, bringing their produce to market and standing around chattering. The *ton* would put in an occasional appearance here. They would sneer and complain about the lack of style and dull provincial tastes, but local as it was, needs must bring them here on occasion.

Isabella was enjoying herself, though. She dawdled a little, perusing the shop windows as Belle walked forward to greet a friend. Belle had been right. She'd noticed a few judging faces who recognised her and walked on, quickening their step, but she found she didn't care as much as she might have believed. So, it was a cruel stroke of luck that brought Isabella face to face with her mother.

The two women started, and Isabella wasn't sure which one of them was the most shocked. As ever, her mother recovered first, a look of disgust filling her narrow face as she looked her daughter up and down.

"I wonder you have the nerve to show your face here, you little slut," she hissed, turning to see if the people she was with had seen Isabella yet. "Just because you got some half-wit to marry you doesn't mean you've a right to return to society."

"He's not a half-wit!" Isabella retorted, fury replacing the numbing shock that had held her immobile on first seeing Lady Scranford. "Henry is a good-man, and a great artist. I'm happy, mother, not that I expect you to care."

"Keep your voice down," her mother hissed, her bony fingers curling around Isabella's arm and dragging her out of sight of her companions.

"Let go of me, you're pinching," Isabella snapped, trying to drag her arm free. The woman might be scrawny, but she had a vice-like grip, her nails digging into Isabella's flesh with deliberate cruelty.

"You're right about one thing, Isabella," her mother said with a sneer. "I don't give a damn if you're happy with your madman, or if your bastard child lived or died. I do care that you not sully my good name any further. So, get out of this place before anyone sees you, and don't come back."

"No."

Her mother stared at her, her shock plain, and Isabella realised she'd never defied her before. Never.

"What did you say?" that bitter mouth demanded, her eyes glittering with malice.

"I said, *no*, mother." Isabella's heart was beating in her throat, combined fury and embarrassment scalding her cheeks as heads turned in their direction. "I'm Mrs Barbour now, and you have no right to tell me what to do. I'll carry on shopping here for as long as I wish, and there's not a single thing you can do about it."

Her mother jolted like someone had slapped her, and Isabella felt a surge of satisfaction. "By the way," she added, raising her voice loud enough, so it carried. "You're the grandmother to a beautiful little girl. I'm sure that knowledge will please you." She laced the words with amusement, vindictive as they were, and Isabella snorted as she saw her mother's friends put two and two together.

She walked off with her chin up, to discover Belle hurrying towards her.

"Oh, Isabella, my dear. I'm so sorry, I didn't see her or …"

Isabella shook her head as Belle took her arm. "It's all right," she said, letting out a breath, though she discovered she trembled as the force of her anger subsided. "I'm glad I faced her."

"You were very brave," Belle said, her tone approving.

Isabella snorted and held out her hand to show how much it shook. What possessed her to look back, she didn't know, but she saw two young women gossiping, and pointing in her direction as another gaped, scandalised by whatever she was being told. They laughed, their eyes wide as though looking at a bizarre and shocking exhibit at a fair. A flush stained her cheeks as Belle followed her gaze.

"Head up, Isabella," she instructed. "Spit in their eyes, remember."

"I think we must get closer for that," Isabella muttered, walking in the opposite direction as fast as she could. Bravery was best accomplished in small doses, she decided. For now, all she wanted was to run back to Henry, and the peace and safety of the sanctuary they'd found together.

***

"How's my little lady, then?" Jack crooned as Isabella handed Marine into his arms from the carriage. He kissed the baby's head before reaching out to help Isabella down.

"Where's Henry?" she asked, desperate to see him now. Though the shock of seeing her mother had worn off a little, her cruel words struck her hard now she'd had time to relive them.

Jack snorted, shaking his head. "Sulking in his studio, of course," he said, chuckling. "Good God, if the man asked me the time once today, he did it fifty times. I sent him off with a flea in his ear."

"Oh dear," Isabella said, hurrying down the steps.

"Oh, don't you fret," Jack said, as Isabella juggled her purchases into a pile she could carry. "He's fine, just missed you, that's all, and that won't do him no harm." He gave Isabella an assessing look. "You can't hide yourself away here forever just because it suits Henry. Won't do little Marine any good."

Isabella sighed as they walked out of the sun and into the cool gloom of the entrance hall. "That's what Belle said."

Jack nodded. "Wise lady, that one," he said, his tone approving. "I like her." He shot Isabella a sideways glance, his eyes on her assessing. "It go all right, then?"

She swallowed, avoiding his eyes. "I … I saw my mother."

"Did you now?" Jack said, his eyes full of concern. "Bet she had a word or two for you, eh?"

"You could say that," Isabella replied, the longing for Henry growing now.

To her surprise, Jack put an arm around her and kissed the top of her head. "You're a brave girl, Isabella. I'm proud of you, and everything you've done. You've made Henry happier than I dared ever hope, and …" His face softened as he glanced down at the baby in his arms. "And this little princess is a wonder and a blessing." He sniffed and cleared his throat, his voice growing stern. "So, don't you let nothing that miserable bitch said make you feel anything less than you are. You're a good girl, and we love you. Right?"

Isabella swallowed hard, touched beyond words that Jack should say such things to her.

"Right," she whispered, blinking back tears.

"Run along and find poor Henry, then," Jack instructed. "Before he frets himself to death. I'll look after little lady muck here."

On impulse, Isabella ran forward and kissed Jack's whiskery cheek, amused to see a blush stain his cheeks as she turned and did as he commanded.

Isabella tip-toed into Henry's studio, wanting to surprise him. To her disappointment, he wasn't standing at his easel, the work covered with a sheet. That meant he was planning something new he didn't want her to see. The temptation to peek was strong, but she was content to wait, knowing it was worth the anticipation. Where, though, was Henry?

It was growing late now, the sun sinking fast, and the room filled with shadows as no candles had been lit. She found him at last, sitting hunched in a dark corner of the room, head bowed, threading the blue ribbon back and forth through his fingers. He was muttering to himself, low, anxious words she couldn't make out.

"Henry?"

He looked up then and let out a breath. "Isabella!" She smiled, holding her arms out to him as he scrambled to his feet. He swept her up in his arms, holding her tight as she squealed.

"Can't breathe, Henry," she gasped, pushing at his huge chest.

"Sorry." He released his hold, just a little, looking sheepish. "I'm so glad you're home."

"You can't possibly be as glad as I am," she retorted, resting her head against him. "Oh, Henry. What a day. I missed you."

"You did?"

The surprise in his voice tugged at her heart and she tutted him. "Of course I did," she said, shaking her head. "How can you think otherwise?"

He shrugged, ducking to lean his head on her shoulder and avoiding her eyes. "I was afraid you wouldn't come back."

Isabella frowned at him, forcing him to lift his head and look at her. "You think that of me, Henry? You think I would run off and leave you?"

Henry swallowed, anxiety in his eyes now as he heard the annoyance in her voice. Isabella remembered what her plans had once been as she saw that anxiety, her plans to run off to France when the baby was old enough to travel. Shame flooded her, and she held Henry tight.

"I'll never leave you, Henry. Never."

She reached up, her arms about his neck as she pulled his head down for a kiss and felt the tension leaving his heavy frame.

"Promise," he whispered against her lips as she smiled at him.

"I promise, with all my heart."

She held him, stroking his face, his hair, as stared down at her. "Where's Marine?" he asked.

"She's sleeping," Isabella said, an amused smile curving over her mouth. "Jack's looking after her."

Henry sighed with relief and took her hand, tugging her towards the door. "Good."

"Where are we going?" she asked, though she didn't need to hear the answer.

He didn't even turn back but dragged her into the hallway, heading for the stairs. "I missed you, Isabella," was all the answer he granted her, but she rather thought it was enough.

***

Later that evening, once Marine was bathed and fed and sung to sleep, Isabella turned to find Henry waiting for her in bed.

She clambered in beside him, collapsing against his chest. "Babies are tiring," she murmured. Henry tugged at her nightgown with a scowl.

"Take it off," he said, trying to tug her arms free.

"Did you hear what I said?" Isabella grumbled, knowing better than to argue with him.

"Yes, but I want to hold you," he protested, grumbling. "Not a nightgown."

She snorted, struggling out of the capacious garment, and then thought he had a point as she snuggled into his chest with a sigh.

"That's better." The words were contented, smug, and Isabella smiled, tangling her fingers in the hair that trailed down his abdomen.

"It is," she said, happy to agree with him. "Blissful," she added, turning her head to kiss his skin. Unbidden, her mother's face drifted before her eyes, the cruel words and the taunting laughter that had followed her down the street. Her eyes blurred a little, though she said nothing, but Henry turned onto his side, moving down the bed so he could see her face.

"What is it?" he asked, cupping her cheek with one large hand. Isabella covered it with her own, turning into it and kissing his palm. She shook her head, not wanting to talk about it, but she could see Henry growing anxious, and so she took a breath.

"I saw my mother today."

Henry frowned, his thumb stroking her cheek. "She wasn't kind to you." It wasn't a question. Henry knew well enough. Isabella found her throat too tight to reply, so she returned a smile that quavered, and shook her head.

"They laughed at you," he said, tension and desperation in the words now as he moved away from her. He sat up, against the headboard, clutching his knees to his chest. "They laughed at you for marrying me."

Isabella opened her mouth to deny it, realising at the last moment she couldn't. That wouldn't work with Henry. She couldn't lie to him. He knew what people said about him. That they were so wrong made her heart break. That it hurt Henry made her furious.

"Henry," she said, her voice soft and coaxing as she moved to sit beside him. She tried to lift his arm, to get close enough to hold him, but it remained rigid, and he refused to move. "They don't know you, they don't know the slightest thing about you."

He put his head on his knees, his face turned away from her. "They know I'm mad." The words were muffled, heavy with misery, and Isabella's heart clenched.

"No, they think it because they don't know you, because they don't understand you and they're too ignorant to try." Isabella could not keep the rage from her voice and Henry turned towards her.

"Am I mad, Isabella?" The fear in his words broke her and she threw her arms about him.

"No!" she said, the word fierce and honest. "They're the mad ones for not seeing the shallow world they live in." She pressed kisses to his lips, his cheeks, holding his face between her hands. "My mother is mad. She's alone and miserable, despising everyone and wanting more, always more, though she has so much. We could have been happy, she and I, but she will never know what that means." She took a breath and pressed another kiss to his lips. "You were right, Henry. She will die alone and unloved because she lives only on the surface of life. She lives for lies and material things which will never satisfy her. You told me that, Henry, and you were right."

He took a shaky breath and Isabella prayed that he would heed her words.

"Before I met you, I was just like her." Her voice trembled as she heard the truth and remembered all the cruel things she'd said and done. "I was hateful, Henry, full of spite, and I hated myself as much as everyone else." She stroked his hair, wanting to tear anyone apart with her bare hands who would dare to hurt her husband. "You taught me kindness and showed me I didn't have to be that person, that I could be better. *You* did that, Henry, you made me a better person, you taught me how to love."

He looked up at her, his eyes shining, and Isabella held out her arms to him. He came to her then, clinging to her as Isabella stroked his back, wondering at the gentleness in this powerful man.

"I love you," she said, kissing his lips. Henry sighed, a heavy shuddering sound as he allowed his fears to fall away. She feathered kisses along his jaw, down his neck, determined to worship him as he deserved. Henry showed his devotion to her in his work, with the beauty of his skills. Isabella would give him hers with her body.

He reached for her and she smiled at him, shaking her head. "Lie still," she whispered. "Let me love you."

She kissed her away across his chest, teasing his nipples into taut little peaks with her tongue. With satisfaction, she watched the rise and fall of his chest increase, his eyes darkening as he watched her. Isabella smoothed her hands over his body, revelling in the warmth of his skin, of the muscles that twitched and grew hard with tension as her lips and hands moved over him. She didn't have much clue about what she was doing, guided only by instinct, by a desire to please him and chase the sadness from his eyes, by the need to love him. He moved, restless now, his breathing growing harsh as she followed the coarse trail of hair across his stomach.

Henry made a sound of disbelief as her mouth found him. She pressed kisses down the length of his erection, still surprised by the silk of his skin. Returning with her tongue sliding over him, he groaned, and it thrilled her, making her own desires burn hotter. Emboldened by how he clutched at the bed clothes, by the increasing desperation of the sounds he made, she took him in her mouth.

"Isabella." Her name tore from his lips, a harsh cry on the heated air, the summer night still and silent around them. Isabella smiled against his skin, exhilarated by his reaction to her touch. She repeated the action over and again until he was writhing, helpless, his skin slick. That his release was close was obvious to her and she moved to take him again, but he pushed her away, onto her back. Henry sought her hands and pressed them into the mattress at either side of her head as he found his place between her legs.

Isabella arched as he slid inside her, a sense of completeness, of perfection with this man, that she refused to believe most people found. It was too extraordinary, and that was because of Henry. He tensed, his hands gripping hers harder as he cried out, his body hot and heavy as he shuddered with pleasure, collapsing on top of her.

Isabella smiled, content, as she stroked his shoulders, his skin overheated and sweaty, not that she cared. He was faultless. His breathing evened out and he moved, bracing himself on his arms and looking down at her.

"That was nice," he said, the devilish grin at his lips suggesting *nice* didn't quite cover it.

"Was it?" Isabella asked, all innocence.

Henry nodded and sat back, kneeling between her legs. "I want to do it to you."

Isabella's eyes grew wide. That hadn't occurred to her. "Oh, but ... but, Henry, I don't ... d-don't think ... *oh!*"

The rest of the night was a revelation. They forgot thoughts of cruel mothers and vicious people as they remembered what was true, and truly important.

Chapter 17

"Wherein Henry faces a battle of sorts, and a villain raises his head."

Isabella stared at herself in the mirror, turning this way and that. She hadn't tried this gown on before, deciding the order for it ought to wait until after she'd regained her figure, or as near to it as she thought possible. Not that she minded the loss of her rather angular form. Henry seemed pleased with her fuller curves, and if she kept up her baking skills, she saw no chance of them diminishing any further. The bustline had been underestimated, though, and her breasts pushed against the bodice, spilling over like freshly baked loaves. Well, this was for Henry alone to enjoy, so what did it matter.

It was Henry who had asked her to wear it, though it was midmorning and unsuitable for the hour. She suspected the large canvas he'd been hiding from her had something to do with it.

He confirmed her suspicions as she entered the studio, to discover Jack helping him to move a red velvet chaise longue. All his work, his tables crammed with paints and brushes and oddments which he collected on his walks, were shunted to one end of the ballroom. They had swept the floor and polished it, too, which likely accounted for the fact they both looked sweaty and dusty and irritable. The easel now stood at the centre of the room, tables bearing painting materials arranged to one side.

Both men sighed as they lowered the heavy piece of furniture and Jack pulled out a hanky, mopping his brow. "Bugger me, it's too damn hot for this malarkey," he grumbled. He looked up as Isabella walked towards them and gaped. A moment later Henry spotted her, and an identical expression crossed his face, too.

Jack cleared his throat. "Right, well, I'll … go check on Marie," he said, hurrying off.

"She's still sleeping," Isabella called after him, amused.

"Let him go," Henry said, still staring at her, a hungry look in his eyes that made Isabella smile. "I want you to myself."

"As you wish, husband." She moved towards him, her smile growing, but Henry held his hand out, stopping her in his tracks.

"No," he said, his voice uncharacteristically stern as he shook his head. "I want to paint you and I'll won't be able to if you come any closer."

Isabella tilted her head to one side, observing the desire in his eyes. "Perhaps I'd prefer if you didn't paint me," she said, her voice teasing.

Henry stared at her, eyes wide, rubbing the back of his neck, and she laughed.

"Oh, all right, I'll be good, but I expect you to make it up to me."

He shot her a grin, pleased and mischievous, and she knew there would be no problem holding him to that. She sat on the chaise longue, assuming it had been placed there for her, and Henry moved forward to arrange the skirts of her dress. It was the colour he had chosen for her, a vivid, blazing orange silk that flickered gold in the light. Isabella would never have dared to wear the colour out, but for Henry, it was a pleasure, to see the awed look in his eyes.

"I love this colour on you, Isabella," he said, sitting back on his heels and staring up at her. "I knew it was right as soon as I saw it. You are the goddess Juno, queen of the gods, and this is your month, named for you."

Isabella laughed, looking down at her handsome husband. "I think Mrs Isabella Barbour is enough for me to live up to."

Henry moved closer to her, shaking his head. "No," he said, his voice grave now. "You are my warrior goddess, come to save me from the dark. You burn like a flame, beautiful Juno."

Isabella stared at him, tears prickling at her eyes. "You make me feel like a goddess, Henry, that's all I care about."

That smile came again, swift and as devastating as ever, and she leaned forward, unable to resist pressing a kiss to his lips. The touch of his mouth was enough for desire to burst to life, and he moved closer, crushing the skirts he had arranged with such care, deepening the kiss. Eyes still closed, he sighed against her mouth before trailing his lips down her neck. Henry brushed his lips over the creamy flesh that spilled from her dress, setting fires beneath her skin. His tongue painted their own masterpiece as her heart sped and she gasped as he dipped into her décolletage. With a ragged sigh, he moved away, casting her a look of reproach.

"Stop distracting me."

"Yes, Henry," she said on a sigh, the words laden with disappointment as he rearranged her skirts. If she had any say in the matter, he'd have to do that often. He was smiling as he returned to his easel, though, and Isabella decided that tormenting her husband was an enjoyable pastime.

***

Isabella looked up from Marie's smiling face, across the carriage to her husband. He was as white as a winter sky despite the heat of the day.

"Henry?"

He looked up from the ribbon he was threading back and forth between his fingers for a moment, and the determination in his eyes tugged at her heart. They were christening Marie today. Belle and her husband Edward would be godparents, a gift that Isabella could never have hoped for. Having such a powerful man as the Marquess of Winterbourne stand for Marie would go some way to diminishing the stain of illegitimacy she would always bear. That

Henry had to endure the ceremony, however, was a problem they could not get around.

He was determined to do it, to christen *his* daughter, and Isabella wanted to weep for the effort he was making.

"I have something for you," she said, reaching one-handed for her reticule and tugging out the silky length of ribbon she had bought for him. Isabella moved to sit beside him and placed it across his outstretched palm. The bronze ribbon glinted in the light, shades of copper and bronze catching the sun.

"That's the colour of your eyes, Henry," she said, smiling at him.

Henry looked up at her with surprise and pleasure in his expression before returning his attention to the ribbons. He folded the blue one with care and tucked it in his pocket before resuming threading the silky bronze length back and forth between his fingers.

"Thank you," he said, his voice low. Isabella leaned over and kissed his cheek, praying the day would pass without causing him too much distress.

Jack hurried inside the church as soon as they arrived, while Henry and Isabella waited in the carriage. Henry was sweating now, his breathing harsh as he cast anxious glances out of the window. Isabella moved Marie to her other arm, reaching out to clasp his hand and finding his palm damp.

"Henry, I'm here, love. Marie and I are both here. There's nothing to fear."

Henry made a sound of anguish and shot Isabella a look filled with panic and shame.

"I know," he said, the words angry, as he took his hand from her and wrapped his arms around his chest. "I know, I know, I know but ..." The *but* was the crux, that one word filled with terror and dismay, and Isabella didn't know how to comfort him.

Marie whimpered, perhaps sensing Henry's agitation, and Isabella looked up with relief as Jack ran back to the carriage. They needed this done, and fast.

"Belle and his lordship are inside already," he said, giving Henry a worried glance and turning back to Isabella. "We'd best get it done."

Isabella nodded and allowed Jack to hand her down before he turned back to the carriage to coax Henry out.

"Come on now, lad. I know you don't want to go in there, but Marie is depending on you. Can't let your little girl down now, eh?"

Henry exhaled a shuddering breath and nodded, climbing out of the carriage as Isabella moved closer to him, taking his arm.

"Jack and I are here, love, and Marie. We'll all go in together."

Henry stared at his feet, silent, but allowed Isabella to move him towards the church. As he got to the door, he dug his heels in, wrenching his arm free and shaking his head.

"C-can't," he said, fighting for breath as he stared at the door. He made a sound of distress and paced, casting glances at the church, his hands clutched in his hair. To her dismay, Isabella saw a husband and wife walk from the graveyard, perhaps having paid their respects to a dead relative. They stopped and stared at Henry, open-mouthed and whispering as they walked away, casting him horrified looks over their shoulder as they went.

Jack and Isabella exchanged anxious glances, both wondering how best to calm him, when a deep and commanding voice came from inside the church.

"Mr Barbour?"

They looked around to find the marquess on the doorstep, Belle holding his arm. She smiled at Isabella, her expression full of sympathy and understanding.

Henry froze, and for a moment Isabella thought he might run, but he remained.

"I'm Winterbourne," the man said, holding Henry's gaze. He was neither as tall nor as broad as Henry, but he exuded strength, a figure men would follow into battle.

Henry nodded, sweating and trembling but holding his ground.

The marquess took a step closer, never looking away from him. "You want to give your daughter your name, before God. Is that correct?" he demanded.

"Y-Yes," Henry stammered, standing a little straighter now.

"Right," Winterbourne said with a sharp nod. "Snap to it, then."

Isabella watched with her heart beating in her throat as Henry swallowed, his hands clenched so tight that the knuckles showed white as he moved to take her hand. He clutched at her, his grasp hurting her fingers.

"Sorry," he whispered, head bowed as they moved to the door. "I'm s-sorry."

Isabella raised his hand to her lips and kissed it. "I love you, Henry," she whispered.

Henry gave her a sideways glance, his expression filled with despair and wonder, and together they went to christen their daughter.

***

Isabella stared down at her baby daughter before leaning down and blowing a raspberry against her stomach. Marie gurgled with laughter, kicking and beaming up at her mother, and Isabella's breath caught. She'd never known it was possible to feel such love for another human being, but Henry and her daughter had taught her otherwise.

With a rush of sadness, she wondered if her own mother had ever known such overwhelming emotions, and knew she had not. She would have handed Isabella to a nurse maid within minutes of the birth, and her mother would be as little occupied with her as possible. To her surprise, it was not resentment that swelled at the realisation, but pity. Her mother had missed this. The woman had never known the joy of the bond between a mother and her child, and for that, Isabella could only feel sorrow for her. Marine was her world, and she knew Henry felt the same. That her husband could open his heart to a child that wasn't his, only showed what a strong and wonderful man he was. She was blessed.

Once she'd dressed Marie, she took her downstairs, to find Jack slamming about in the kitchen. That he was in a temper was plain, and she hesitated for a moment before walking in, aware that he hadn't seen she was there.

"Jack?"

He jumped a little and she saw the effort he took to arrange his face into something less furious.

"I didn't see you there," he said, coming over to smile at Marie. "And how's my little princess today?"

"Giggly," Isabella replied, smiling as Jack offered the baby his little finger. "And you, Jack? How are you?"

A troubled look entered the man's eye and he avoided her gaze. "Fine and dandy," he replied, the words light-hearted. Isabella knew him well enough to know his tone was forced.

"And how are you, really?" She narrowed her eyes at him as he sighed. The kettle sang on the stove and he turned away.

"You want tea?"

"Yes, please," Isabella replied, sitting down at the table and wondering why he was being so evasive. He'd been into town this morning to fetch supplies, she knew that. "Now tell me what has you in such a bad skin this morning."

Jack shrugged as he poured hot water into the teapot. As he brought it to the table, he cast Isabella a look filled with anxiety and she knew he was thinking about fobbing her off again.

"Jack," she said, reaching across the table to squeeze his hands. "We're friends, surely you can tell me if something troubles you."

"Course, Isabella," he said, shaking his head as he sat down opposite her. "I ... I didn't want you worrying, too, if there were no need, but ..."

"But?" Isabella repeated, a tremor of unease worming its way under her skin.

Jack sat forward, lowering his voice. "There was a deal of gossip this morning," he said, anger underlying the words. "About you and Henry and ... and Viscount Treedle."

Isabella's blood chilled under her skin, her heart growing cold. She had put the man from her mind and resolved never to think of him again. Mere gossip was not enough to make Jack look as though he feared something, though.

"What else, Jack?"

Before the man could answer, they jumped as a hammering sound came at the front door.

Jack's eyes widened with fear. "Reckon that's him, Isabella," he said, the words panicked. "I thought perhaps it was all talk, but ..."

"But what, Jack?" Isabella cried, leaping to her feet.

She watched, fear growing in her heart as Jack said the horrifying words, "He's come for Marie."

Chapter 18

"Wherein ... war."

Jack's words spun in Isabella's head, making her dizzy and nauseated, but they made no sense.

"He didn't want her, he cast us out ... Why ... w-why now?" she stammered, clutching Marie to her chest.

"Because of the talk," Jack said, his voice angry. "He's being pilloried for allowing a *madman* to raise his bastard child."

Isabella jolted as the hammering at the door grew louder, alongside shouted demands that they open up. The bastard. Fury filled her veins, chasing away fear, though it lingered in her heart. Viscount Treedle had taken enough from her for one lifetime, he'd not take anything else.

"Jack," she said, her voice firm. "Take Marie and get out of here. Go down to the woodsman's hut where you found Henry. One of us will come for you when it's safe."

Jack nodded, taking the baby into his arms. "You sure, Isabella, what about you? P'raps you should hide with her."

Isabella gave him a grim smile and shook her head. "I know how to deal with a snake like Treedle. I'll be fine, Jack. Don't you worry. Now go."

She watched him hurrying towards the back of the building before she turned around. Isabella took a moment to compose herself, smoothing down her skirts and searching out what remained of the cold, disdainful woman her mother had bred her to be.

She stalked to the door and swung it open, glaring with contempt at the man whose fist was raised to knock again.

"Do you wish to smash my door to pieces, sir, or is this your usual display of manners when paying a call on a lady?"

The fellow dropped his fist, taken aback for a moment, and then Viscount Treedle stepped forward.

"A lady?" he queried, his tone insulting. "We were not calling upon a *lady*, dear Isabella."

Isabella snorted, wondering at the fool she'd been. A marriage to this man would have destroyed her, how could she have longed for such a thing with such desperation? Now *there* was madness.

"I see your manners have improved none," she said, shuddering at the memory of his hands upon her. "You always were a boring fool, and without the first idea about fashion. What in the name of God are you wearing?" she demanded, looking him over with a sneer, knowing this would rile him more than any other comment she could utter.

One of the two men beside him smothered a grin and Isabella knew they held the ridiculous creature in as much contempt as she did.

Treedle blushed with fury, turning as best he could to glare at his companion while the outrageous heights of his collar impeded his movement. Isabella knew he considered himself a pink of the *ton,* a trendsetter, when he was actually a laughingstock, but so vastly wealthy that no one would say it to his face.

"Stand aside, you vicious bitch," he snarled. "I've come for my daughter."

Isabella's heart kicked in her chest, but her face remained impassive. "You have no daughter, my lord. Henry Barbour is my husband and the child's father. She's none of yours."

Treedle laughed, a contemptuous sound that made Isabella burn with shame and fury.

"Everyone knows I had you that night, believe me. I told enough people. Low and behold, you bear a child nine months later. Even your half-wit husband should be able to figure that out."

Isabella took a moment to turn the sapphire ring she wore on her finger. It had been a birthday gift to her on her sixteenth birthday, and the trick, one she'd learned from her mother. She slapped him, putting the full force of her fury and regret behind the movement. Her palm burned with pain and her fingers ached, but she smiled with satisfaction at the blood that ran from the cut on Treedle's cheek where the ring had struck him. It dripped onto his perfect cravat and collars, and he raised his fist to strike her.

Isabella cried out, but the blow never landed and Treedle was felled to the ground. She gasped as she saw Henry standing over him, rigid with fury.

"Stand up, damn you," he said. Isabella opened her mouth in shock, her gentle, loving Henry sounded ready to do murder. Treedle stared up at the huge figure looming over him and scrambled away.

"Get him, you fools," he commanded the two men beside him.

They moved towards Henry, and Isabella watched in astonishment as Henry knocked one out cold with a blow that snapped his head back, and left the second doubled-up in pain. He advanced on Treedle, who was now on his feet, and hit him again, the blow sending him sprawling, and broke his nose, if the crunching sound was anything to go on.

"You dare come here and raise a hand to my wife?" Henry shouted, as Treedle screamed for the man who was not unconscious to come to his aid, to no avail. He clutched at his nose, staring at Henry in terror as her husband reached down and pulled the man to his feet by his lapels.

"You think I'm mad, do you?" Henry demanded, shaking the man like a rag doll. "Well, unless you get out of here now and never come back, I'll show you how true that is."

Treedle whimpered, blood dripping from his nose in a steady stream.

Henry lifted the man so that their faces were level, the viscount's toes no longer touching the ground. "Who does the child belong to?" he said, the words growled rather than spoken.

"Y-you," Treedle replied, shaking and weeping. "The girl's yours, all yours."

"And don't you forget it." Henry dropped him in the dirt, the desire to do further harm blazing in his eyes. "Now get off my property, before I decide you'll not leave at all."

Isabella watched, torn between astonishment and amusement as Treedle left his companions bleeding on the ground and ran. The one still conscious was a little more heroic and roused his sleeping friend before they, too, ran for cover.

Henry stood like a sentinel, rigid with fury, long after the men were out of sight.

"Henry?" Isabella moved towards him, her steps slow, her voice calm, sensing his distress. As she faced him, she saw the anger had leached away, replaced by terror that shone in his eyes as he trembled.

"They'll take you away from me," he said, the words anguished as Isabella ran to him, throwing her arms around his waist.

"No, Henry. No one can do that. Never. I won't let them."

Henry shook his head, his distress growing now. "He will," he said, the certainty in his voice breaking her heart. "He'll make them lock me up. They'll say I'm mad and they'll lock me up. I'll never see you … or Marie … They'll take me away."

"Henry! Henry, no," Isabella cried as he shook with fear.

"Don't let them," he pleaded, clutching at her and holding her tight. "Don't let them take me away."

"Never. Never, my love," Isabella promised, even as terror built in her own heart. Viscount Treedle was a powerful man, and a vindictive one. He'd not dare face Henry again himself, but he'd delight in seeing him locked up. Henry's words seemed less like paranoia and more like inevitability, the truth of them filling her heart with ice. She held him tight, kissing him and murmuring reassurances. "No one will take you from me, Henry Barbour," she said, her voice full of fury. "You and Marie are mine, and anyone who thinks to take what's mine … I'll make them regret the day they were born."

***

The more Isabella thought on Henry's words, the more she knew he was right. She didn't believe the viscount would press to take Marie from her again. That he'd only done so because of the pressure of gossip was obvious enough. He had no interest in her child further than removing an embarrassment. Removing Henry from the child would suit his purposes just as well, and had the added incentive of wreaking vengeance on both her and her husband.

The fury with which Henry had defended them both shocked and touched her. Such fury was long since gone, though, as she dragged him through the woods, down to the river, in search of Jack and Marie. He had retreated into himself and silence, numb with misery and terror, and Isabella wanted to rip Treedle's heart from his chest with her bare hands for causing it.

"Jack!" Isabella called as they grew closer, and felt a surge of relief as his dark head appeared, the baby still cradled in his arms.

He hurried towards them, his eyes taking in Henry's hunched figure with concern.

"What happened?" he demanded as Marie cried, her wails tugging at Isabella's womb, her breasts prickling with the desire to feed her child. She took the baby from Jack, shaking her head, implying they could not talk yet.

"Henry saved us," she said, smiling at her husband who would not now meet her eyes. "But now he's worn out and he needs peace," she said, looking instead to Jack, who took in the blood on Henry's shirt and fists and understood her meaning. "I think perhaps you should stay here for a while where it's quiet," she said, addressing this to Henry, who didn't respond.

"Come along, now, lad," Jack said, his voice coaxing. "Me and your missus have got things to sort out, and that little princess is hungry again, if I know anything. So, you settle yourself down here until you feel more the thing, eh? We'll come and fetch you for dinner."

Henry still didn't respond, staring at the ground, though his fists remained clenched.

"Henry," Isabella said, stepping closer to him. She touched his face, turning his gaze towards her. "Do you trust me?"

Henry's eyes slid to hers, dark and afraid and troubled, but he nodded.

"Then believe in me," she said, reaching up to press a kiss to his mouth. "Jack and I love you, and we won't let anyone take you from us."

He nodded again, and they watched as he walked to the little hut, ducking under the low opening and into the dark within.

Isabella cast Jack a pleading look and they hurried back to the house.

"He beat the viscount until he was bloody, Jack," she said, her voice desperate now. "He knocked one man unconscious and flattened the other with one blow apiece."

Jack gaped at her as they strode through the undergrowth. "Bugger me," he said, shaking his head. "I thought I ought to have warned you after I'd gone, but it was too late. Only time I ever saw Henry raise his fists was when a fellow shouted at his father. He was only a lad, barely sixteen, but he was already big and strong. It was quite a sight."

Isabella snorted. "I think Treedle would agree with you," she said, her tone dry. "Henry broke his nose, and he's such a preening fop, he will want Henry's blood for it."

"You reckon he'll try to get him locked up?"

Isabella felt fear prickle down her back and nodded, unable to speak her agreement out loud as her throat grew tight.

"Over my dead body," Jack growled, full of fury at the idea.

Isabella reached out a hand to him and squeezed the calloused palm he placed in hers.

"Together, Jack," she said, her voice firm. "No one will take Henry away."

"What are we gonna do, then?" he demanded, surprising her by looking to her for advice.

Isabella took a breath, determination a burn in her blood. "I will feed Marie, and then you will take her to her godparents' for safety and explain that we need help, at once. Tell them what happened, Jack," she said, turning to him. "Belle knows Treedle is the father. Tell them I'm begging them, and I'll be forever in their debt," she added, her voice breaking. "Tell them whatever you need to. Just make them send help."

Jack nodded, his face grim. "Oh, I'll bring help, don't you worry. But what about you?"

Isabella cursed as her dress snagged on a bramble and snatched the material from the thorns, heedless of the tear it made. "I have one last thing I need you to do for me before you go," she said, breathless now as the grand house came into sight at last.

"Oh?" Jack stopped for a moment and braced his hands on his knees to catch his breath. "What's that, then?" he demanded.

Isabella turned back to him, taking his arm with her free hand and dragging him on as Marie fretted again. "I need you to teach me to fire a gun."

Chapter 19

"Wherein our heroine takes a stand."

Isabella watched for a moment until the carriage bearing her daughter was out of sight. Jack would lock the gates at the entrance to Henry's land as he left. It would buy them some time. She imagined it would take a while for Treedle to gather the men he needed to come back for Henry. How long it would take Belle to persuade her husband to send help, she didn't know, so every moment counted. There had been understanding in the marquess' eyes for Henry during the christening, though. Perhaps he would not need much persuasion. She sent a silent prayer to the heavens, praying it was true, praying her family would be safe, that they could live in peace. Perhaps she didn't deserve such a life after her behaviour over the past years, but Henry did, Marie did. God could not punish them for her sins.

Her heart thudded now as fear insinuated itself beneath her skin, a living thing that made her tremble.

"Head up, Isabella," she murmured, trying to steady her breathing. "This is for Henry, for your daughter. You can do this."

She hurried into her bedroom, gathering the bag of powder and shot that Jack had given her after a brief demonstration of how not to blow up a gun in her face. They'd loaded two pair of duelling pistols, along with two rifles. That gave her six shots before she needed to reload. Isabella reached for the powder flask with shaking hands and then paused. She had cast aside the orange gown that Henry loved over a chair. It had lain there since Henry had stripped it from her with something close to desperation the last time she'd sat for his painting. She smiled.

Juno, the queen of goddesses. That's what Henry had said she was. Goddess of love and of marriage, yet Juno was a warrior, too.

She would have defended her family from all comers, Isabella felt sure.

It was foolish perhaps, but as she struggled into the dress alone and with fingers that would not cooperate, she found a strange sense of tranquillity. Her heart still thudded in her chest as she reached once more for the powder and shot, but her hands no longer shook.

Isabella moved with quiet calm to the window at the front of the house, which had the best view of the tree-lined alley that led to their door. She flung the windows open wide and reached for one of the duelling pistols that Jack had left primed and ready. It was a beautiful thing, inlaid with mother-of-pearl and silver scroll work. Juno would approve, she thought with a wry smile.

The night lay hot and heavy, the month of her goddess fierce, scorching the landscape where most years she was a gentler presence. Sweat prickled down Isabella's back, heat and nerves combined, pressing down on her as she waited.

It was almost full dark when she heard them, and Isabella thanked providence that a bright full moon hung fat and full in the sky. A silvery light touched the gardens before her, casting eerie shadows as Isabella knelt before the window, her wrists propped on the sill as she raised the pistol.

The muted clatter of hooves on dusty ground grew louder, the sound of men laughing, as if they were out for a pleasurable sporting event. Fury grew in Isabella's heart and the sound of a pistol firing rang out across the darkness as the riders emerged from the tree-covered alley. The first horse reared with a scream of fear as the bullet hit the tree beside it, sending splinters flying. The rider of the horrified beast tumbled to the ground with a curse as the others scattered, their mounts plunging into the dark garden as the men shouted and tried to regain control.

"Who the devil is firing up there?" shouted an angry voice from beneath the canopy of the trees.

Isabella fired again, just to make a point, before standing in the light of the window.

"I am Lady Isabella Barbour, and you, sir, are trespassing. I demand you remove yourselves from my husband's land before I shoot you." Isabella heard her voice carry in the darkness, the imperious, high-handed tone of the woman her mother had bred to marry a marquess.

"Lady Isabella," came a cultured, soothing voice. "There is no need for such histrionics. We have come for your husband, not for you. He's a danger to himself and others and needs keeping in a place of safety. We mean neither of you any harm, madam. Hand him over and you will be mistress of Barcham Place."

Rage such as Isabella had never known lent her an icy calm. She picked up the rifle, taking her time to aim, keeping her breathing steady and even. The toe of a gleaming hessian boot was visible, peeping out from behind the tree the man sheltered behind. Isabella spared a moment to send a prayer, to God, or to Juno, whoever was listening … and fired.

The scream echoed around the gardens and Isabella gave a little shout of triumph, exhilaration fizzing in her blood like champagne. "I warned you, sir," she shouted over the din of the man's screams. "I will aim a little higher at the next man to approach this house, so I hope you all have an heir and a spare, for you'll not sire another if you make the attempt."

Isabella held her breath as she heard shouts of rage and indignation as the man continued to scream. Good Lord, what a white-livered cur. "He should try having a baby," she muttered to herself as she reached for the next gun. Three shots left. "Hurry, Belle. Please hurry." She whispered the words, her palms sweating as she tried to hold the weight of the pistol steady. The gardens grew quiet, the stamp and huff of unsettled horses the only sound, save that of an owl on the hunt. She knew they'd not be fool enough to approach the front of the house now.

Isabella closed the window, gathered the loaded rifle and the two pistols with care, carrying the shot bag in her teeth and the powder flask under her arm as she ran to the back of the house. All doors and windows were secured, but she was damned if she'd allow them close enough to find out. Besides which, this was a waiting game now. If they realised Henry was not inside the house, they'd widen their search. She prayed her husband would stay where he was and not move.

She threw the window open just in time to see a shadowy figure cross the lawn. Without bothering to take the time to aim, she fired. Dirt flew up a bare foot in front of the man who yelled in surprise.

"Damnation, madam!"

He stilled as Isabella threw down the pistol and took the rifle in hand. She smirked at the fellow who had covered his crotch with his hands. Who knew she was such a fine shot? Perhaps her warrior goddess was looking down at her after all. Here she stood, illuminated by moonlight, her figure clear and bright to those down below, defending everything she loved.

"The next one will make you a eunuch, sir," she shouted. The figure ran for cover. Isabella snorted, laughing with disdain. "I have more loaded guns, and enough powder and shot to play this game for days, gentlemen. Might I suggest you leave before I grow bored and make my next shot count? I won't be aiming for your toes, I promise."

The night grew still around her, and Isabella took a deep breath, training the rifle on the gardens below. "Hurry, Belle," she said, the words pleading as she glanced up at the moon. "Please hurry."

***

Henry jolted as the sound of a shot firing pierced the night. His heart leapt in his chest, fear, cold and burning like ice as it surged beneath his skin.

"Isabella!"

He scrambled to his feet, hurrying outside when the terror of what awaited him stilled his movements. Guns didn't frighten him. Dying and leaving his family if it meant they would be safe was a risk he would take with a glad heart ... Yet his own terrors lurked, tangling in his head, pressing down on him like a weight until his heart felt it would burst with frustration and fear.

Another shot, and dread for Isabella and Marie's safety overrode all else.

He plunged into the darkness, running like a wild creature, the taste of life and death on his tongue, fuelling his blood and pumping his heart as he ran to protect what was his. The distance between him and his home seemed that of the earth to the moon as he covered the ground with all the speed he possessed.

Henry slid to a halt as a third shot rang out, and then a scream rent the air. His heart beat in his throat, so fierce it hurt. A man's scream, he assured himself, pushing on once more. As the pitiful wails howled to the moon, he knew it wasn't Jack. Jack would never make such a fuss. Which meant Jack was there, he was defending the house. His terror calmed a little and he moved with more stealth now.

The great house appeared through the tree line and Henry slowed. He could hear men's voices, cursing his wife. Rage and indignation boiled inside him, and then he saw her.

An upper window flew open, Isabella lit up in the moonlight. With astonishment, he saw her raise a pistol without hesitation and fire. The man trying to approach the house yelled and cursed as the bullet struck just inches before him. Henry stared.

"Juno," he murmured, his heart filled with pride and awe. He noted that she wore the dress he'd chosen for her, the moonlight turning it to gold. She'd done that for him, the embodiment of an ancient deity come to earth.

"The next one will make you a eunuch, sir."

Henry swallowed a laugh of wonder and surprise. His love for her swelled in his chest along with a desperate bitterness they should force her to defend him in such a way. Yet what kind of man was he that he would hide in the dark while his wife fought for him alone? For she was alone, Jack nowhere in sight.

The murderous rage that had wanted Treedle's blood simmered beneath his skin. Isabella would not face this alone for his sake.

He stalked through the undergrowth until he found someone on whom to vent his rage. It was too easy, though, as his large hand covered the man's mouth, his arm squeezing his throat until it cut his air off.

"Make a sound and I'll snap your neck like a dry twig," Henry growled in his ear. He could feel the terrified thud of the man's heart, his breathing harsh over Henry's fingers as he gave a slight nod. The desire to break his neck anyway was tantalising, but Henry stilled his bloodlust. There was a rope at the man's feet, no doubt intended for him, and Henry took satisfaction in tying him up so tight the rope bit into his skin. Stuffing the fellow's handkerchief into his mouth, Henry left him wide-eyed with terror as he moved forward.

Two men lingered on the edge of the lawn, their voices low, but carrying on the still night.

"Bitch is as mad as he is," one of them muttered.

"Treedle said as much," replied his companion, sounding amused. "Reckoned she was mad for it, practically begged him to take her. Her husband must be a half-wit, to marry her when she was full of another man's bastard."

Henry's fist smashed into the side of the dark figure's head and he dropped like it had felled him, crashing to the ground as his companion turned with a gasp, raising a pistol. Henry smacked it from his hand and the pistol tumbled, exploding to life as it hit the ground and the mechanism fired. His hand clamped around the man's neck as his eyes grew wide, the white startling in the moonlight.

"Say it again," Henry dared him, squeezing now as the man choked.

His victim shook his head, scrabbling at Henry's massive hand, to no avail as his face grew purple. Henry turned him, his arm about the man's neck still as he reached down for the pistol his companion wore. He tugged it from the man who lay as still as the dead. Henry didn't much care if he was.

Pressing the gun to the man's temple, he moved into the open.

"Henry! *No!*" Isabella's cry pierced the night and his heart as he looked up at her.

"It's all right," he said, his voice calm and strong, though terror was licking at his mind. "I love you, Juno," he added, the words just for her as men moved from the darkness.

"Stay back!" his wife screamed, raising the rifle she carried. The men stilled, seeing her now for the threat she was. Treedle wasn't here, Henry noted with contempt. Still hiding in the dark like a coward, like *he* had. Self-disgust bit deep, and Henry turned to the men who would come for him.

"If you leave now, I'll let him go unharmed," he said, facing the one man who seemed the ring leader here. No doubt he was in Viscount Treedle's employ. Henry watched as the fellow held out his hands in a placating gesture. It might have been more reassuring if his companions weren't armed to the teeth.

"Now then, Mr Barbour," the man said, his tone patronising. "We don't want to hurt you, just to take you for a little ride so you can have a talk with us, that's all."

Henry snorted. "Yes, I know that. A one-way ride to the asylum. Mad I may be, but not stupid, I'm afraid. So, I think I'll pass, if it's all the same to you."

"Ah, but is isn't all the same," the man said, his voice still soothing, though his eyes glittered with malice. He was the kind of man who loved to hunt, Henry realised with a thrill of fear shivering down his spine. Henry was his prey. "You've caused a deal of damage and embarrassment to my employer, sir. If I don't return the favour, it'll be me with my head on a pike. I don't like that idea."

"Sounds a fine idea to me," Henry shot back, glancing up at Isabella to give him courage. She stood rigid in the moonlight, her rifle still trained on the man he spoke with. "And if your employer hadn't trespassed on my land, threatened my daughter, and raised his hand to my wife, he'd still be in one piece." As he remembered Treedle raising his fist to Isabella, Henry's rage grew. "You can tell him I'll come for what's left when I get around to it. Which will be all the sooner if he ever speaks my wife's name again."

"Really?" the man sneered as he spoke, his voice dripping contempt as his hand slid to draw a pistol from beneath the folds of his coat. "How will you manage that when you're too frightened to leave your own home? Hiding behind your wife's skirts."

Humiliation burned as the words found their mark. Henry sucked in a breath, his concentration wavering as the man he held sensed his distraction and thrust his elbow into Henry's stomach.

Henry doubled over as the fellow ran, and then everything happened at once.

Isabella's scream rang out as he saw the man before him raise his pistol, and a shot rang out. Shouts and yells filled the moonlit garden as more men thundered towards them on horse-back.

By the time Henry could make sense of what had happened, he saw the man who'd gone to fire upon him cradling his hand to his chest, blood dripping in a steady stream. His pistol lay where it had fallen in the grass.

A moment later and Henry got to his feet, only to be almost knocked flat again as Isabella burst from the house and threw her arms around him.

"Henry, *Henry!*"

She still carried a pistol and her eyes darted around the dark garden as Henry thrust her behind him, raising the gun he still carried.

"Henry, be careful. It's Winterbourne," she said, her voice urgent. "He's come to help us."

As she spoke, a dark, cold voice sounded in the garden. "Lower your damn guns before I shoot you myself."

"That's not Winterbourne," Henry said, keeping Isabella at his back.

The riders moved forward, and Henry felt a rush of relief to see Lord Winterbourne was indeed there, though it was not him that had spoken. That fellow looked like the devil himself, his hair black and tied back in a style long gone, his eyes glinting in the moonlight.

"Calm yourself, Gabriel," Lord Winterbourne's voice was clear and strong and the man beside him snorted. Henry watched as the marquess dismounted and walked towards him.

"Henry?" he said, his tone cautious as he held out a hand to him.

Henry stared around the garden, at men on both sides who were armed, still unsure of whom to trust.

"We won't let them take you, Henry," the marquess said. "They have no right, and Treedle will get what's coming to him, I assure you."

"He will indeed." The man who looked like Satan out for a midnight ride sounded amused at the prospect.

Edward glanced back at him before returning his attention to Henry.

"My cousin," he said with a wry smile. "Viscount DeMorte." DeMorte flashed a devilish grin, saluting with the pistol he held.

Isabella gasped behind him, as did the men who'd come to take Henry to the madhouse. Whoever he was, they knew him and feared him, too.

"Who here says this man is mad?" DeMorte demanded, his voice harsh and angry in the darkness. "For I say, he's as sane as I am." He laughed, a wicked, almost deranged sound as he turned his horse in a circle, staring at each man in turn. "Would anyone like to argue that?"

There were murmurs and head-shaking, and that disturbing laughter sounded again. "I thought not," Lord DeMorte said, the sneer on his face audible in the words. "Be off with you then, and anyone wanting to remove my friend here from his property will answer to me. Make sure Viscount Treedle knows, and tell him to expect me on the morrow. We can breakfast together."

Even Henry felt the shiver of apprehension that followed those words. Whoever DeMorte was, Treedle would not enjoy his visit. He looked back at the marquess as Edward held his hand out once more. The men who would have taken him were dispersing now.

Henry looked at the man's outstretched hand and felt Isabella grasp his arm, her touch reassuring. He looked at her and took a breath before taking Edward's hand and shaking it.

"Good man," Edward said, his voice approving. "Now, is there any chance of a drink before we leave? I feel I need one."

Chapter 20

"Wherein demons are confronted."

Isabella passed the generous glasses of brandy to Lord Winterbourne and Lord DeMorte. She avoided DeMorte's eye, finding the man an unsettling presence. He seemed as ill at ease as Henry, but far more threatening.

"I've sent word back to the house," Lord Winterbourne said with a smile as he accepted the drink. "Your little Marie will be back with you soon enough."

"Thank you, my lord," Isabella said with relief.

Winterbourne shook his head. "Call me Edward, please."

He seemed far more relaxed than Isabella remembered him. At the Christmas party, he'd appeared rude and unpleasant, unapproachable. Belle must have done this, she thought with a smile. Belle's innate kindness and understanding shone from her. Even a big, angry fellow like the marquess must be no match for that depth of sweetness. She glanced back at Henry, her heart aching as she wished she could help him in the same way.

He was sitting with his head bowed, avoiding everyone's eye and threading the bronze ribbon she'd given him back and forth and around his fingers. DeMorte watched him, his glittering eyes fascinated, though she sensed no judgement in his gaze.

"My wife has told me a great deal about your work, Henry," Lord Winterbourne said, disregarding that Henry was ignoring everybody. "In fact, I've heard little else from her. I am tasked to persuade you to paint our son. God help you," he murmured, though the pride in his voice was obvious.

"I'm not sure it's possible to paint a moving target," DeMorte remarked as Edward snorted. "She also said Mr Barbour was terribly handsome, did she not, Edward?" his cousin observed, the flicker of a taunting smile at his lips that looked cruel and hard.

Edward glowered at him, deciding the comment was beneath him as he turned back to Henry. "I would be honoured if we might view some of your work?"

"Henry?" Isabella prompted, her voice gentle.

Henry didn't look up, but shrugged, hunching into himself.

"May I show them, Henry?" she asked, hoping it was just the two men in the room whose presence disturbed him. He looked deeply unhappy and she feared the events of the night had left a mark on him.

He nodded, the movement almost imperceptible. Isabella turned back to the two men to discover DeMorte was engaged in arranging the items on her sideboard with a depth of concentration that was a little unusual. She turned to Edward instead.

"Excuse me one moment, please."

She hurried to Henry's side, crouching beside him. "Won't you come, too, love?" she said, taking his hand. He pulled it from her grasp, continuing to study the ribbon. She knew by now it wasn't done to hurt her, more that he was hurting and didn't know what to do about it. She laid her hand on his arm, her voice low and soothing. "Please? Henry, for me?"

His hands stilled, his breathing picking up. The scowl on his face troubled her, but he gave a sharp nod and got to his feet, stalking out of the room without another word.

Isabella stood up. "I'm afraid it's been a trying evening, and … well, Henry doesn't like people much. Just being in a room with the two of you …" She took a breath, shaking her head. "You do not understand how much effort that is taking him."

"I think you'll find we understand better than most," Edward said, and Isabella saw the truth of his words in his eyes. "Gabriel," he said, turning to his cousin, who seemed to still be arranging the items to his satisfaction. "Come along." The words were calm but firm, yet it seemed to take DeMorte a moment to wrench himself away from the sideboard. He avoided Isabella's eye as he followed Edward from the room.

Henry occupied himself lighting candles, ignoring them all still as they walked in. Edward paused, his face one of astonishment as he took in the paintings.

"Belle was right," he said, sounding more amused than surprised. "Henry is a genius."

"I know that," Isabella replied as Edward crouched to inspect a painting. To her dismay, it was one of a dead rabbit, its intestines showing, maggots writhing under the flesh. Edward seemed fascinated, however.

"The detail," he said, shaking his head in wonder. "It's astonishing. I could reach in and touch the fur, it's so ... *real.*"

She smiled as Edward moved on, to her relief, to inspect a portrait of Henry's father. Turning, she sought Henry, to find him staring at Lord DeMorte with consternation and something that might have been concern. As she followed his gaze, she saw why.

The huge figure who still frightened Isabella, despite his help tonight, was sweating, staring around the room with distress. He tugged at his cravat, looking as if he might be sick.

"Excuse me," he said, the words rough. "I ... I can't stay in here."

Isabella looked to Edward as the marquess got to his feet, watching his cousin almost run from the room.

"He means no disrespect," he said, his expression troubled. "It's just that, Gabriel ... he likes order. No, it's more than that," he said, shaking his head. "He *needs* order. Everything in its place.

I'm afraid this room as ... vibrant and charming as it is..." He hesitated, looking around at the roughly stacked canvases and disarray of paints and brushes, and Isabella smiled at his diplomacy.

"It troubles him," Henry said, his voice quiet.

Edward nodded. "Quite so," he replied, moving to lay a hand on Henry's shoulder. "We all have our demons, Henry."

That Henry didn't move away from him made Isabella smile with quiet pride.

"I'll leave you now," Edward said, rightly judging the tension in the room. "I expect our nursemaid to be here with your daughter any time now." He turned to leave and then paused. "I don't imagine you'll have any further trouble with Treedle, not once Gabriel has finished with him," he added with a sardonic smile. "However, I hope you will count me as a friend, and call on me if ever you should have need."

"Thank you," Isabella said, touched by his assurance. Edward nodded his goodbye and left the room.

Isabella turned back to Henry. He had returned to lighting candles and she knew he intended to paint.

"Henry," she said, dismayed by the rigid set of his shoulders. He ignored her, the dark expression on his face betraying the depth of his troubles. "Henry, don't shut me out. Talk to me."

But Henry would not speak to her. Marie returned with Jack and Belle's nursemaid, as promised, and the baby occupied Isabella, feeding and settling her down. Jack, too, wanted to know everything that had happened, and it was the early hours of the morning before she made her way back to Henry's studio.

He was painting, that intense concentration she had not seen for some time surrounding him. He'd been less obsessive about his work of late, the draw of spending time with her and Marie enough to make him break away, albeit for short periods of time.

"Come to bed, Henry," she said, laying her hand on his arm. To her dismay, he shook her off, his face a mask. "Are you angry with me?" she asked, hurt and troubled by his reaction after the events of last night. There was a pause, the paintbrush hovering over the canvas before he gave a slight shake of his head, and then he returned to his work, and Isabella knew she'd not coax another word from him tonight.

Exhaustion tugged at her mind and body, the fears and excitements of the evening dulling her ability to find a way through to him. So, she reached up and kissed his cheek, and left him to his work.

***

"Don't worry so," Jack said as they sat at the breakfast table two days later. "You know how he gets when he works."

Isabella shook her head. "This is different, Jack, I know it is." She remembered the first day she had sat for him in the orange dress. He'd painted for several hours, and then dragged her up the stairs to make love to her, unable to concentrate any longer as heat simmered between them. Now Isabella felt as though she had disappeared, as though she only existed on the canvas, as Henry would not see her. "He's upset."

"Well, after the other night ..." Jack shrugged, frowning into his mug. "Hardly surprising, I suppose."

Isabella nodded, knowing Jack was right, it was something to do with that evening, but what?

"Perhaps leave him be for a day or two," Jack said, his tone sympathetic. "Maybe he'll snap out of it on his own. Seems to me sometimes he needs time to think things over with no distractions. He'll come around."

Except Henry didn't come around. Isabella sat for him, wearing the dress he so loved, though he didn't ask her to. He observed her as he worked, as dispassionate as if he regarded a bowl of fruit, all the heat and love and passion shuttered up somewhere Isabella could not reach it. Days turned into a week, and Isabella's worries only increased.

It was late at night, a full ten days since Treedle had come for Marie. Isabella lay in bed, alone, fear in her heart that whatever had hurt Henry had changed him for good. She assured herself that wasn't true, but the idea lingered, making tears prickle at her eyes.

"Enough, Henry," she said, the words determined as she swung her legs out of bed. She checked on Marie, who she'd fed not long ago, and seeing the baby fast asleep, she tiptoed downstairs, leaving her door open in case Marie should wake.

The door to Henry's studio opened with ease, nothing to announce her presence, and for a while she stood and studied her handsome, troubled husband. His beard had grown thick again, and she could see he'd lost weight. He had touched none of the food they'd brought. He'd left the cakes she'd made, too. That he was locked in misery showed in the shadows under his eyes, the defeated air that clung to him, where before when he worked, he'd blazed with energy.

She walked towards him, her footsteps silent. As she grew closer, Isabella noted the work he'd done was almost all the room behind where she'd sat. He had made little progress on her figure. Her heart ached with fear and longing. Had Henry changed his mind about her? Had she done something that night to make him think about her differently? Treedle, perhaps, or his men, the things they'd said about her ... Had he heard something?

Isabella swallowed down her own misery, refusing to allow Henry to run from her any longer. If he didn't love her anymore, she didn't know how she would live with it, but she would not ignore the truth and not know why or what had happened.

"Henry," she said, her voice low, filled with sadness. There was the briefest pause in his work as he registered her voice, but that was all. She walked up behind him, wrapping her arms about his waist, her head against his back. "Henry, please. Please, love. I miss you so much." His body was rigid with tension beneath her touch, but he carried on painting. "Henry, I'm unhappy," she said, her voice wavering now. "You're making me unhappy."

His arms dropped to his sides, his breathing picking up. She could feel his heart as it hammered in his chest, his distress and panic obvious, though he said nothing. He dropped to his knees, startling her, and threw his brush away from him in fury, putting his head in his hands.

"Henry!" Isabella sat beside him, trying to hold him. "Henry talk to me, please," she begged, as her emotions ran out of control and tears gathered. "Did someone say something to you? Did they say something about me? Don't you love me anymore?" Anguish coloured the last question, her tears falling unchecked now.

Henry made a sound of such pain that she gasped, watching as he shook his head, and he clutched his arms about himself. It tore Isabella in two, needing to know what had hurt him so. She laid her body over his back, holding him, kissing him wherever she could reach, stroking his hair.

"Do you want me to go?" she asked him through her tears, holding her breath until he shook his head with such vehemence she knew it wasn't what he wanted. "Marie misses you." The words struck him hard and Henry sobbed, the sound so heart-rending that she almost wished to take the words back.

"Henry, talk to me!" Isabella pleaded, the words almost shouted as desperation clutched at her heart. "I can't let you shut me out like this. Tell me why, dammit!"

He stilled, his breathing harsh as he forced himself to calm. With anguish, she saw that tears still streaked his face as he sat with his head bowed.

"Talk to me," she said, her voice softer now. "Please, Henry. I love you, so much. It's killing me to see you in such pain."

He shook his head. "Don't deserve it," he mumbled, almost incoherent.

"Don't deserve what?" Isabella demanded, perplexed and wanting to understand.

"You. Marie, *anything!*" Henry shouted as he pushed to his feet, anger rolling off him in waves now.

Isabella scrambled up, rushing after him and grasping his arm, afraid he'd run off into the woods if she let him go. "Whatever are you talking about?" Her own words were angry now as she wondered who had put such thoughts in his head.

"I'm a coward!" She stilled as he roared the words, his fists clenched. "I hid in the dark while you … you and Marie …" His voice broke and he turned away from her, his arms clutched about himself.

"Oh, Henry," she said, wondering how he could think such a thing. "You did nothing of the sort."

He spun around, his eyes wild now, pointing a finger toward the woods. "I was there, cowering in that hut when I heard the shots, and even then … even then …" He stopped, his throat working. "I was scared, Isabella."

"Henry Barbour," Isabella shouted, her voice hard and angry now as she grasped his arms, wishing she had force enough to shake him. "Listen to me, and you listen good. You saved me from drowning when you might easily have been swept away yourself. You didn't even know me then!" she exclaimed, her fury growing with the moment. "You half killed Treedle and his men when they came for Marie, and you didn't stay in the dark, Henry. You were frightened but you came for us. You came, and you defended us, and you put yourself in danger to do so."

He shook his head, avoiding her eyes, refusing her comfort, so Isabella took his head in her hands, forcing him to look at her. "If you aren't frightened, you can't be brave, Henry. You … are the bravest person I've ever met. I don't know what you face every day, my love, but you *do* face it, and with such generosity of spirit. I love and admire you for that."

He looked up at her then, a little hope in his eyes though sorrow still lurked. "I should have confronted Treedle again," he said, guilt lacing the words. "Not Lord DeMorte."

Isabella made a noise of amusement, shaking her head. "If you'd have shown up, the man would have likely run to France or expired on the spot, after your first meeting." Henry frowned, and she sighed, taking his hand and putting it to her face. "These hands were made to create beauty," she said, turning her face and kissing his palm. "Not for violence. I know you would defend us if we required it." Henry opened his mouth, a stubborn look in his eyes, but Isabella pressed a finger to his lips, silencing him. "You've proved that." She glared at him, daring him to contradict her, and he let out a breath. "You're everything I want or need. I wouldn't change a thing about you, other than those things that make *you* unhappy, and that's for your sake alone, not mine. You are perfect to me, just as you are."

"You had to defend yourself," he said, his voice low. "To defend me. You had to take a gun and ..."

"Yes, I did," Isabella retorted, angry with him now. "Do you have a problem with that, because I don't."

Henry's expression grew cautious, a little startled by her vehemence.

Isabella let out a breath, exasperated now. "Let me save you, too, Henry. At least once in a while," she said, struck again with the urge to shake sense into his massive frame. "It's only fair."

He made a sound of surprise that might have been a laugh, and Isabella sighed with relief, hoping she'd drawn him out of the dark place that night had trapped him in. She moved closer, putting her arms around him, and this time he held her in return.

"I want to go out with you, Isabella. I want to go out into the world with you and Marie, but ... but I can't."

Isabella smiled and looked up at him. "I believe you can do anything you want, if you want it enough." His expression remained doubtful and she raised up on her toes, pressing a lingering kiss to his mouth. "But that is something we can talk about. For now…" She kissed him again and then moved back, undoing the tie that fastened her nightgown and allowing it to fall from her shoulders, a puddle of white cotton at her feet. "For now, I need you with me, close to me. I've missed you so much."

He pulled her into his arms, his grasp on her hard and desperate as she realised that he needed this more than she did. Isabella clung to him, pulling his shirt from his trousers, sliding her hands underneath to touch his skin.

To her dismay, he pushed her hands away, a look of regret in his eyes. "I haven't washed in days," he said, as he rubbed at his beard.

Isabella chuckled, astonished that he'd believe such a thing would put her off at this moment and after all they'd been through. "As if I care," she retorted, sounding a little frantic and tugging at his neck, urging his head back down. "Now shut up and kiss me."

Chapter 21

"Wherein our hero is set a tricky task."

Isabella turned onto her side, watching Henry as he slept. It had been days since he'd broken down, and things were returning to what they'd been. That it had shaken his confidence was obvious, though, and she had tried and tried to think of a way to help him.

She reached out, pushing his dark hair from his eyes. It needed cutting, his beard still needed shaving, too, yet she'd told him to leave it for now. There was something a little wild about him like this, something raw and powerful that made her blood heat.

A warm breeze fluttered through the curtains, all the windows opened wide as the heatwave continued. With a smile, she pulled back the sheet that covered him, admiring that powerful body and wondering at the gentleness of the man that possessed it. She sighed as Marie stirred, soft little mewling noises that would become fractious at any moment. How did the girl always know when Isabella's thoughts followed such a path? Isabella sat up, swinging her legs out of the bed. The baby could not need feeding yet, it was only half an hour since the last time. She tiptoed over to the cradle and wrinkled her nose. Ah, that was the problem.

Isabella went to reach for her daughter when something stopped her. The idea caught and held, and she turned to stare at the bed where Henry slept. He still hadn't picked his daughter up, despite the fact that Isabella knew he longed to. With a prayer she was doing the right thing, she ducked her head, pressing a kiss to Marie's downy head.

"Forgive me," she whispered. "It's only for a little while. Papa will look after you. He'll have to," she murmured with a smile, as she crept from the room, snatching up her wrapper as she went.

Isabella hurried to the kitchen where Jack was making breakfast.

"Jack," she said, her voice urgent. "Quick, we need to hide."

"What?" Jack replied, staring at her as if she'd gone mad. "What the devil for?"

"Because Marie needs changing," she said, tugging at his sleeve now. "And she's going to lose her temper if someone doesn't do it very soon."

Jack stared at her, none the wiser, and Isabella rolled her eyes at him.

"If I'm not here, and you're not here, who will do it, Jack?"

A slow smile curved over Jack's mouth as he returned an approving expression. "That's crafty, that is," he said, chuckling.

Isabella frowned at him, suddenly anxious. "You don't think …"

"No," Jack said, his voice firm as he ushered her out of the kitchen and towards the door that led to the cellars. "I think you've struck gold. Henry won't let the poor babe suffer. He doesn't have it in him. He'll figure it out."

Isabella sighed and nodded, and they hurried down the stairs to hide in the dark of the cellar.

***

Henry rubbed his eyes, yawning and scratching at his beard as he woke to the sound of Marie's protests. He blinked, surprised to find the curtains opened and the sun streaming in, but no sign of Isabella.

"Isabella?" He frowned as there was no response and swung his legs over the side of the bed. "Where's your mama?" he asked Marie, smiling at her over the side of the cradle. She stopped crying, mollified for a moment by the sight of his face. The desire to reach out and stroke the soft fuzz of hair on her head, to allow her tiny hand to grasp his finger, caught at his heart, but fear still held him back. She was so tiny, so delicate, and he was big and clumsy, too inept to be of any real use to her.

He watched in dismay as her little face screwed up and a wail of fury erupted from her tiny body. As her small fists clenched and her legs kicked, a familiar and unpleasant smell assaulted his nose.

"Oh." He turned and ran for the door, swinging it open and running for the bannister. "Isabella!" he yelled, anxiety growing in his chest as Marie wailed with greater enthusiasm. *"Isabella!"*

He took the stairs two at a time, running towards the kitchen and bursting through the door. The table was laid, a pot of tea brewing on the side, but no one was around.

"Isabella? Jack?" Henry ran back into the hall where Marie's cries were still audible. The poor little thing was getting furious now. He could hardly blame her either, but … but he couldn't do anything about it.

Henry ran, searching the few rooms they used now, and a few of those they didn't. He even ran outside and bellowed across the gardens. Where the devil had they gone?

The terrifying idea that Isabella had up and left him struck him hard, only to be dismissed a moment later. He wasn't so mad as to believe she'd do that to him, not and leave Marie. Then perhaps something had happened to them? That idea stopped him in his tracks until he forced himself to think how unlikely this was. No.

This was a test.

The idea made his heart leap to his throat.

Henry ran back up the stairs to where Marie was now red-faced with fury.

"Don't cry," he pleaded, grasping the back of his neck as sweat prickled down his spine. He picked up the little silver rattle that Jack had given her for her christening and shook it, but the sound of the tinkling bells only seemed to infuriate her more.

Isabella had done this on purpose! For a moment, anger and frustration swept over him at being forced into such a position, but as little Marie wailed, he realised the truth. Isabella trusted him. She trusted him to look after his daughter as a father ought to do. If he couldn't do that, he might just have well as handed her over to Viscount Treedle. The idea made him feel sick to his stomach.

"All right, Marie," he said, sucking in a deep breath. "I … I will change you." The words were for himself as much as her as he rushed about the room. He laid a towel upon the bed and gathered up a clean clout and pilcher. After watching Isabella change her countless times, he ought to manage. It looked simple enough when she did it. How hard could it be?

Once he had everything ready and a bowl of lukewarm water to hand, he returned to the cradle. Marie was beside herself, kicking and screaming, and Henry hesitated, terror flooding him at the idea he might hurt her or drop her with his clumsy hands.

"Come along, then, my little love," he said, his heart beating so hard he felt nausea roil in his guts. He lifted her, astonished by how light she was, and yet so solid at the same time. Her skin was sweaty after screaming in the heat, and he hurried to lay her down on the bed.

Removing her clothes wasn't too tricky, though what lay within the clout made him retch and cover his nose with the back of his hand. He turned his head away and took a deep breath, not breathing at all as he wiped up the worst of the mess. With hasty hands, he wrapped the revolting clout up in a square of muslin and cast it across the room.

Thank heavens.

As he washed the baby, with such care and attention to detail he suspected Isabella would laugh at him for taking so long, Marie calmed and ceased her crying. Once she was dry and clean, he took a moment to watch her. Happy now, she gurgled and cooed, kicking her little legs in the air. He huffed out a breath of relief and reached out a finger, tickling her round belly. She squealed, and Henry grinned.

"Ticklish like your mama," he said, amused as she blinked at him. Those eyes would stay that colour, like Isabella's, he was certain. "Beautiful little Marine," he said, his voice low. "You'll break hearts with those sea-blue eyes."

His hand rested beside the child, her little arms and legs kicking as she enjoyed the freedom of being without her clothes on such a warm day. Henry started as her tiny fingers curved around one of his. He stared, an all-consuming sensation filling his heart to the brim as he watched her clutch his finger. Trusting him.

He leaned down and pressed a kiss to her forehead, stroking the soft fluff of blonde hair with wonder as he had wanted to do since the moment she'd been born.

"Right then, beautiful girl," he said, determined now. "Let's put you back together."

He took exactly seven tries to get the clout on and tied up. He thought it didn't look too bad, if not as neat as when Isabella did it. The pilcher, however, after all the practise on the clout, was a piece of cake.

"Ha!" he exclaimed, beaming at Marie as she gurgled at him, as impressed by his triumph as he was. "We did it, Marie." He sighed, pleased with himself, and then forced himself to reach for her again, taking the tiny baby in his arms. He lowered his face, allowing her to pinch his nose and making a muffled sound of protest as her sharp little nails dug in.

"Ow."

He looked up, laughing as she released her hold, and found Isabella staring at him, blinking hard.

"Hello," he said, feeling flustered all at once. "She … she was crying so …"

"So I see," Isabella replied, beaming at him, her voice sounding unsteady.

"I didn't do too badly, I think?" he said, lifting her a little to show the clout and pilcher, which promptly fell off her tiny form and hit the floor. Henry scowled. "I think I need more practise," he said with frustration.

Isabella smothered a laugh. "I don't think that will be a problem," she said.

He snorted and looked down at their daughter with a smile. "No, I don't suppose it will."

***

Henry paced outside the door to his studio, rubbing the back of his neck. He looked around to find Isabella watching him. She didn't speak, didn't hurry him or tell him he was being ridiculous. She waited until he was ready.

He *was* being ridiculous though knowing it didn't change a thing. Henry took a deep breath and forced himself to a halt before reaching for the door handle. He walked in, not stopping or looking up until he got to his easel, busying himself with selecting a pencil to sketch out his painting.

Belle waited, silent and patient, and he knew Isabella had told her what to expect. She wanted a portrait done of herself as a present for her husband for Christmas. It had taken Isabella weeks of persuasion before he'd agreed. Belle came to the house often now, sometimes alone, sometimes with Edward, and often with their son, Eli. Henry was trying his best to get used to having them around. Some days he managed better than others, but they never reproached him for getting up and leaving them without a word if things got too much.

Henry liked Eli. He was seven months old now, a strong and sturdy little lad who looked like he'd be a mischievous little devil as soon as he found his feet, though even crawling, he caused chaos. He'd bitten Henry's finger the week previous, which had made them both laugh even as Belle exclaimed with remorse.

Just concentrate on the painting, Isabella's voice sounded in his ear, even though she sat quiet and still in the far corner, a book in hand. She'd promised to stay with him, but she would not interrupt while he worked. With a sigh, he stared at Belle, avoiding her eye for now but taking in the proportions of the pose and sketching in the rough image. He approved the vibrant blue of her gown, the colour of which would be striking, the silk sleek and gleaming in the sunlight that lit the scene. Little by little, Henry relaxed, consumed by the work and forgetting it was someone he did not know well who sat for him, as the desire to paint took him over.

Chapter 22

"Wherein an unlikely friendship is struck."

"Henry, just speak to him, please. You've spoken to him before. If you don't wish to do as he asks, then you have every right to say no. It's your decision."

Henry huffed out a breath, irritated. He'd painted Belle and now it seemed everyone and their blasted mother was clamouring to be next. Isabella turned people away almost daily and the post stacked up in the library. Henry refused to look at it. He painted for himself, not for others.

Never had Isabella insisted he speak to someone himself, but this time she was adamant.

"Why can't you tell him no?" he demanded, knowing he sounded sulky as a child and hating himself for it.

"Because I think you should, and ..." Isabella hesitated. "And he unnerves me a little," she said, looking sheepish. "Besides, after what he did for us, I think it only polite you try to talk to him. Just try, please. For me?"

Henry muttered under his breath and stalked out of the studio. It was childish and ungracious of him, but he hated being forced to do things, even when he knew she did it for his own good. He flung the door of the parlour open, to find Lord DeMorte engaged in rearranging the items on the sideboard. The man froze, looking as uncomfortable as Henry was about having to speak to him.

"It's all right," Henry said, his voice gruff as he gestured to the ornaments. "Put them how you want them."

He waited until DeMorte had arranged everything to his satisfaction, and the man turned to look at him. Henry avoided his eyes, hoping he'd hurry and get it over with.

"My wife saw the painting you did for Belle," DeMorte said, the words stilted, sounding as though they'd been pulled from him with a deal of reluctance. "My wife has ... *requested* I get one done of myself."

Henry looked up, a little intrigued to discover the intimidating figure of Lord DeMorte sounding as though his wife's request had been as good as putting a gun to his head. He regarded his guest with amusement.

"You don't want to sit for me," Henry said as DeMorte grimaced.

"I'd rather have my teeth pulled," the man muttered, glowering a little.

Henry's eyebrows shot up. "Why are you here then?"

DeMorte returned a withering look. "Good God, man, you're married, aren't you? I assume the only reason you're talking to me is because it was *requested* of you?"

Henry nodded, seeing no reason to deny it. DeMorte gave a snort of amusement.

"Well, then," he demanded, his voice brusque and impatient. "Will you do it or not?"

The question made Henry pause. It had been on the tip of his tongue to refuse, but ... He looked again at DeMorte. He was fierce, his features harsh, cruel, even, yet there was something else, a vulnerability that glinted from time to time. If you didn't look hard, you'd miss it, too unsettled by the glowering stare that could pierce you to the core. Capturing that uncompromising character, and that sense of something more ... something hidden - that would be a challenge.

"Yes," Henry said, and walked out of the room.

***

"Where's Henry?" Isabella asked as she walked into the kitchen.

"In his studio," Jack replied, looking up from the piece of bread he was loading with jam. "Preparing for Lord DeMorte."

Isabella frowned. "He didn't come to bed last night. He rarely does that unless he's painting." She worried at her lip, reaching for a slice of plum cake and juggling Marie to a position where she could eat it without dropping crumbs on her. "Perhaps this portrait wasn't a good idea. If he's worrying about it …"

Jack shook his head and Isabella waited until he stopped chewing. "Not worrying," Jack said, reaching for his mug of tea. "He's preparing."

"Oh?" Isabella replied, surprised by his answer. "Preparing what?"

Jack chuckled and shook his head. "Go and see. Then you'll understand why he's been up all night."

Isabella got to her feet and gave Marie to Jack, who beamed at the little girl.

"Ah, there's my little princess. Give old Jack a smile, then, treacle." Isabella watched for a moment as her baby daughter dissolved Jack into a puddle of mush before going to discover what her husband was up to.

The change to come over the studio was dramatic, and Jack was right, now she could see what had taken so long. All the canvases had moved, arranged by subject and by size. Henry had arranged the tables which had been stacked and overflowing, piled with paints and brushes and jars and rags around the easel. He'd sorted brushes in jars by type and size, and the paints by colour, each one laid out neat as soldiers on parade.

Henry looked up as Isabella walked towards him.

"What a lovely man you are," she said, beaming at him as Henry flushed, though his eyes betrayed his pleasure at her words. "You spent all night doing this for Lord DeMorte."

Henry shrugged, rubbing the back of his neck. "Not entirely," he said, looking awkward. "He'll never relax in here if it's messy, and I don't want to paint somewhere else, so ..."

Isabella kissed his cheek. "I still say it's very thoughtful."

She looked up at the sound of a throat clearing and Henry tensed.

"I'm afraid I'm rather early," Lord DeMorte said, sounding uncomfortable and rather cross, and then stopped, staring around the room. His jaw grew a little tight and for a moment Isabella wondered what his reaction might be. They watched as he let out a breath, a little of the tension leaving his shoulders.

"Er," Henry said, staring at the floor and avoiding DeMorte's assessing gaze. "If there is anything ..." He gestured around the room and Gabriel stared at him, astonished by the trouble Henry had taken to put him at ease. "Please move anything that disturbs you, my lord."

"Gabriel." Lord DeMorte cleared his throat, stared at Henry, unblinking, as though he would try to figure him out. "My name is Gabriel." He moved closer, holding out his hand.

"Henry," Isabella prompted as Gabriel waited.

Henry rubbed the back of his neck and then reached out, shaking the man's hand before dropping it again.

"Shall we begin?" Gabriel asked. Henry glanced at Isabella and then nodded, moving to his easel as Gabriel sat down at the chair Henry had arranged for him.

Isabella looked between the two men, wondering which of them was the most ill at ease.

"Well, I'll leave you two gentlemen to it," she said, hiding a smile as she returned to finish her breakfast.

***

Gabriel was interesting to paint. He sat still without fidgeting, for one, which even Isabella couldn't do. Once he'd found a pose and Henry approved, he'd barely moved a muscle, his gaze locked on something in the far distance. The problem was that Henry could only see the mask he wore. His expression was fierce, uncompromising and rather unsettling. Henry had seen a glimpse of something intriguing beneath that mask though, and that's what he wanted to paint.

He looked up from his painting to see that Gabriel was no longer staring straight ahead, but focused on something close at hand. He was sweating.

Henry followed his gaze to see that a paintbrush had fallen on the floor and he hadn't noticed. He moved forward, picking it up and placing it on the table next to the others he'd laid out ready. It wasn't quite straight, so Henry took a moment to twitch it parallel with the others. Gabriel exhaled.

"You should have just picked it up," Henry said, returning to his work.

"I didn't want to interrupt your work," Gabriel replied, his voice gruff, though Henry sensed he was embarrassed.

Henry looked around the canvas. "I don't mind."

Gabriel frowned at him. "Belle, said it was better not to talk to you, or … or to move."

Henry cleared his throat as a recollection of storming from the room when Belle had stood up to stretch her legs returned to him. "Yes, well … I'm … working on it," he muttered, feeling awkward himself now.

"You and me both," Gabriel replied, his tone amused.

Henry snorted. He painted in silence for a while longer until Gabriel spoke again.

"I have a portrait by Reynolds."

Henry looked around the canvas.

"He painted my grandmother," Gabriel added, a cautious look in his eyes. "I also have several Gainsborough's and a Lawrence. I've just acquired an interesting piece by Turner, too."

Henry had never been envious of another man's possessions, but in that moment, he was. He'd seen paintings by the great men in catalogues but never in the flesh. Going out and visiting a gallery had always been an impossibility, though the longing to do just that struck him hard.

"Would you like to see them?" Gabriel asked, interpreting the look in Henry's eyes.

Henry dropped his brush, moving out from behind the canvas as Gabriel raised his eyebrows in surprise.

"Now?" he said, as Henry nodded.

"Yes, now." Nervous excitement jittered down Henry's spine, leaving his home and going somewhere new made nausea roil in his belly ... but a portrait by Joshua Reynolds ... "Now," he repeated, forcing down the fear as the desire to look upon the work of a master overrode all else. He watched, impatient as Gabriel got to his feet.

"Why have you never bought paintings yourself, Henry?" he asked, his expression quizzical. "You're a wealthy man as I understand it, you could have filled the house with paintings."

Henry frowned, pausing as he faced Gabriel. "Because art should be seen, shared and enjoyed, not locked away. There was only me here, and Jack, before Isabella came."

Gabriel nodded, his face troubled. "Yes, I believe Crecy - my wife - would agree with you. However, I don't like visitors and I am not as altruistic as you. I would not deny myself the pleasure for the good of others."

"You don't like visitors?" Henry repeated, watching as Gabriel shook his head.

"I don't like people," Gabriel clarified, his tone dry as he gave Henry that glittering, intense look once again. "I feel I am about to make one more exception, however, come along."

Henry took that for the compliment he recognised it to be, hurrying after Gabriel as he strode out of the studio and towards the front door.

"Henry?" Isabella called after him, as she came down the stairs. "Henry, what's wrong? Where are you going?"

Henry turned, though he kept moving, walking backwards, anxious now to see such works of art that Gabriel had. "He's got a Reynolds, Isabella!" he shouted, grinning now. *"A Reynolds!* And two Gainsborough's and a Lawrence and a Turner. He's going to show me."

"Oh!" Isabella replied, astonished as she watched him leave the house in the company of Gabriel DeMorte.

***

"Oh, Belle, what shall I do if he's angry?" Isabella demanded, worrying at her lower lip.

Belle laughed, shaking her head. "I'm sure you'll think of something," she said, placid as ever. "Besides, you've done it now," she added, patting the sealed envelope on the seat beside her. She grinned at Isabella as she put her teacup down.

"I can still take it back again," Isabella muttered, wondering if she was doing the right thing. Going behind Henry's back seemed a terrible thing to do, but … but the world deserved to see his genius, and he deserved recognition for his talent. She had put submitting his work to the Royal Academy to him some time before, only to throw him into such a panic at the idea she hadn't dared broach the subject again. He didn't like the thought of his work being judged, his painting scrutinised by those names in the art world he revered so. His painting *was* him, it was personal and left him feeling exposed. Yet allowing him to live his life without ever knowing the great talent he possessed, without sharing it with the world, that seemed a worse crime than doing something he might reproach her for.

When Belle had said Mary Moser, one of the founding members of the Academy, had seen Henry's portrait of Belle and demanded to know everything about the artist, Isabella had known she must act.

"What did Mary Moser say again?" Isabella demanded, hoping to reassure herself.

Belle shot her a sympathetic smile. "She was all for visiting Henry that moment," she said, reaching out and patting Isabella's knee. "Although she is no longer a young woman and had just walked in the door after a fatiguing journey. I talked her out of it, thank goodness, but she was astonished that no one had ever heard of him or seen his work. The woman practically ordered me to get him to submit a painting for the summer exhibition."

"Do you think we chose the right painting?" she asked, still fretting. It would be next year before they heard if they had accepted him. She'd be a nervous wreck by then. Making excuses about the whereabouts of the piece had almost given her a break down.

"Well, Gabriel was adamant," Belle reminded her. "And he's the most discerning of all of us where art is concerned.

Isabella let out a breath of relief. "Surely Henry will be pleased if he's accepted? Don't you think?" she asked Belle, anxiety forming a knot in her stomach. "And they will accept him, won't they?"

Isabella knew Belle couldn't answer the questions with any real certainty, but she allowed her friend's reassuring smile to sooth her fears.

"I certainly think he'll be accepted if Mary Moser has anything to do with it, and as for Henry, you know your husband better than I, Isabella. I think the approval of the great names he holds in such regard should make up for any reproaches he may have towards you for acting without asking his permission."

Isabella nodded, but continued to chew on her lip. She prayed that Belle was right.

Chapter 23

"Wherein a lie is revealed."

Isabella stared at the envelope on the table in front of her as Jack bounced Marie on his knee. The little girl squealed and giggled.

"'Gain, 'gain!" she demanded, her little golden curls bouncing as she beamed at Jack. Jack, of course, obliged her at once. At a year old, she could wrap the burly man around her tiny finger. Jack could no more deny his *little princess* than Henry could. The child would be horribly spoilt if Isabella didn't watch them both. Right at this moment, however, the contents of the envelope before her was of greater concern.

"Just open the damn thing," Jack said, shaking his head with frustration. "You've been staring at it for the best part of forty minutes."

"Damn," Marie echoed, grinning at Jack, who blanched.

Isabella rolled her eyes at Jack, glowering a little. "I told you that you needed to mind your tongue in front of her."

Jack cleared his throat, looking sheepish. "I forgot, sorry." He gave Marie a stern look. "That's a bad word, princess. Jack ought not to have said it. Try doggy. Remember, we saw a doggy. Woof, woof." Isabella hid a grin as Marie watched, entranced. "What did the doggy say then, princess?"

"Damn!" Marie replied, squealing with delight.

Jack pulled at his neck cloth, giving Isabella a rueful glance. "I'll work on it," he muttered.

Isabella sighed and reached for the envelope. She slid her finger under the seal and held her breath.

"He did it!" she exclaimed, jumping from her seat. "Henry did it! They accepted him for the summer exhibition. Oh, and Jack," she said, her excitement bubbling over now. "His painting will hang on the centreline! That's a place of honour."

"Well, I should think so, too," Jack replied, though she could see he was brimming with pride just as she was.

"Oh!" Isabella squealed with delight as her daughter stared at her, bemused. She ran to Jack, kissing his cheek and then kissing Marie. "See what a clever papa you have, Marie. I must tell him."

"Here, Isabella," Jack said, hefting Marie onto his hip as he stood. "Hold your horses. Just go easy, eh? Remember, we don't know how he'll feel about it."

Isabella nodded, forcing her excitement down, as she knew Jack was right. "Yes. Yes, of course," she said as she remembered why she'd been so worried. "I'll tread carefully."

***

"Oh, Eli, do stop squirming, dear," Belle said as her little boy wriggled to the floor and ran off across the studio. "I'm so sorry, Henry. It's like trying to hold on to an eel."

Henry gave an absent nod, too absorbed in his work to worry. Henry's oil paints were bought in walnut-sized pig's bladders to keep them fresh, and Eli had tried to eat one during his last sitting and had been promptly sick. Everywhere. Henry felt he could cope with anything else the little devil could do after that revolting episode.

He looked up as Isabella came in, wondering if it was time to take a break already. The slippery Eli had barely sat still for two minutes together and painting him was akin to grabbing for snowflakes. Just when you thought you had one, it melted away. The last thing he needed was interruptions.

"H-Henry," Isabella stammered, looking nervous and ill at ease. "May I speak with you for a moment?"

"Marie?" he asked, his heart plummeting at the serious look in her eyes.

"Oh! Oh, no, Henry, it's nothing bad," she said, hurrying towards him. "Actually it's … it's rather wonderful, at least I think so."

Henry's heart leapt this time and he held his breath.

"I'll leave you in peace for a moment," Belle said, casting Isabella a significant look and running to grab hold of Eli before he took a bite from a bladder of burnt umber. "Come along, my paint-devouring monster," she called to Eli, sweeping him up and hauling him from the room. "Let's visit Marie."

Henry turned back to Isabella, his hopes soaring.

"Henry," Isabella said, her breathing rather rapid. Why was she so nervous? "I … I have something to t-tell you."

Henry set down his brush and moved closer to her. "Yes?"

"Y-you've been accepted by the Royal Academy for the summer exhibition. They want to hang your painting on the centreline, Henry," she said, sounding breathless now. "That's the best position, love. They will show the world your talent, Henry. Everyone will see what a genius you are."

Henry frowned. That was not what he'd been expecting or hoping for her to say. He stared at his feet, perplexed.

"You sent a painting?" he said, as his emotions lurched. He hadn't known that.

Isabella nodded, apprehension in her eyes as she twisted her hands together.

"I know you told me not to, Henry, but Mary Moser, she's one of the founders of the Academy …"

"I know who she is," Henry muttered, folding his arms and glowering a little now.

"W-well, she saw your painting of Belle and she practically ordered her to get you to submit a work, and so I spoke to Gabriel and … and …" She swallowed, looking like she might cry now. "And so, we sent a painting." Her words trailed off, rather faint.

His jaw tightened. "Juno," he guessed, anger sparking now. She'd told him she'd packed it away, as they were having work done. Another thing he'd forced himself to allow, strangers in the house again. Not only that, everyone else had known. Jack, Belle, and Edward, *Gabriel!* That Gabriel hadn't told him …

The two men had become close since Henry had painted his portrait. Gabriel found Henry's acceptance of his need for order soothing, and Gabriel was one of the few people Henry didn't feel ill at ease with, as he was every bit as odd as he was. It appeared the people Henry trusted most in the world had gone behind his back. They'd lied to him.

Henry left the room, slamming the door on his way out.

***

"Thank you for coming, Gabriel," Isabella said, ushering the man inside. She was at her wit's end, and the idea of facing a silent and angry Henry for many more days was wearing her down. Asking Gabriel to come was her last resort. She had no idea if he could help or not, but she had to do something.

Gabriel nodded, placing his hat and gloves down with precision. "Where is he?"

"In his studio," she said, remorse a weight in her chest. "Oh, Gabriel, I wish I'd never done it. He's not spoken for three days, and …" She blinked back tears, struggling to compose herself. Gabriel hated visible displays of emotion and as she'd begged the man to come and speak to Henry, the least she could do was keep a hold of herself. "He thinks we lied to him. Well, we did," she said, throwing up her hands in despair. *"I did!* He'll never trust me again."

"Nonsense," Gabriel retorted, his tone brusque. "He's just sulking. Leave him to me."

Isabella nodded, wringing her hands together, glad to let someone else try where she had failed.

***

Henry glanced up from his painting as Gabriel opened the door. He sighed. He'd wondered how long it would take.

"Henry," the man said, staring at him with those piercing eyes.

Henry glowered and put down the paintbrush he was holding so it laid at an awkward angle across the paints on his table. Gabriel twitched.

"I see. Like that, is it?" Gabriel said, reaching out and putting the paintbrush straight.

Henry reached for another brush and returned to his work.

"Now, listen here, you pig-headed fool," Gabriel said, folding his arms and turning his back on the tables of paints and brushes which were nowhere near as tidy as when he'd sat for his portrait. "All of us know and see your talent, Henry. We know you're a blasted genius, even if you are an awkward devil."

Henry ignored him.

Gabriel huffed out a breath and Henry saw him twitch as his eyes drifted to the table again. "A wise and generous man once told me that all great art ought to be shared, not shut away in the dark where no one could appreciate it."

Henry froze, his paintbrush suspended over the canvas. He frowned, turning back to Gabriel, who looked a deal too smug.

"I don't want to go," he said, the words angry, still irritated for no good reason he could think of.

"Fine," Gabriel replied, shrugging as he gave into the desire to rearrange the paints which were making him anxious. "We shall listen to everyone praise you to the skies and come back and tell you all about it."

Henry glowered harder. It wasn't true that he didn't want to go. Not even a little. The more he thought about it, the more he wanted to see his work hung upon those lofty walls, surrounded by the great names of the art world. He'd even begun to feel glad that Isabella had done what she had, though damned if he'd admit as much, but he couldn't face all the people.

"I've heard your painting of Isabella is between a portrait by Thomas Lawrence on one side and a work by Turner on the other."

The words were casual, careless, but it was enough to make Henry start, staring at Gabriel in shock. He swallowed as those famous names made his heart pick up, the longing to see them for himself tangible.

"Truly?" he said, his voice hesitant.

"Of course, truly!" Gabriel snapped, looking up from the table. "What do you take me for? Certainly not a sulky school boy who is punishing his wife for doing something wonderful for him."

Henry rubbed the back of his neck, guilt warring with indignation. "She lied to me," he muttered, feeling every bit the sulky child Gabriel accused him of being.

"Because you were being an idiot!" Gabriel rolled his eyes at him and Henry stamped down the desire to run from the room with difficulty. "You refused because you were afraid, despite all our assurances of your talent. For heaven's sake, man, on the one hand, you accuse us of being untrustworthy, but you wouldn't trust our judgement you should enter the competition."

Gabriel's expression softened a little and he stepped forward, grasping Henry's arm. "Isabella is upset, you damn fool."

Henry held his gaze and let out a breath. "I know, and ..." He shook his head, feeling wretched. "I know." Henry shrugged, rubbing a hand over his face. "To be honest, it wasn't just that."

"Oh?" Gabriel said, releasing his arm and waiting for Henry to continue.

"She came in, all excited, saying she had something to tell me and ... and I thought ..." Henry shook his head, staring at his feet, embarrassed now. He didn't know why he'd admitted as much, but a weight lifted from his chest with the admission.

"Ah," Gabriel replied, his tone sympathetic. "You hoped she was with child?" Henry nodded and then frowned as Gabriel gave a dark chuckle. "So rather than try to ensure she *could* tell you that news soon enough, you blame her and sleep in your studio? Bravo." His tone was mocking, though not unkind, but Henry flushed anyway.

Gabriel patted Henry on the back in a brotherly fashion. "My work here is done," he said, grinning. "It's good to know I'm not the only damn fool where my wife is concerned." He strode away, relief in his expression at being able to leave Henry's studio, having done his duty.

Henry waited, knowing Isabella would seek him out soon enough. He ought to find her, apologise, but he felt stupid and indignant and childish enough to want to avoid her a little longer.

He was painting when she appeared at his side, and the desire for her to hold him and tell him he was forgiven warred against his stubborn nature.

"Do you forgive me, Henry?"

Her voice was quiet and uncertain, and Henry cursed himself for being a wretched creature. He didn't deserve her. It was him that needed forgiveness.

She waited as he set down his brush and turned, head bowed, staring at his feet. "Not your fault," he muttered, the words a little ungracious. "My fault. Sorry."

The breath left him in a rush as she flung her arms about his waist. "Oh, but I'm so sorry. I should never have done it without your permission. I never will again, I swear. Please don't think you can't trust me."

Henry sighed, wrapping his arms about her waist. "I was foolish not to listen to you," he said, lowering his head to rest upon hers. "You were right."

She sighed, and he stood straight, looking down at her as wonder swept him up with excitement. "The painting is beside one by Thomas Lawrence, and Turner on the other side."

Isabella nodded, her eyes bright, her expression fierce with pride. "I know, Henry, on the centreline where everyone will recognise you for the talent you are. It's where you deserve to be."

Henry smiled, his heart swelling with the pleasure she took in his success. "Is Belle still here?" he asked, his tone cautious.

"No, I'm sorry, Henry. We thought perhaps she ought to leave, as …"

"As I was sulking?" Henry cut in, rubbing the back of his neck with a grimace.

"As you might not feel like painting anymore today," Isabella corrected, making excuses for him as always.

"I don't," he said, and worry lit her eyes at the determination behind the words. He grinned at her as he grasped her hand, tugging her towards the door.

"Where are we going, Henry?" she exclaimed, almost running into him as he stopped and tugged her into his arms for a kiss.

"To the orchard," he said, desire leaping beneath his skin. Gabriel had been right. He was a bloody fool not to have spent the last three nights ensuring that Isabella bore another child instead of regretting that she did not. Fool no more, however. There was no time to lose.

Chapter 24

"Wherein a new master is discovered by the ton."

Isabella clung to Belle's arm.

"Just look!" she exclaimed, bubbling over with pride and joy.

"I am looking," she laughed, patting Isabella's arm, her pleasure in Isabella's happiness making her eyes shine. "It's breath taking."

Isabella stared at the painting, wondering how Henry captured her but made her look so much lovelier than she was. The orange dress sang out, catching the eye and tearing everyone's attention from what she saw as dull landscapes and muddy-coloured portraits. To her mind, Henry's work outshone everyone's here, though she admitted she might be just a little biased. Not that she cared.

She looked around as Gabriel returned, his beautiful wife at his side. Isabella smiled at her. Crecy appeared to be an original and free spirit, full of laughter and surprising comments. Isabella had taken to her immediately and found the way that her terrifying husband melted into a puddle in her company intriguing. Gabriel was a deal less frightening since he had befriended Henry, but he still emanated a dark air that made the crowds part before him.

"Did you buy it?" she asked, knowing the answer as Crecy beamed and Gabriel returned a *what do you think* expression. Crecy had fallen in love with a tiny engraving by William Blake, so naturally Gabriel would stop at nothing to get it for her.

"How is Henry faring?" Gabriel asked, concern in his eyes now.

Isabella's smile faltered a little. "The journey here was … trying," she said, though that didn't really cover it. Henry was stressed and exhausted, the trials of the journey pitting against his determination to see his work hung in the New Somerset House alongside the others he so revered. To her astonishment, Edward had arranged that Henry have a private viewing, this evening, once the crowds had gone. He'd said there was little point in being a marquess if you couldn't get your own way occasionally. It had made the entire trip possible for Henry, who could never have faced the great and the good *en masse* as they were at present.

The cream of the *ton* was here on this first showing of the new works. It had frightened Isabella to attend herself, knowing she would face censure and the likelihood of being sneered at and cut in public. Yet through Henry's work, she had become a rather romantic, if scandalous figure, and to her bewilderment, people were falling over themselves to talk to her about her reclusive husband. Somehow, rumours of his madness and his astonishing good looks had combined to create a Byronic persona which everyone wanted to know more about.

More than happy to speak of her husband's hitherto undiscovered talents, Isabella indulged them, despite feeling contempt for such fickle friendships as people would now offer her. Now she had seen Henry's success, seen his work recognised for what it was, all that remained was for Henry himself to see the work where it sat. Then they could go home. She smiled with relief as the thought buoyed her.

In a moment of respite, Isabella turned to Belle and rolled her eyes.

"Good heavens, these people ask the most ridiculous questions," she said, looking with sympathy at Gabriel, who was looking a little grey and worn. Edward had already gone, the crowds too much for him to cope with, though he'd congratulated Isabella on Henry's success. Before she could ask if Edward was all right, or if they should return Belle to their London home to check on him, a familiar voice made Isabella spin around.

"Isabella, darling."

Isabella froze, torn between disbelief and fury as her mother bustled up to her, her cousin Jane and the rest of their fashionable coterie in tow. That the selfish creature who had hoped Isabella might die to save her from embarrassment would now try to insinuate herself back into her life made rage a living thing beneath her skin. She would profit from Henry's fame, when she had denigrated him and called him a half-wit. Well, not if Isabella had any say in the matter. That the woman would believe Isabella shallow enough to want to return to the fold now that she'd retrieved her reputation from utter ruin made Isabella itch to slap her face. The desire was so strong she had to clench her fists to repress the urge to act on it.

"Darling, I just had to bring a few friends to see your clever husband's work. He's the talk of the *ton.*"

For a moment, words jostled on Isabella's tongue, furious tirades full of accusation and gossip enough to fuel the rumour mill and keep her mother in hiding for years to come.

No.

She would not detract from Henry's work and his success. She would not allow her mother to make this about her, no matter how appealing it was to destroy her in public. That did not mean to say she would not punish her.

"Forgive me, madam," she said, her tone icy as she stared at the woman who had thrown her from her home to starve along with her unborn child. "You seem to be under the mistaken assumption we know each other."

Her mother's smile set on her face, the colour leaching from her powdered cheeks as her companions made audible gasps of shock.

"Lady Isabella?" Isabella looked around to find Gabriel at her side. He delivered a scathing look to Lady Scranford before turning back to her. "I believe Thomas Lawrence would like to speak with Henry and visit his studio. Come, you have a more convivial company awaiting you."

Isabella turned without a backwards glance, leaving her mother mortified and alone as her companions disappeared. Her fair-weather friends vanished in an instant, keen to distance themselves from her disgrace, and to dine out on the story.

There was no victory in her triumph, no glory in vengeance for Isabella, though, only a sense of sorrow that her mother had never loved her. The longing to return to Henry and Marie was an ache beneath her skin. Still, she allowed Gabriel to present her to the famous Mr Lawrence, her pleasure in Henry's triumph only tinged with the regret she could not leave at once to be with him.

***

Henry stared up at the vast walls of New Somerset House, the paintings skied one on top of the other, side by side with a bare inch of space between them. Each work of art jostling for space and attention as light flooded in from the huge windows in the ceiling. He took a shaky a breath, finding it overwhelming, too many great works clamouring to be noticed, as his eyes tried to settle.

"I wish I could look at them one at a time," he whispered to Isabella, whose hand he was clutching so hard he must be hurting her. He tried to unlock his fingers a little, his palm sweaty with nerves, but Isabella just held his hand tighter still. "It makes my head spin."

"It is rather overwhelming," she agreed, sounding somewhat breathless. "But magnificent, too. Oh, Henry, yours is by far the best work here."

Henry smiled, sending her an indulgent look that spoke of his adoration. Isabella would think anything he did was the best in the world. It was a humbling feeling. Just as well, as seeing his work displayed so might go to his head. Already Gabriel's reciting of his own words was coming back to him. Art ought to be displayed, enjoyed, not hidden away in the dark. That constant refrain circled his brain and was one he would previously have rejected out of hand. It was too frightening, too outside of the realms of his experience and what he could cope with, yet it lingered. He pushed it to one side for now, content to stand and stare at the hundreds of paintings clamouring for his attention.

As the light waned, someone came and lit the huge chandelier that the Prince Regent had gifted the academy to illuminate its evening exhibitions. It had recently been converted to gas and Henry stared with wonder at the invention.

"It smells," Isabella said, giving the new-fangled device a sceptical glance. "Frightening, too, how it burns with no candle or wick."

"It's the future," Henry murmured, watching the blue flames for a moment longer, before returning his attention to the artwork.

"You're the future," Isabella whispered in his ear. "You're famous now, Henry."

Henry snorted and ducked his head to kiss her lips. "Famous and eccentric?" he queried, one eyebrow raised.

Isabella chuckled, having told him the things that were being said about him. It seemed ridiculous and unlikely, but then he'd never understood people. He doubted he ever would.

"Certainly," she said with a grave nod and a twinkle in her lovely eyes.

He sighed, taking one last look around the great building and its works of art. "Good." He stared around, satisfied and ready to leave. "Then I can go home," he said, grinning at her and lifting her hand to his lips. "And stay there."

Chapter 25

"Wherein life is picture perfect."

Isabella lay back, her head resting on her arm as she stared up at the branches of the apple tree. It was a glorious summer's day, the sun hot yet a light breeze stirring the leaves above her.

Jack had taken Marie to visit Eli, the two of them thick as thieves now, though Jack complained the boy led his princess into mischief. It was ever thus, Isabella thought with a smile. She looked up to see Henry focused on yet another drawing of her.

"Will you ever get bored with drawing me?" she asked, staring at her handsome man's dark head as it bent over the page.

"No."

She smiled, used to his lack of conversation when he was intent on something. It would take something out of the ordinary to break his concentration now. She lay back, amusement tugging at her lips as an idea occurred to her.

Isabella got to her knees, eliciting a tut of disapproval from Henry as she broke the pose.

"Isabella!"

She grinned at him and tugged at the fastenings of her dress.

"What, Henry?" she asked, her voice low and sultry.

Henry opened his mouth and closed it again, surprise lighting his eyes.

She stripped off the muslin gown, tossing it to hang from the branches of the apple tree as she removed each layer. To her delight, Henry's eyes were dark now, his gaze on her hotter than the sun that gilded the surrounding landscape. As she lay down again, Henry put aside his paper and moved towards her.

"Ah, ah," she said, wagging a finger at him. "You wanted to draw me like this, remember?"

Henry sucked in a breath, the desire to capture her form on paper warring with a more instinctive need that blazed in his eyes.

"Well, now's your chance," she taunted, enjoying her power over him. "Take it or leave it."

Henry swallowed, reaching for his paper again with more reluctance than she'd ever seen. She allowed him to work for a while, feeling decadent and scandalous as the warm breeze fluttered over her naked skin. As she turned her head, she saw that the artist in him had won out, intense concentration in his eyes now as he sketched, his hand moving rapidly over the page. She closed her eyes, imagining his hands tracing the contours he now followed with his eyes and his pencil, committing the curves and valleys to paper. Desire rose, a heat that warmed and burned beneath her skin as the month of June heated her from above.

Isabella allowed her imagination to wander, thinking of what would happen once Henry had completed his sketch. Anticipation thrilled her, shivering over her flesh, tightening her nipples to taut little peaks. Though she was spoiling the pose, she raised her hand, allowing one lazy finger to circle the tight bud. The sound of pencil on paper faltered. She smiled, her eyes still closed as she imagined the rapt expression on her husband's face. Her finger repeated the motion in slow circles and then drew a line down between her breasts, across her stomach. She reached the springy thatch of curls between her thighs and allowed her fingers to thread back and forth. One finger sought lower, touching the source of her pleasure and making her mouth open with a silent sigh of desire. Henry's breathing was audible now, though he didn't move, spellbound by her.

She opened her eyes, her eyelids heavy as she watched Henry watching her. He swallowed as she parted her legs a little, the warm air still cooling the damp fire of her skin as his breath caught, snagging in his throat.

He still gripped the pencil, though the paper and board had slid from his lap.

Isabella tutted at him, amused. "You're supposed to be drawing me," she scolded him.

"C-can't," he stammered, clearing his throat as he watched her finger dip in and out of the hidden spot between her thighs. "Can't concentrate." She laughed at his expression, entranced as he watched her.

"That's a shame," she whispered, arching her body and allowing the pleasure of her own touch to consume her as Henry's hot gaze devoured her and sent her arousal spiralling higher. "You so wanted to draw me like this ... didn't you?"

Henry didn't answer.

"Didn't you, Henry?" Henry tore his gaze away from her caressing fingers and stared at her.

"What?" he said, blinking as though dazed.

Isabella chuckled again and then closed her eyes as the pleasure built inside her. She sighed as he pushed her hand aside and a warm, wet heat slid over her, pushing her closer to the edge. As she looked down, Henry's dark head bent over her, his concentration as absolute as when he painted as he strove to bring her pleasure.

Isabella closed her eyes, the sunlight turning the world a heated red as pleasure enveloped her and Henry stole her breath, her ability to think, her heart, all over again.

***

Henry looked up, fascinated and enthralled as pleasure shook Isabella's beautiful frame, her gasping, breathless pants a sound he would never tire of as her fingers clutched at his hair. He kissed his way up her body, painting with his tongue that which he could never reproduce to his satisfaction on a canvas. Nothing would ever replace or capture her ability to captivate him.

Young men sent poems to her, inspired by the beauty he'd shown the world in his portrait. Sonnets and love poems dedicated to the embodiment of Juno, his fiery goddess. He'd been angry at first, jealous of their ability to put words to their feelings when his tangled up in his head. Isabella had laughed, though, throwing their extravagant words into the fire as she made him remember why she loved him, and him alone.

She opened herself to him now and pleasure overrode the will to think of anything outside of the two of them, the perfect slide of their bodies in unison. Her hands moved over him, caressing his skin as he looked up and found himself caught in the desire in her eyes. Perfection, this was, *she was* ... perfection.

A jay echoed his cries, out in the woods, the raucous sound still not as harsh as the exclamation he made as he lost himself inside her, with Isabella holding him tight and urging him on.

They lay together, sated and indolent, his limbs heavy with heat and the boneless sense of contentment that came after the excess of pleasure she brought him. He ran a hand over her breast, down her side, resting over her stomach. Henry's eyes were closed as her hand covered his and she turned to him.

"Henry," she said, her voice low and as sleepy as he felt. He opened his eyes, smiling and dazed as he found her blue eyes. Ultramarine, like Marie's.

"Hmmm," he replied, too tired to form words. They might have to sleep out here, he wasn't sure he could move.

"I'm having a baby."

Henry blinked. The words circled his brain and he knew their meaning was significant, important, but for a moment the meaning eluded him.

"A ...?" he began, the words stalling somewhere between his mind and his tongue.

"A baby," Isabella repeated, her expression placid, waiting for him to understand what she was telling him.

He sat up all at once, the movement sliding her head from his arm to the blanket with something of a thud.

"Henry!" she exclaimed, laughing as he stared at her, appalled by his clumsiness.

"Sorry!" he exclaimed, rubbing her head and earning another reproach as he mussed up her hair. She fussed, pushing the blonde locks from her eyes until he could take no more. He took her wrists, pinning her hands, one each side of her head.

"Say it again," he demanded, not yet daring to believe he'd heard correctly.

She smiled up at him, the expression beatific and knowing all at once. "I'm having a baby, Henry."

Henry let out a breath, releasing her wrists and sitting back, staring at her stomach. There was a gentle curve to it he had noted when he'd sketched her, but he'd not begun to hope that ...

Scurrying backwards, he leant down over her, kissing her stomach. Isabella laughed and squealed, and Henry smiled against her skin while her hands tried to push him away as he tickled her.

"Henry, stop, *stop!*" she gasped, laughing and fighting for breath. He obeyed this time and looked down at her, his heart ready to burst.

"Another baby?" he said, awestruck still. "You're sure?"

Isabella nodded, reaching for him. "I'm sure."

"A boy," he said, his tone confident, knowing it would make her laugh. "A brother for Marie."

She grinned at him then, pulling his head down for a kiss. "Whatever you say, Henry."

Epilogue

"Wherein ... happily ever after."

"Eli, no! Don't you dare ... Oh, my Lord!"

Isabella laughed as Belle picked up her skirts and ran after her troublesome son. At almost eight years old, the child had an independent spirit and a nose for mischief. Little Leo, three years his junior, ran to keep up with the older brother he idolised, refusing to be left out. Marine crowed with laughter, spilling the ice she was eating down the pretty blue dress she wore.

"Oops, sorry, mama." She gave Isabella a rueful grin, shovelling down the last of the melted strawberry ice before running off to see what trouble Eli was in now. Isabella smiled, watching as her beautiful daughter ran off to cause trouble of her own, blonde ringlets bouncing as she went. Though Isabella suspected she was biased, the girl was stunning, with the widest, bluest eyes she had ever seen. Marine indeed. Henry had been right again. Those eyes had the power to devastate, something she practised often on both her papa and her adored Jacky, neither of whom could deny the child anything.

Isabella looked around her with satisfaction. Edward was ignoring his son's antics in favour of reading the book that Belle had just abandoned. Crecy dozed on a picnic blanket, having been kept up all night by their newest arrival, a baby boy. Henry and Isabella were godparents, and the adorably chubby babe was making Isabella broody. Helping herself to one of her own cakes, Isabella chewed, contented, and noticed Crecy and Gabriel's eldest daughter, Hope, had climbed to the top of an apple tree. The child was giggling and refusing to come down. Gabriel looked like he would have a heart-attack if she didn't return to the ground immediately and was dithering at the bottom of the tree, torn between shouting at her to do as she was told and climbing up after her. He was a terrible worrier.

Thinking it would be a good moment to steal a cuddle with her godson, Isabella hurried off to the wicker basket in a quieter corner of the orchard, in the shade of an apple tree. Too late. She gave a little huff of disappointment, looking around to find who was there first. Her eyes discovered Henry, sitting in the shade, his little namesake in his arms. That Henry and Gabriel's friendship had grown over the years was something that had become a strength for both men. They each had their demons, things that set them apart from the world and made them feel different, outsiders. Together, however, they had found a bond, a friendship that was deep and respectful, and made them both stronger.

Isabella sighed, her heart turning to mush as she looked at Henry cradling the baby, the child so tiny against his massive frame. Their own son, Gabe, leaned over his shoulder and Isabella could not keep the smile from her lips. There could be no one more contented in the whole of England than she. Isabella returned to retrieve the plate of cakes and hurried across the orchard to join the idyllic scene.

"When will he be old enough to play with me, papa?" Gabe demanded, the frustration in his voice clear.

"Soon enough," Henry replied, his voice amused. "Don't be impatient. You have lots of other friends to play with."

Gabe folded his arms, looking a little mutinous. "I don't like Hope." He kicked one boot in the dirt, scuffing the already worn toe further and glowering across the orchard. "She's so bossy."

Henry looked up, meeting Isabella's eyes as she joined them. "I'm sure that's not true, Gabe."

"Is too," the boy insisted.

"Well, you like Leo," Henry said, trying to mediate.

Gabe shrugged. "He's all right, but Eli is too loud, and he thinks Marine is pretty." An eye roll that illustrated his feelings on this point followed the statement.

Isabella bit her lip as Henry scowled. "Does he, indeed?"

"Cakes!" Isabella sat herself down beside her men as Gabe snaffled two and ran away before anyone could protest.

Isabella held out her arms to Henry. "I'll take the baby while you eat yours."

Henry shook his head and popped the cake in his mouth in one go. "I can manage," he mumbled, earning himself an impatient look.

"It's my turn!"

Her stubborn husband just shook his head, grinning down at baby Henry, who gurgled and kicked. Isabella sighed and leaned into the larger version, who put his arm around her.

An aching sort of sensation tugged at her womb and she sighed again, dewy-eyed. "Isn't he lovely?"

Henry nodded, giving the baby his finger to hold. He turned his head, kissing Isabella's cheek. "Shall we have another, do you think?"

Isabella hid a smile, leaning her head on his shoulder. "I might be persuaded," she said, a doubtful tone to her voice she didn't think would fool him for a moment. "But you must be *very* persuasive."

He snorted, a rather smug look in his eyes that told her just how much resistance he expected to encounter. They looked up as Jack called to them and Isabella waved.

"Hello mama! Look papa, look at me!"

They both laughed as their youngest daughter grinned at them, perched as she was upon Jack's shoulders. To Isabella's delight, their little girl, unlike Gabe, favoured Henry. Thick dark curls fell to her shoulders and she had extraordinarily coloured eyes that were always full of laughter. They were almost a golden brown, the colour of autumn leaves. Henry was convinced she'd inherited his talent. Isabella thought it was too early to tell yet, but the girl loved to draw. She would spend hours in Henry's studio either watching him paint or trying to herself.

Jack sat down with a groan as Sienna slid from his shoulders, kissed his cheek, and ran off again, stealing a cake as she went.

"Oi, you little minx, where's my cake?" Jack protested as the child disappeared to find her playmates, moving like quicksilver.

"Here you go." Isabella offered Jack the plate and he helped himself with a grin.

"Henry!" They looked around as Gabriel approached. He was carrying a parcel under his arm. Isabella watched, hiding her amusement as Gabriel regarded the picnic blanket with misgiving. Picnics were not his favourite events, but he hid it far better now than he used to. He sat down, cross-legged, and looked a little ill at ease before his gaze fell on his son.

"Swap." He held out the parcel to Henry, who obliged him by handing his son over.

"But it was my turn!" Isabella said, glaring at Henry, who shrugged, tugging the string that held the brown paper closed.

"It's his son."

She folded her arms, huffing, until he drew back the paper to reveal a painting.

"Oh," she said, intrigued. "That's lovely."

Gabriel nodded, watching Henry's face as he studied the picture. "I thought so. I have two more by the same artist at home."

"Who is it by?" Isabella asked, admiring the rather unusual portrait. A young girl stared from the painting, perhaps eight years old. She was a pretty girl, but unlike most portraits of young ladies, it was not of a sweet, fresh-faced girl in a pink dress and bonnet, charming and innocent. This girl was defiant, her arms folded, glaring from the canvas with an uncompromising look that spoke of her displeasure.

"It's remarkable," Henry said, staring at it with delight in his eyes. "Honest."

Gabriel nodded, approving Henry's words. "Exactly what I thought myself. Uncommercial, however. No one would commission a painting of their child looking like that."

Henry snorted, and Gabriel grinned at him. "Yes, well, no one outside of our circle," he said, amending the statement correctly. Isabella thought it would be wonderful to capture little Gabe's furious pout when he was in a miff. "The painting itself shows skill, but I would say this is a young artist. Someone learning their craft, untutored, if I'm not mistaken. A talented amateur."

"You have more like it?" Henry looked up at him and Gabriel nodded.

"I got them for a song," he said, his eyes flicking to the plate on which one lonely cake remained. "I've been trying to track down the artist, but as you will see, they are unsigned, and so far, I've been unsuccessful."

"You're thinking of the gallery?" Henry asked, excitement in his eyes now.

Gabriel nodded, swiping the cake. "It's untidy," he said, his tone amused as he caught Isabella's eye.

Isabella smiled, pride swelling her heart for everything they had achieved and would do in the future. Henry, with his business partners, Gabriel and Edward, had opened an art gallery in Bath. It had been Henry's idea, but he'd known it would be impossible for him to undertake many aspects of the business himself. Like finding a venue.

Gabriel, however, was a tough businessman and had taken the more practical aspects of the endeavour in hand. The gallery had opened just over a year ago. Under Gabriel's eagle eye and with Edward's patronage, it was fast becoming a fashionable and respected venue. Especially as it displayed Henry's most recent works. That his name had grown and grown in the art world did not surprise Isabella. The pride she took in him and his work was unmistakable.

Not that he'd changed. He was still reclusive, though he now found pleasure in their close-knit circle of friends and children. It was more likely that you would find him sat on the periphery of their gatherings, watching rather than joining in, but he seemed content. Everyone understood and knew him by now, and he was happy to talk to people individually. The children were different. He loved them all, and didn't care how many ran up to him, chattering and making noise and demanding his attention. That didn't bother him in the least. Isabella thought it was perhaps because children had no side to them, no hidden agenda or care for propriety and manners and rules. They were honest and had not yet learned to wear the masks that troubled him so.

He rarely visited the art gallery himself, but he vetted all the works exhibited there, and his opinion was final. His passion, however, and one that Gabriel shared, was discovering new talent, young artists. They had even spoken about sponsoring someone who would not have the opportunity to develop their skills in normal circumstances. This mystery artist was intriguing to them for just such a reason. Isabella smiled at their enthusiasm, thinking whoever it was had no idea of the luck awaiting 'round the corner for them.

She wondered who they were and what their life was like. Were they rich or poor, young or old, happily married with family, or alone and friendless and in dire straits? That Henry and his friends could change a life that was unhappy and wretched and bring a new artist to the attention of the world was one that caught at her heart.

She was becoming a romantic at last. Though, what else could she be, with Henry in her life?

He'd been her saviour, as she'd been his. There was nothing more romantic than that.

Life was like that, if you were lucky, she realised as her eyes met Henry's. He smiled at her, his eyes full of warmth and love and the adoration he'd never hidden from her. Not so long ago, she had been standing alone, on the edge of disaster, the world around her bleak and dark and frightening, and there he'd been. He'd saved her from the river, from the dark, from a life where she'd not known what it was to be loved, to be happy, to belong, and she'd saved him right back.

The next book in the Rogues & Gentlemen series (keep reading for a sneak peek!),

Charity and the Devil
Rogues and Gentlemen Book 11

Charity Kendell needs a miracle. She's already hanging on to her family and their farm by her fingertips when her despised landlord, Viscount Devlin, sells her home from under her.

Though she's never met him, Charity knows Lord Devlin to be a gambler, a rogue, and a wastrel. Unprepared to allow such a man to throw her family from the only home they've ever known, she prepares to fight back.

Baxter Linton, Viscount Devlin is in trouble. He owes a gambling debt to a dangerous man who doesn't appreciate waiting for his payment. To raise the money, Dev tries to sell off land, but an unfortunate riding accident leaves him injured before the deal can complete, and with no memory of who or where he is.

When Dev's amnesia disappears, he discovers himself at the tender mercy of Miss Kendell, the bossy virago whose furious letters still litter his desk. In the circumstances, Dev keeps his mouth shut.

But when the handsome Viscount falls under spirited Charity's spell, revealing the man he truly is becomes a daunting prospect.

Chapter 1

"Wherein the devil is in a dark place."

Mr Phillip Ogden had served the Devlin family all his adult life. He had worked his way up to his position as steward, the pinnacle of his career. The previous viscount had been an admirable man, the kind it made you proud to work for. He'd been politically active and well respected throughout England. A voice of reason in the House of Lords.

Mr Ogden looked up to regard the current viscount and gave an inward sigh. He pasted a smile to his face and hoped his expression remained one of sympathy, though sympathy was not an emotion that came to mind.

"I understand your predicament, my lord. However, as I've explained, the Kendall family live at Brasted Farm." Mr Ogden looked down at the papers in his hand, noting the fact he had crumpled them in his agitation. "They are excellent tenants and the family have lived there for close to a century."

He remembered the lovely Miss Kendall's devastation as he'd outlined the viscount's intentions when he'd first realised them, two weeks earlier. He'd rather enjoyed being a comfort to her. It had been all he could do, though, to give them a little warning of the fate in store for them.

"They have nowhere else to go and—"

"What of it?" The words were cold, callous, devoid of interest in the plight of a family who had already experienced their fair share of suffering. "I need the funds and that fat old squire has been nosing after that farm since I was a boy. It will be a quick sale—you said so yourself—and I'll be out from Blackehart's grasp once and for all."

Until next time. Mr Ogden bit back the words with difficulty. Luke Linton, the sixth Viscount Devlin had a devil of a temper. He would not welcome such observations. Not for the first time Ogden wondered if the old viscount's wife had taken the fellow for a fool, for there were not two more different men in the whole of England than the present and the late viscount. While his father had been prudent, serious and the model of propriety, his son....

Ogden gritted his teeth. He'd worked every second of his whole damn life for what he could claim now, while circumstance had handed this man everything on a gilded plate... and he'd thrown it all in his father's face.

Devlin turned to him and Ogden had to fight to hold his gaze. It was unnerving: crystalline blue, cold, and cruel.

"They'll have a little over two months to vacate," Devlin said, the words clipped, indicating that further observations on the welfare of the inhabitants of Brasted Farm would not be met with pleasure. "I leave first thing in the morning. I'll ride the first stage and stop off with Lord Jenson, before accompanying him into town. My valet went to London this morning and you may also send my belongings direct. Jenson's man will see to me for a day or two. I'll return in eight weeks, by which time I expect this affair to be in order. Is that clear?"

Mr Ogden inclined his head to acknowledge that it was indeed clear. The less he said the better at this point. At least he could tell Miss Kendall that he had done his best to help her with a clear conscience. He hoped she'd be grateful to him for his efforts and sighed, remembering her lovely face.

The viscount had turned away to stare out of his study window, giving Mr Ogden a view of a coat from the finest tailor in the country clinging to broad shoulders and a lean, muscular frame. Jealousy stirred, and Ogden fought it back with difficulty. Lord

Devlin had everything: money, title, and looks that made women sigh with longing, and what had he done with it? The fool had run through his fortune in little more than a decade, whoring and drinking and gambling. Sometimes Ogden believed he'd done it on purpose, out of spite for the old man, knowing it would have him turning in his grave, but even Devlin wasn't that vindictive… was he?

The viscount turned back, an amused curl to his cruel mouth suggesting he knew exactly what Ogden was thinking. Ogden fought the flush that rose to his cheeks and wished that Devlin, thirteen years his junior, couldn't unnerve him with quite such ease.

"What are you waiting for?" Devlin challenged, irritation threading his precise, sharp edged voice. "You have your instructions, now get out."

Ogden swallowed his anger and his pride, bowed, and retreated to brood in private.

***

Lord Devlin snorted as Ogden closed the study door behind him. Poor Ogden, trying so hard to give good advice and wringing his hands as everything fell apart. His father's man. Loyal to his last breath and still trying to pass on the old bastard's advice from beyond the grave. Dev wondered why he kept him on. Some masochistic tendency, perhaps, or perhaps he just enjoyed watching the man's distress as he descended further into the dark. His father had missed that; he'd died just as Dev was getting into his stride, though most people had blamed his excesses for the old viscount's demise. Pity. He'd loved to have seen the horror and distress in his father's eyes as he saw what little was left of the great fortune he'd worked so hard to amass.

Dev poured himself a drink. He lifted the fine crystal to his lips and savoured the quality of the liquor. How long before he was finding oblivion in cheap liquor in some seedy gin palace He almost welcomed it. Almost. A run-in with Mr Blackehart had made him question his own quest for self-destruction. Perhaps he valued his life a little more than he'd imagined. Blackehart was not a man to be taken lightly. The truth was he'd made Dev's blood run cold, and that was no easy task, hence the sudden need to divest himself of property. The man had demanded payment in full and Dev had to make good on it, or he might fulfil his father's prophecy about his inevitable demise sooner than anyone had anticipated. The only way to meet such a sum quickly was to sell land and property, with the added advantage that his father would have despised him for it.

Brasted Farm wasn't large, but it had good soil. Good enough for growing wheat and barley, something which was rare around Dartmoor which was only fit for grazing.

Tomorrow, Dev was meeting the dreadful Blackehart himself, to show him the papers that had been drawn up between him and the squire. While the idea occurred to him, Dev removed the heavy gold signet ring which bore the Devlin seal and put it in his desk drawer. He wouldn't put it past Blackehart to have the shirt from his back in lieu of payment, but he'd not be able to take what wasn't there. He only hoped that the proof of the sale being set in motion would be enough to make the man wait a little longer, knowing payment would be made in full.

Freeing himself of the man's grasp on his throat was tantalising. He'd been looking over his shoulder for weeks now. Perhaps after this meeting he'd be able to breathe again. He snorted. Perhaps not. He wasn't fool enough to believe his debts alone had caused his misery. They were merely symptoms of it.

He still wasn't sure what he hoped to achieve, or what left the hollow ache gaping in his chest. A desire to grind his father's hopes and dreams into the dirt? Oh, yes. He wanted that. Yet it had been more than that, once at least.

A knock at the door sounded and had Dev turning on his heel. He barked at whoever was fool enough to disturb him to come in.

To his irritation, Ogden entered once more. There was an uncharacteristic, challenging look in the fellow's eyes that Dev could almost admire.

"A letter for you, my lord," he said evenly. "I thought perhaps you should see it before you left in the morning."

"Leave it on my desk," Dev muttered, pouring himself another drink. He suspected he knew who the letter was from and he knew damn well Ogden would recognise the precise lettering of the woman in question. It wouldn't be the first he'd received. No doubt Miss Kendall had thought of another colourful stream of invective with which to assassinate his character. One had to admire her vocabulary if nothing else. She'd even come to the house herself on more than one occasion. Dev had refused to see her. The last thing he needed was some overwrought female vacillating between fury and tears. Besides, it would change nothing. Dev's heart was a dead thing, blackened and shrivelled from lack of use. No feminine tears had the power to move him, as many had discovered to their cost.

He sat brooding for hours. The tray brought to him for dinner sat untouched while the decanter at his elbow emptied. His mind turned, going over the past as it often did and fuelling his despair. By the time the first glimmers of daylight lightened the skies, his mood was as bleak and pitiless as a frozen sea.

More from boredom than interest, Dev reached for Miss Kendall's letter. The last one had made him laugh out loud at her audacity, and entertainment of any variety would be welcome at this moment. He picked up the missive, sliding his finger beneath the seal and settling down to read the dreadful creature's words. He wondered what she looked like. As Dev's experience of women was of the perfumed and pampered variety, a woman who would live in isolation and run a small farm was outside his experience. He conjured the image of a short, dumpy figure with large, capable hands, a squint, and a moustache. Mr Ogden knew her, but he'd never commented on her outside of expressing sympathy for her and her family's predicament. If she'd been pretty, the fellow would have married her himself, wouldn't he? He must be pushing forty. It wasn't as if there were many options for a fellow in this backwater, either.

Dev scanned the missive in his hand and any amusement he might have felt fell away as Miss Kendall dissected his character with a surgeon's dexterity. Something like fury fired in his blood. How dare she? How dare she write such… such….

Dev took a breath, getting himself under control. As he got to his feet, he swayed a little as the contents of the decanter made its presence known. The insolent baggage. Well, enough was enough. She'd wanted to see him, to put her case to him in person and he would damn well give her the opportunity. This time, however, he'd have a few choice words of his own.

He sent the stables into chaos, yelling with fury for someone to ready his horse even though it was not yet daylight. Men stumbled into the yard, bleary eyed as they pulled on breeches and boots and scurried to do his bidding.

Dev had not been to Brasted Farm since he was a boy, dragged about by his father to show him the responsibilities he would one day face. He had a vague recollection of a handsome stone building and thought he remembered where it was. It had been a long while, but he'd ridden the moors as a young man and had a good sense of direction. It was at least two hours ride from here, taking the road. If he cut across the wild moors, then he might do it in an hour. He'd arrive early enough to give the woman the shock of her life. She'd still be in her nightgown at such an early hour, and if she thought he'd wait for her to dress and prettify herself to face him she'd be sorely disappointed. The thought satisfied him.

With fury and indignation still burning in his blood, alongside a skin-full of cognac, Dev rode off to meet his nemesis.

***

Charity Kendall stared at her bedroom ceiling. It was the same ceiling she'd stared at as a little girl, dreaming of all the things of which little girls dreamed. At least, she assumed she'd dreamed like that. It was hard to remember. It seemed a long time ago she'd been a girl at all. She knew she should be up and about already, but she felt worn down. The weight of her worries seemed heavier at his hour of the morning, filling the room in the hours before the daylight crept in. Worries snuck under the curtains ahead of the first fingers of daylight, stealing the air from the room, smothering her in its suffocating grasp, pressing down on her. She took a breath, forcing the air into her lungs even though her chest protested, unwilling to expand. Such wallowing was beneath her. Dramatics and hysteria had never been her style. She left that to her twin, Kit. He was the dramatic one in the family, full of romance and fire and dark musings. Charity had little enough energy to consider what they ought to have for dinner, let alone find anger enough that her 'art' was misunderstood. Not that she had any art. She hadn't a creative bone in her body.

In her spare moments, such as they were between running a farm and raising a family, she had been considering their options. There were two abandoned farms in the region. Charity had hoped to move the family to whichever one of them suited best. On visiting however they'd discovered the buildings in a state of decay, the land sick from neglect, and a raft of jobs so overwhelming it would take years to turn them around. Years and a great deal of money they didn't have.

The only solution was to go to Bristol as their Uncle implored them to do. He lived there with his own his family but was fond of his nieces and nephews. The man worried for them she knew. As a doctor he could keep a closer eye on Kit's poor health too. Yet living in a city, leaving the moors and this place which had been her home since birth … it cut her heart to ribbons.

Charity's fist hit the pillow as she pummelled it into a more comfortable shape and turned onto her side with a huff. There was one thing she *could* get angry about, no matter how exhausted she was. Anger was a hopeless, fragile description for the fury which filled her veins. Far more than mere anger. It was just possible she might even do the hateful man bodily harm, should the two of them ever be in a room together. Lord Devlin must know that too, as he'd refused to see her, despite the many times she'd called.

Frustration had burned so hard that it had reduced her to writing vitriolic letters to let off steam. Her last letter was keeping her awake. She suspected she may have gone a little too far.

Just a little.

She swallowed, unable to move the heavy bricklike sensation that seemed to lie somewhere in her throat. Well, all right then, more than a little. She pressed her hands to her cheeks. They were scalding beneath her rather sweaty palms. Oh, dear Lord. What had she done? It wasn't as if the wretched man cared a jot for what happened to her and those she loved. No amount of rage or tears or begging or screaming would have changed his mind. She'd known that, yet the impotence of being able to do nothing as he tossed her family onto the street like rubbish... well, it had unbalanced her mind. Temporarily of course, Charity added, imagining putting her case before a magistrate. Which was all too likely if Devlin ever saw that letter. Nausea roiled as her stomach clenched and twisted, but before she could indulge in a rare display of self-pity and bawl her eyes out, her bedroom door flew open.

"Charity, oh, Charity!"

Charity started and flung back the covers as her seven-year-old sister flew into her arms, clutching her about the waist. Their brother, John, three years' Jane's senior, hung back, white faced and solemn as the little girl sobbed her heart out.

"Whatever is all this?" Charity demanded "What's happened?"

"Oh, oh, don't let them take him away, Charity," Jane pleaded, fisting Charity's nightdress in her hands. "It was an accident! He didn't mean to kill him."

"What?" Charity gasped, noting with horror that John just swallowed instead of leaping in and telling Jane not to be such a silly goose as she might have expected. "Killed who? Whatever has happened?"

"It was an accident, Charity," John said, his voice trembling with the effort of keeping calm. "I swear it."

"Well, of course it was," Charity murmured. "There's no question of that."

She sat up, her mind working overtime as she swung her legs out of bed and grabbed a faded pelisse to pull on over her night rail.

"What were you doing out at this time Wait... no. Don't tell me."

She lifted her hand to halt his reply and groaned. She could see it now. John was determined to be the man of the family as Kit spent most of his time with his head in the clouds and his mind on poetry. She could see it now. The boy had crept out to go hunting rabbits and his devoted little sister had foisted her company upon him despite his protests.

"I got two," John replied, a little defiant despite the circumstances and the fact that she had expressly forbidden him to leave the farm before daylight and never, ever, alone.

Charity sighed and sat down again as Jane returned her arms to her waist, clinging like a limpet and sobbing. She stroked her little sister's hair. "You'd best tell me, and quick."

"He came out of nowhere," John said, looking like he might be sick at any moment. "I was just lining up a shot and suddenly this huge horse came out from behind the tor. It gave us such a fright that my finger squeezed the trigger."

Jane sobbed harder as John recounted the sorry tale. "The horse reared up, screaming and the fellow tried to hold him, but he couldn't. He fell a-and h-h-hit his head on a rock and there was blood everywhere and h-he was s-s-so still, Charity." John swallowed, tears in his eyes, his narrow chest heaving.

Charity got to her feet and gave John a reassuring hug, her expression calm. "Don't fret. Head wounds can bleed prodigiously, it doesn't mean the fellow is dead. Jane, fetch Kit, tell him to get Mr Baxter and bring the cart, and then go finish your chores, everything will be all right. John, you'd best show me."

John nodded, looking a little braver as he led her out of the room and down the stairs.

Chapter 2

"Wherein a body lies alone on the moor."

Charity was not a fanciful girl. Legends abounded on this part of Dartmoor, full of ghosts, fairies, and spirits, but none of them had ever stirred her imagination. She'd been too busy trying to keep her family fed and the farm running to have time for a fit of the vapours or indulge in flights of fantasy. As she walked the moor now, however, looking for a possibly dead body as the mists rose in the early morning sunlight, her flesh prickled with foreboding. There was some sixth sense tugging at her conscience, warning her that what happened today would have consequences beyond anything she could imagine.

She shivered, though it wasn't cold, and clutched her coat around her. As John gave a shout, Charity turned and gestured to Kit who was following behind with the cart. Her twin ought not be out in the damp of the morning, his health was too frail, but there was nothing to be done. If there was a body she'd not get it in the cart with just Mr Baxter their handyman to help.

To her dismay, as she hurried towards her little brother, she discovered his words were not those of a hysterical boy, frightened by the dark and an overactive imagination.

He was a big man, handsome too, despite the blood and his dishevelled appearance. His hair was black, his skin a rather olive complexion that was striking despite his current pallor. With relief, Charity found his heart beating strong and regular beneath his broad chest.

"He's far from dead, John," she said, casting her brother a reassuring smile.

John sat down on the damp ground with a thud and put his head in his hands. Charity ruffled his hair but said nothing, giving the young man a moment to gather himself.

"Knocked out cold, eh?" Kit said, observing the body as he strode nearer.

Charity nodded as Kit and Mr Baxter got closer. Ralph Baxter and his wife Beryl had been at Brasted Farm since before Charity was born and had worked for both her grandparents and parents. The farm was all they knew. Mr Baxter was as skinny and spare as his wife was round, and the dark cloud to her sunshine. They were an odd couple but as much a part of Charity's life and the farm as the ancient stones of the building itself. She wondered what would happen to them now but shook the maudlin thoughts away and returned her attention to the problem at hand.

"Mr Baxter, you take his shoulders, Kit and I will take a leg."

Baxter glowered at the body. "Fellow will cause trouble, mark my words," he said, his voice heavy with foreboding as he spat on the ground at his feet. "There was a dead crow in the courtyard last night. 'Tis an ill omen."

Charity held back the desire to roll her eyes and curse with difficulty She looked up to see Kit's lips twitch with amusement. Her brother knew of her scepticism for anything she couldn't see with her own eyes. "Jolly good," she said briskly. "Now, let's get him home and see if we can't patch him up."

They had the devil's own job getting him into the cart they used to go to market. The fellow weighed a ton and between Charity, Baxter's skinny frame, and Kit's poor health. they made a wretched mess of it. With chagrin, Charity observed that if the man hadn't had a concussion before they'd got him in the cart, he damn well would have after.

"Charity," Kit said, staring at the stranger at their feet as they jolted back to the farm, "look at his clothes."

Charity nodded. The fine silk waistcoat and beautifully tailored coat the man wore hadn't escaped her. She'd noted his hands, too: softer than hers despite the bulk of him. Not a man who laboured for a living. He was a fine gent, whoever he was. She hoped he wasn't the vindictive kind, hell bent on causing trouble.

"What on earth was he doing out here at this hour of the morning?" she wondered.

An isolated place, Brasted Farm was the only dwelling in the area and on the road to nowhere, the nearest village being an hour away. They'd had neighbours a scant half hour's ride away until two years ago, when the old couple had given up and moved to be closer to their children and civilisation. Life on Dartmoor was harsh and unforgiving, and the winters were cruel. You had to be tough to survive here. Tough, stubborn, and stupid, Kit would say with his crooked smile.

"Lost more than likely," Kit said, his expression thoughtful. "Did you catch a whiff of his breath? The fellow was drunk as a wheelbarrow, likely why he couldn't control that flashy mount of his." He cast a rather covetous look at the huge black horse tied to the back of the old cart. It was no wonder it had startled John, appearing out of the mists like an ebony monster. "Prettiest piece of horseflesh I've ever seen," Kit added with a sigh. "Must have cost an arm and a leg."

"You'll be able to afford such things too, when you're a famous poet," Charity said, solemnly.

Kit grinned at her, his handsome face lighting up at the familiar joke, and her heart ached for him. Poets spent their lives starving in garrets and they both knew it all too well—that and dying young. That Kit was probably doomed to do exactly that was something Charity refused to contemplate, hence the jokes about him being wealthy and successful. Kit would be different. He had to be.

As Brasted Farm came into view, for once the skies showed a glorious blue. The high moor was a dramatic landscape, with far-reaching views, and the farmhouse was a large determined granite building with a grey slate roof. It huddled into the countryside, stubborn and a little grim, presiding over a cluster of outbuildings, daring the moors to do their worst. A few stunted firs clustered in the meagre shelter of the low, gnarly, grey stone wall that surrounded the farm, facing the north wind.

Charity loved it.

"Look!" John cried out from his position at the front of the cart beside Mr Baxter. "There's someone at the farm."

Charity angled her neck to look and gave an exclamation of joy. "Uncle Edward!"

"It never is?" Kit questioned, standing up in the back of the cart to get a better look. "Well, I'll be damned."

Mr Baxter snorted, turning his head to give the still unconscious body in the cart a look of deep distrust. "Aye, we'll all be damned I reckon. Whoever that fellow is… he's got the luck of the devil."

***

Once his patient had been seen to, Uncle Edward—who by happy circumstance was a doctor—settled down to a jovial breakfast with his nephews and nieces.

"Well, well, isn't this a welcome sight," he said, the white whiskers at his cheeks bristling as he beamed at the laden plate of bacon, eggs and fried bread that Mrs Baxter set before him.

"No one makes breakfast like old Batty," Kit agreed, stuffing his mouth with bacon as the lady herself clouted him about the ear.

"Mind your tongue, you dreadful young scape grace," she scolded, though there was amusement in her eyes and no heat behind the words.

"Sorry, Batty," Kit mumbled through his bacon, his brown eyes glinting with mirth.

Mrs Baxter snorted and returned her attention to frying more bacon as Charity filled her uncle's cup with tea.

"You really think he'll be all right?" she asked, still anxious that their guest had not yet awoken.

Edward cast her a sympathetic glance before reaching for his tea. "Head wounds are tricky things," he said, repeating his words from earlier that morning. "They can do odd things to a fellow, but he's young and fit and strong. As I said, he badly bruised his arm and shoulder in the fall. Nothing was broken, from what I can tell, but he'll be feeling pretty sorry for himself when he comes to. I've left laudanum for the pain and you've got the other instructions written for his care." He set down his teacup and picked up his knife and fork again, spearing another piece of bacon. "I'm afraid you have a house guest for a good few days, though, depending on how he recovers."

Charity nodded, biting her lip. They had been fortunate that the man had landed in their midst during one of their uncle's visits. It was a long journey from Bristol for their closest relative, who was not as young as he once was. He was a kindly man though and he worried for Kit, placing about as much faith as they did in the local doctor.

"And how are you, Kit?" Edward asked, striving for nonchalance. "I'll have to be off again tomorrow, but I'll give you a once over before I go."

There was a flash of irritation in Kit's dark eyes before he pasted a smile to his face.

"I'm in fighting form, Uncle," he replied, his smile stretching into a grimace. "You know the summer is always better for me."

"Hmph," Edward replied, his voice noncommittal. "Until it rains."

Kit sighed and gestured to the cloudless skies beyond the window. "I have it on good authority it will be a long, hot summer," he said, winking at Charity.

Another of Mr Baxter's predictions, though he'd said it would be too hot and too dry, the fruit would be no more than little bullets, and their garden would die of thirst. Ever a shining light in the darkness was Ralph Baxter.

"There's a first time for everything I suppose," Edward said, chuckling as he returned his attention to his breakfast with gusto.

***

The sound of conversation and laughter filtering through his clouded mind was the first inkling Dev had that he wasn't at home. *Laughter* and *home* were words that did not go together. Pain seared through his tender brain as he tried to open his eyes and an unfamiliar room swam into view: white painted, with heavy oak beams. He hissed at the sunlight that flooded through a small leaded window and shielded his eyes with his arm.

"Oh, I'm so sorry!"

A feminine voice made him start with surprise and he tried to focus his gaze on the blurry figure that hurried to the window. Whoever she was, she tugged the curtains across, blocking out the daylight.

"I just came up to check on you. I had no idea you were awake."

Dev swallowed and tried to sit up, but his head swam, and pain lanced through his arm, which felt heavy and peculiar.

"Oh, don't do that," the woman admonished him, her voice rather stern. "Here, you must be thirsty."

A slender but surprisingly strong arm slipped behind his neck. She supported his throbbing head and brought a glass of water to his parched lips. Dev drank deeply, grateful despite the indignity of being at some strange woman's mercy. What the devil had happened to him?

"Forgive me," the voice said, becoming increasingly disembodied. "I'm afraid there was a little laudanum in that. My uncle is a doctor, you see, and he said you must rest as much as possible for the moment. I'm Miss Charity Kendall, by the way," she added. "What's your name, sir?"

Dev blinked, confusion flooding his tired mind. Where was he?

"I'm...." He paused, feeling daunted, and shocked at the roughness of his voice. A name lingered, just out of reach on the tip of his tongue. It was an important name but....

Damn it. Who was Charity Kendall?

He found a pair of wide brown eyes watching him, filled with concern. Well, he could sleep a little if those eyes were watching over him. The perplexing question of why he of all people needed charity circled his brain with no clear answer until sleep, and the laudanum, pulled him under.

***

"Anything?"

Charity raised her head as Kit poked his head around the door.

"No. He awoke for a moment, but he seemed rather disorientated. I put a drop of laudanum in his water, so he'll sleep awhile now." She bit her lip, looking at the big figure with some misgiving and no little curiosity.

Kit stepped into the room and gave the fellow a dark look before putting his hands on Charity's shoulders. Turning her around he guided her out of the room.

"He's not a motherless lamb that needs feeding, nor the runt of the litter, nor a lame duck," he said, as he closed the door on the sleeping figure. "So don't go trying to fix him. Uncle Edward has done that and, as soon as he's fit enough, he's on his way."

"Kit," Charity began, folding her arms and turning to face him. "I have no intention—"

"Of course you do," Kit said, a pitying look in his eyes. "You can't help yourself. You've made it your life's work to look after this farm, Mr and Mrs Baxter, me, John and Jane, and whatever else lands in your lap. For heaven's sake, Charity, what about you?"

Charity glowered at him, the familiar argument poking at fears and uncertainties she did not wish to face.

"You know being thrown out of this place might be the best thing that ever happened to you," Kit continued, relentless now. "You might actually be forced out into the real world, you might even begin to live for yourself, instead of hiding yourself away here, buried alive."

"Oh, don't give me your dramatics, Kit," Charity hissed, turning in the narrow corridor to scowl at him. "I've neither the patience nor the stomach for it." She tutted and shook her head. "Buried alive indeed," she muttered, rolling her eyes at him before stomping down the stairs. Kit might have longed for London, for fame and notoriety, for the society of fellow artists but not her. She had given up on any fanciful notions of marrying and raising a family of her own. At twenty-five and with a farm and two young children to support, she had family enough and no time for day-dreaming. "Now if you'll excuse me," she added tartly, "I have work to do."

She didn't see the glimmer of concern in her brother's eyes as she closed the door on him, but she didn't need to see it. It was always there; the worry about how she would manage without the money he provided from his writing, meagre as it was. He seemed well enough now, and she prayed it might continue, but they were neither of them as romantic as all that. Consumption, or tuberculosis as her uncle referred to it, was a wicked hereditary disease and one that life here at Brasted Farm did nothing to hinder. It had killed their parents and Kit believed he'd not make old bones. Little they'd experienced in the past contradicted that assumption.

So, he wanted her to go out into the world, to find herself a husband who would support her and be kind to John and Jane. How in the world he supposed she could accomplish that without leaving them all to fend for themselves ...? She snorted at the idea. They wouldn't survive till the end of the week without her. The thought was reassuring, vindicating her lack of enthusiasm to face the real world. The world here was quite real enough for her, thank you very much.

With that argument settled, in her mind at least, Charity rolled up her sleeves and headed to the kitchen.

Free to read on Kindle Unlimited

Charity and the Devil

Want more Emma?

If you enjoyed this book, please support this indie author and take a moment to leave a few words in a review. *Thank you!*

To be kept informed of special offers and free deals (which I do regularly) follow me on *https://www.bookbub.com/authors/emma-v-leech*

To find out more and to get news and sneak peeks of the first chapter of upcoming works, go to my website and sign up for the newsletter.
http://www.emmavleech.com/

Come and join the fans in my Facebook group for news, info and exciting discussion...

Emmas Book Club

Or Follow me here......

http://viewauthor.at/EmmaVLeechAmazon
Facebook
Instagram
Emma's Twitter page
TikTok

About Me!

I started this incredible journey way back in 2010 with The Key to Erebus but didn't summon the courage to hit publish until October 2012. For anyone who's done it, you'll know publishing your first title is a terribly scary thing! I still get butterflies on the morning a new title releases, but the terror has subsided at least. Now I just live in dread of the day my daughters are old enough to read them.

The horror! (On both sides I suspect.)

2017 marked the year that I made my first foray into Historical Romance and the world of the Regency Romance, and my word what a year! I was delighted by the response to this series and can't wait to add more titles. Paranormal Romance readers need not despair however as there is much more to come there too. Writing has become an addiction and as soon as one book is over I'm hugely excited to start the next so you can expect plenty more in the future.

As many of my works reflect I am greatly influenced by the beautiful French countryside in which I live. I've been here in the

South West for the past twenty years though I was born and raised in England. My three gorgeous girls are all bilingual and the youngest who is only six, is showing signs of following in my footsteps after producing *The Lonely Princess* all by herself.

I'm told book two is coming soon ...

She's keeping me on my toes, so I'd better get cracking!

KEEP READING TO DISCOVER MY OTHER BOOKS!

Other Works by Emma V. Leech

(For those of you who have read The French Fae Legend series, please remember that chronologically The Heart of Arima precedes The Dark Prince)

Rogues & Gentlemen

Rogues & Gentlemen Series

Girls Who Dare

Girls Who Dare Series

Daring Daughters

Daring Daughters Series

The Regency Romance Mysteries

The Regency Romance Mysteries Series

The French Vampire Legend

The French Vampire Legend Series

The French Fae Legend

The French Fae Legend Series

Stand Alone
The Book Lover (a paranormal novella)
The Girl is Not for Christmas (Regency Romance)

Audio Books

Don't have time to read but still need your romance fix? The wait is over…

By popular demand, get many of your favourite Emma V Leech Regency Romance books on audio as performed by the incomparable Philip Battley and Gerard Marzilli. Several titles available and more added each month!

Find them at your favourite audiobook retailer!

Girls Who Dare– The exciting new series from Emma V Leech, the multi-award-winning, Amazon Top 10 romance writer behind the Rogues & Gentlemen series.

Inside every wallflower is the beating heart of a lioness, a passionate individual willing to risk all for their dream, if only they can find the courage to begin. When these overlooked girls make a pact to change their lives, anything can happen.

Ten girls – Ten dares in a hat. Who will dare to risk it all?

To Dare a Duke
Girls Who Dare Book 1

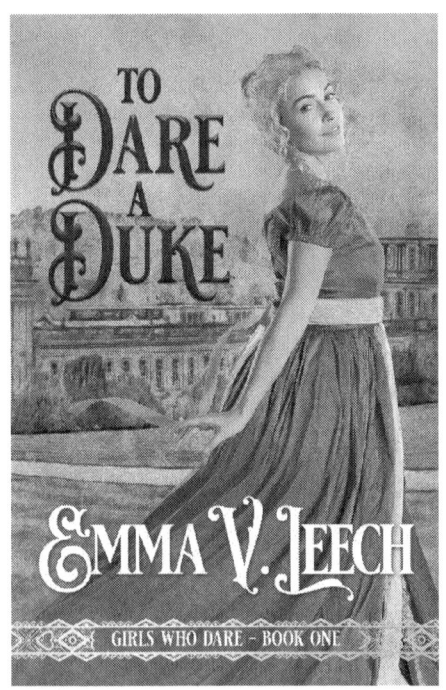

Dreams of true love and happy ever afters

Dreams of love are all well and good, but all Prunella Chuffington-Smythe wants is to publish her novel. Marriage at the price of her independence is something she will not consider. Having tasted success writing under a false name in The Lady's Weekly Review, her alter ego is attaining notoriety and fame and Prue rather likes it.

A Duty that must be endured

Robert Adolphus, The Duke of Bedwin, is in no hurry to marry, he's done it once and repeating that disaster is the last thing he desires. Yet, an heir is a necessary evil for a duke and one he cannot shirk. A dark reputation precedes him though, his first wife may have died young, but the scandals the beautiful, vivacious and spiteful creature supplied the ton have not. A wife must be found. A wife who is neither beautiful or vivacious but sweet and dull, and certain to stay out of trouble.

Dared to do something drastic

The sudden interest of a certain dastardly duke is as bewildering as it is unwelcome. She'll not throw her ambitions aside to marry a scoundrel just as her plans for self-sufficiency and freedom are coming to fruition. Surely showing the man she's not actually the meek little wallflower he is looking for should be enough to put paid to his intentions? When Prue is dared by her friends to do something drastic, it seems the perfect opportunity to kill two birds.

However, Prue cannot help being intrigued by the rogue who has inspired so many of her romances. Ordinarily, he plays the part of handsome rake, set on destroying her plucky heroine. But is he really the villain of the piece this time, or could he be the hero?

Finding out will be dangerous, but it just might inspire her greatest story yet.

To Dare a Duke

From the author of the bestselling Girls Who Dare Series – An exciting new series featuring the children of the Girls Who Dare...

The stories of the **Peculiar Ladies Book Club** and their hatful of dares has become legend among their children. When the hat is rediscovered, dusty and forlorn, the remaining dares spark a series of events that will echo through all the families... and their

Daring Daughters

Dare to be Wicked
Daring Daughters Book One

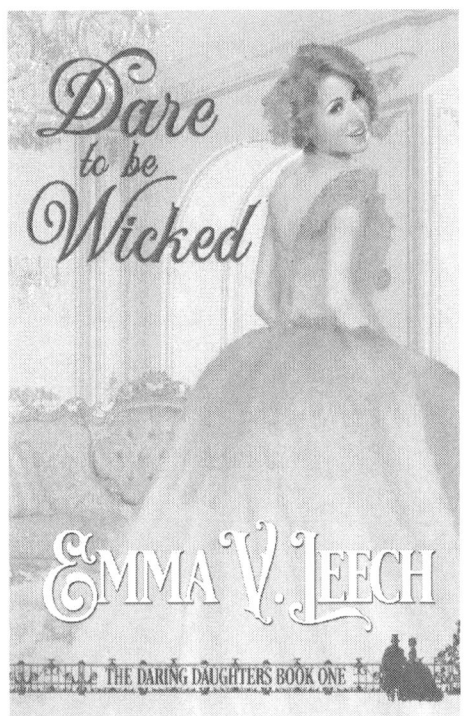

Two daring daughters ...

Lady Elizabeth and Lady Charlotte are the daughters of the Duke and Duchess of Bedwin. Raised by an unconventional mother and an indulgent, if overprotective father, they both strain against the rigid morality of the era.

The fashionable image of a meek, weak young lady, prone to swooning at the least provocation, is one that makes them seethe with frustration.

Their handsome childhood friend ...

Cassius Cadogen, Viscount Oakley, is the only child of the Earl and Countess St Clair. Beloved and indulged, he is popular, gloriously handsome, and a talented artist.

Returning from two years of study in France, his friendship with both sisters becomes strained as jealousy raises its head. A situation not helped by the two mysterious Frenchmen who have accompanied him home.

And simmering sibling rivalry ...

Passion, art, and secrets prove to be a combustible combination, and someone will undoubtedly get burned.

Order your copy here Dare to be Wicked

Interested in a Regency Romance with a twist?

Dying for a Duke

The Regency Romance Mysteries Book 1

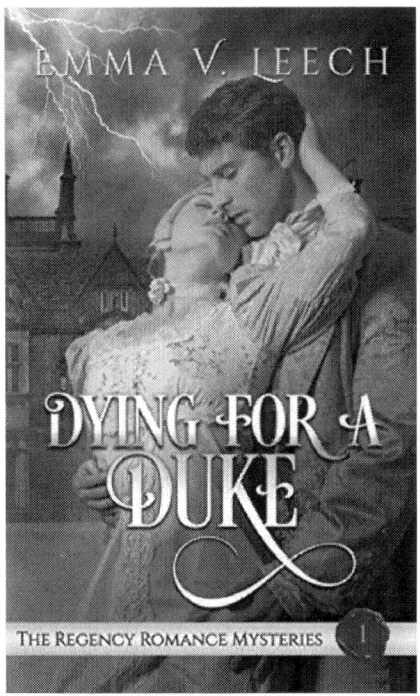

Straight-laced, imperious and morally rigid, Benedict Rutland - the darkly handsome Earl of Rothay - gained his title too young. Responsible for a large family of younger siblings that his frivolous parents have brought to bankruptcy, his youth was spent clawing back the family fortunes.

Now a man in his prime and financially secure he is betrothed to a strict, sensible and cool-headed woman who will never upset the balance of his life or disturb his emotions ...

But then Miss Skeffington-Fox arrives.

Brought up solely by her rake of a step-father, Benedict is scandalised by everything about the dashing Miss.

But as family members in line for the dukedom begin to die at an alarming rate, all fingers point at Benedict, and Miss Skeffington-Fox may be the only one who can save him.

FREE to read on Amazon Kindle Unlimited.. Dying for a Duke

Lose yourself in Emma's paranormal world with The French Vampire Legend series.

The Key to Erebus
The French Vampire Legend Book 1

The truth can kill you.

Taken away as a small child, from a life where vampires, the Fae, and other mythical creatures are real and treacherous, the beautiful young witch, Jéhenne Corbeaux is totally unprepared when she returns to rural France to live with her eccentric Grandmother.

Thrown headlong into a world she knows nothing about she seeks to learn the truth about herself, uncovering secrets more shocking than anything she could ever have imagined and finding that she is by no means powerless to protect the ones she loves.

Despite her Gran's dire warnings, she is inexorably drawn to the dark and terrifying figure of Corvus, an ancient vampire and master of the vast Albinus family.

Jéhenne is about to find her answers and discover that, not only is Corvus far more dangerous than she could ever imagine, but that he holds much more than the key to her heart …

Now available at your favourite retailer

The Key to Erebus

Check out Emma's exciting fantasy series with hailed by Kirkus Reviews as "An enchanting fantasy with a likable heroine, romantic intrigue, and clever narrative flourishes."

The Dark Prince
The French Fae Legend Book 1

Two Fae Princes
One Human Woman
And a world ready to tear them all apart

Laen Braed is Prince of the Dark fae, with a temper and reputation to match his black eyes, and a heart that despises the human race. When he is sent back through the forbidden gates between realms to retrieve an ancient fae artifact, he returns home with far more than he bargained for.

Corin Albrecht, the most powerful Elven Prince ever born. His golden eyes are rumoured to be a gift from the gods, and destiny is calling him. With a love for the human world that runs deep, his friendship with Laen is being torn apart by his prejudices.

Océane DeBeauvoir is an artist and bookbinder who has always relied on her lively imagination to get her through an unhappy and uneventful life. A jewelled dagger put on display at a nearby museum hits the headlines with speculation of another race, the Fae. But the discovery also inspires Océane to create an extraordinary piece of art that cannot be confined to the pages of a book.

With two powerful men vying for her attention and their friendship stretched to the breaking point, the only question that remains...who is truly The Dark Prince.

The man of your dreams is coming...or is it your nightmares he visits? Find out in Book One of The French Fae Legend.

Available now at your favourite retailer

The Dark Prince

Acknowledgements

This book would not have been possible without the knowledge, advice and guidance from my wonderful sensitivity readers. Their help with bringing Henry to life was invaluable and I'm very grateful. They all have personal experience of Autism, either through close family members or in a professional capacity. In no particular order my deep thanks to Julie Eros, Kaila Laila, Hanna Elizabeth and Heather Hammonds, you're all amazing.

Autism did not receive an official diagnosis until 1908 but it has been recently suggested that many important historical figures had the condition. These include Socrates, Isaac Newton, Michelangelo, Charles Darwin, Albert Einstein, Andy Warhol, and WB Yeats.

My thanks also to my Beta readers, the usual suspects, Alejandra Avila, Amanda Corey and Veronique Glotin Phillips, love you guys!

A special thank you to Beta reader extraordinaire, PA and BFF, Varsi Richardson Appel for literally everything. You're an angel and a patient one at that!

Lastly, but certainly not least, thank you to you, my readers. I hope you enjoyed Henry's story. If you did and you have a moment to leave a review, I'd be very grateful.

Emma x

Can't get your fill of Historical Romance? Do you crave stories with passion and red hot chemistry?

If the answer is yes, have I got the group for you!

Come join myself and other awesome authors in our Facebook group

Historical Harlots

Be the first to know about exclusive giveaways, chat with amazing HistRom authors, lots of raunchy shenanigans and more!

Historical Harlots Facebook Group

Made in the USA
Columbia, SC
07 March 2025